Heart of Stone

John Jackson

CROOKED
CAT

Discover us online:
www.crookedcatbooks.com

Join us on facebook:
www.facebook.com/crookedcat

Tweet a photo of yourself holding
this book to **@crookedcatbooks**
and something nice will happen.

For Pamela -
Always

Acknowledgements

Although this is a work of fiction, the main characters are based on real people and events. Robert Rochford and Mary Molesworth were my 5x-great-grandparents. The story I have told in this book is, perhaps, the story of what SHOULD have happened to them.

The picture of Robert Rochfort on the front cover hangs in Belvedere House, Mullingar, Ireland. I must thank Mr Maurice Stenson, the Manager of Belvedere House and Gardens, for his generous co-operation, and Mr Simon Semperski, Photographer, who took the photo for me. Belvedere House, together with the infamous Wall, still stands today on the shores of Lough Ennel, and is open to the public.

I cannot overstate the thanks that are due to the Romantic Novelists' Association. Their support and help has been outstanding, and their "New Writers Scheme" is a marvellous help to newcomers.

In particular, I would also thank Liz Fenwick, Liz Harris and Sue Moorcroft for their unstinting encouragement, support and friendship.

Every writer owes a debt to their editor and publisher; in my case Sue Barnard, who has guided me on the path of good prose, and Laurence and Stephanie Patterson of Crooked Cat Books who accepted my manuscript.

For a writer of historical novels, a Family Tree is truly the gift that keeps on giving. The Rochforts are by no means my only ancestors with a colourful past. Readers can expect more stories based on their exploits.

Finally, I must thank my wife Pamela, who has been a constant source of support and encouragement since I started writing.

John Jackson
York, Summer 2017

About the Author

After a lifetime in the maritime industries, John Jackson has now retired and lives in York. After thirty years of drafting regulations, safety procedures and the like, he has now turned his hand to writing fiction.

An avid genealogist, he found a rich vein of ancestors going back many generations. His forebears included Irish peers, country parsons, and both naval and military officers. They opened up Canada and Australia and fought at Waterloo.

A chance meeting with some authors, now increasingly successful in the world of romantic fiction, led him to try to turn some of his family history into historical novels.

John is a keen member of the Romantic Novelists Association and graduated through their New Writers Scheme. He is also a member of the Historic Novel Association and an enthusiastic conference-goer for both organizations.

He describes himself as being "Brought up on Georgette Heyer from an early age, and, like many of my age devoured R L Stevenson, Jane Austen, R M Ballantyne, and the like."

His modern favorite authors include Bernard Cornwell, Simon Scarrow, Lindsey Davis, Liz Fenwick and Kate Mosse.

Heart of Stone

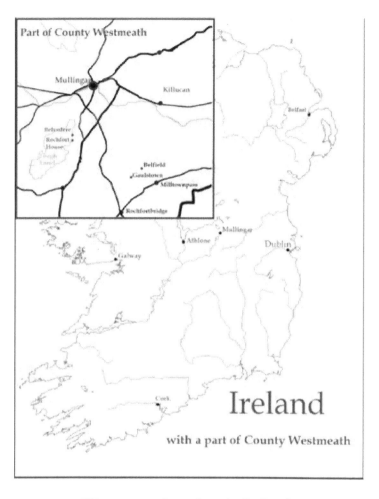

**The story takes place in Ireland,
between the years 1735 and 1752.**

The Descendants of
George Rochfort

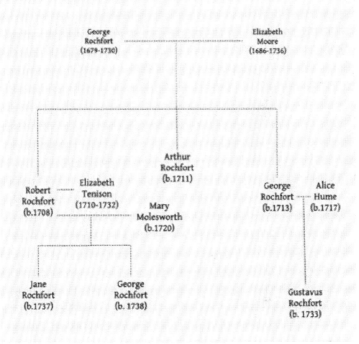

George
Rochfort
(1679-1730) .... Elizabeth
Moore
(1686-1736)

Arthur
Rochfort
(b.1711)

Robert .... Elizabeth
Rochfort   Tenison
(b.1708)   (1710-1732)
                            Mary
                            Molesworth
                            (b.1720)

George .... Alice
Rochfort   Hume
(b.1713)   (b.1717)

Jane   George
Rochfort   Rochfort
(b.1737)   (b. 1738)

Gustavus
Rochfort
(b. 1733)

Chapter One

IN WHICH WE MEET ROBERT & ARTHUR ROCHFORT, BROTHERS, AND KEY TO OUR STORY

"Arthur?"

Arthur Rochfort turned in surprise on hearing his name called out. He had just finished dining in Vauxhall's New Spring Gardens, and now found himself face-to-face with a tall gentleman some three years older than himself, with dark hair clubbed short, dressed in a well-cut blue coat and gleaming Hessians.

Arthur smiled broadly at the sight of his older brother. While they had never been close, they had always got on well.

"Hello, Robert. What in God's name brings you to London?"

"Arthur! How are you? I didn't expect to find you in a place like this."

"My regiment is in London before going overseas. We will be attached to the garrison here for a time before we embark. How is Father? Getting any information from him is like getting blood from a stone."

"Still sick. He is dying, I think," replied Robert, with a sigh. A note of concern crept into his voice, and he spoke quietly. "His illness seems to be eating him up day by day. Are you coming over to Ireland?"

"I have some leave due, so I'll be across as soon as I can arrange it. I'll write to him again."

"Do it soon. I don't believe he will last another winter. If he wants to see anyone, it is you. You were always his favourite, anyway. His temper hasn't improved."

A group of young ladies ran over to Arthur.

"Ladies, allow me to introduce my brother, Robert Rochfort."

Robert bowed to them, as the bevy of worshipping females dragged Arthur away to re-join his party.

"Sorry, Robert," said Arthur with a faux-apologetic air and a broad grin, ruefully shaking his head, crowned with a golden mane of hair. "I will call at the house."

The Rochfort family home in London was a small house in Kensington, a short ride from Whitehall. A few days later, Arthur paid his promised call and found Robert at home. Over dinner and brandies, they brought each other up to date.

"I was sorry to hear of your wife's death," Arthur proffered.

"It's over and done. I have moved on. We didn't deal well together, in any event."

Arthur raised his eyebrows, although he wasn't surprised. Robert's lack of concern for other people was not news to him.

"Do you stay long in town?" Robert asked.

"Some weeks here in barracks, then some months in the country, sorting out the next batch of recruits. I want to get across to see Father as soon as possible, especially as he's so ill, and I will apply for leave of absence."

"And after that? What does the regiment do?"

"We're posted overseas, but we don't know where yet. I want promotion, and the fastest routes to that are a short plague or a bloody war. I want to make Father proud of what I've done. As thanks for him purchasing my Commission, I suppose."

"I mentioned his health was worse. He is dying."

"I didn't realise how sick he was until you told me at Vauxhall. He wrote some months ago. He made light of his condition, but I knew he was getting worse by the way he wrote."

A few weeks after his arrival in London, Robert received a summons to Horse Guards. He was puzzled, and also irritated.

4

What could the army want with him?

He attended the next day and was shown into an uncomfortable anteroom where he spent an impatient hour pacing backwards and forwards; a long wait which did nothing to improve his temper. Eventually, a footman appeared and ushered him into the presence of an elderly gentleman in a full-bottomed and powdered wig, who waved him to a chair. Robert started to protest at the delay, but after one look at his host's eyes, he quickly stifled any complaint.

The elderly gentleman eventually put his papers down and turned to Robert.

"Welcome to London, Rochfort. I'm sure you're wondering why you are here. You may call me Stafford. For now, that is all you need to know."

Robert swallowed, and glanced around at a large office, the walls of which were lined with glass-fronted bookcases, maps and cupboards. The size of the office gave Robert an inkling of his host's importance.

"Rochfort, you are a Member of Parliament for Westmeath. Members of your family hold several other seats in the area, and have influence over several more. The control that your family wields over those seats is what interests us."

Robert nodded his head. At last, he understood why he had been summoned.

"Your father devoted much of his life to our Service," his host went on. "For this, and other reasons of policy, His Majesty is of a mind to ennoble you as a peer. His Majesty has need of your vote in the Lords in his interests. We know your father is in poor health, and we must look to the day when you are head of the family."

Robert smiled to himself. Mr Stafford looked up at him, and Robert immediately assumed a more serious expression; his host was clearly not a person to be trifled with.

"As a young man, you spent two seasons in London, and you formed part of His Majesty's circle. We know, for example, that you attended the Newmarket Spring and Autumn meetings in both 1727 and 1728. We also know you lost some small amounts of money to His Majesty and that you paid your debts when they were due. You also joined His Majesty at cards on occasion. He seems to have regarded you as an amiable person. In short, Rochfort, he liked you."

Mr Stafford rose to his feet and walked over to a large map of Ireland on the wall.

"Your presence here at Horse Guards is due to the other task we have in mind for you. You will no doubt be aware that there are Irish regiments within the French army? We also know they have been recruiting Irish Catholics. This must stop. You are to take over as Muster Master of our forces in the centre of Ireland. This means the garrisons in Mullingar and Athlone." He pointed to these towns and the area between them on the map.

"For now, recruiting is satisfactory, and the garrisons are up to strength. However, with the ban on Catholics joining the army, this may change. You may receive drafts from England, but you shouldn't rely on this. But, first and foremost, there are to be no more recruits from Ireland joining the French army."

Robert looked alarmed. This was not a problem he had ever considered.

Stafford continued, "Up to now, your military experience has been with the Militia. There is a world of difference between the Militia and a Regiment of the Line. You will shortly be gazetted as Colonel in the Dublin Garrison, should your time here in Whitehall be satisfactory."

Robert remained silent. No reply from him seemed to be required.

"It is important that you know His Majesty is a generous monarch. If your service is satisfactory, he will, no doubt, show his gratitude."

This course of action didn't fit in with Robert's own plans at all. He tried to secure what he thought of as his freedom.

"Well, thank you, Mr Stafford. This is all very interesting. May I give you my reply in a few days? I will certainly give it my most earnest consideration."

Stafford turned his gaze on Robert, who quailed under his frown. "Mr Rochfort, you misunderstand me. This is not a request; it is a royal command. You will attend the Horse

Guards and the office of the Secretary of the Army until we send you back to Ireland. That will be some months hence. Now, do you understand me?"

Robert gulped. He had been boxed into a corner, and there was no escape.

"Well, Mr Stafford, if you put it like that, I can hardly refuse."

"Indeed, you cannot."

Stafford rose, and added in a tone that brooked no argument, "Oh, one more thing, sir. We are aware of your reputation in Dublin. I suggest that you moderate your tastes while in London. Keeping a mistress is one thing, but for one in your position, the bawdy houses of Covent Garden are best avoided. Do well in this task, and His Majesty and I will smile upon you. Fail, and it will be as if you had never existed. Do I make myself clear?"

"Abundantly, sir," replied Robert as he took his leave. While he might not like it, he was quick-witted enough to realise where the real power lay.

"Well, what do you think?" asked Lionel Sackville, the Duke of Dorset and the King's Lord Lieutenant of Ireland, now seated in the chair recently vacated by Robert.

"Your Grace, I think we must use the tools we have."

"Indeed, Mr Stafford, we must. I do wish there was an alternative, though. He is a strange man."

"I agree. His father has been a loyal servant and friend of the Crown for many years, but his illness means he won't last long. Robert must be prepared. He has two things to recommend him: he has the favour of His Majesty (although God alone knows why), and his family controls the county. When his father was younger, nothing moved in Westmeath without his knowledge and approval. I do worry about Robert's temper, though. He is a jealous man. He shows no feeling for others and is always ready to take offence. We will be watching him, as I'm sure you will do here. I wish to God Arthur was the eldest. He seems to have all the virtues while Robert has all the vices."

The next morning, and for many weeks after, Robert presented himself at the Army Office. He spent hours each day learning about the army, its composition, and its deployment in Ireland.

Matchmaking mamas seemed to regard Robert as dangerous, and they made a point of keeping their daughters well beyond his reach. This caused him no concern. Widowed for three years, he had no wish to marry again. It took him no time at all to set up another pretty young courtesan as his mistress in an apartment on Harley Street.

Every few weeks he would receive a summons from Mr Stafford. It soon became clear to Robert that someone was watching his daily habits.

"My colleagues tell me your instruction goes well," Mr Stafford remarked during one of Robert's calls. "Oh, and we see you have a new mistress."

Mr Stafford never indicated whether he approved or disapproved, merely that he was aware of everything Robert did. In view of this, Robert was secretly relieved that he had indeed managed to forego the bordellos of Covent Garden.

The following May he received a final call to Mr Stafford's office.

"Rochfort, I am happy to tell you that you have done well in your time here. My officials say you are now aware of the full extent of your duties and the responsibilities of your proposed position."

Robert swallowed hard. "Thank you, sir. I have tried, and your officials have been most helpful."

Stafford handed him a packet sealed in oilcloth and bearing a wax seal imprinted with a crown. "These are your orders. You are to take ship to Dublin and present yourself to the Lord Lieutenant. He is aware of your arrival, and you will hold the rank of Lieutenant Colonel attached to the Headquarters Company in the Castle."

The following week, Robert took a packet-boat from Liverpool back to Dublin. He made his way to Dublin Castle and presented himself to the Lord Lieutenant, Lionel Sackville.

"Welcome to Dublin Castle," said Lord Sackville, in a friendly and welcoming tone. He opened Robert's papers and read them with care, before letting a smile play across his lips. Mr Stafford had briefed him in depth, although he knew Robert in person and was aware of his reputation. Mr Stafford had concluded his letter with the words, "*Such a shame, in such a fine figure of a man, and with such a background. Still, as I said, we must play the cards we have in our hand, and he and his family control several boroughs.*"

"It's good to see you again, Mr Rochfort – or should I say, Colonel Rochfort! Mr Stafford has written to me and briefed me on your duties."

"I'm looking forward to starting, my lord. I must write to my father and my brothers to let them know the news."

That night Robert wrote to them all and told them when he would be home. His father lived on his estate at Rochfort House, near the garrison town of Mullingar. There he lived the quiet life of a country gentleman as a widower, now with rapidly failing health, having lost his wife several years before. Rochfort House itself, although large, was crumbling around him and his small retinue of servants.

George, his youngest son, had married and was bringing up a family in a wing of the house. Always complaining that he was short of funds, he was building a reputation in the area as a hard landlord, forever increasing his rents. An advantageous marriage had brought many tenanted farms into his possession. A large square-set man with a florid face and black hair, he looked – and was – a hard man to cross. Heaven help any tenant farmer who was late with his rent.

Every year a fresh crop of marriageable maidens and scheming mamas came to Dublin for the Season. While they knew of his previous marriage, Robert found himself receiving more and more attention from those with daughters.

Among those whose attentions were becoming more and more enthusiastic was Lady Jane Molesworth. Mary, her sixteen-year-old step-daughter, was pretty, dark-haired, and vivacious. Her youth was no object for her step-mama, who had three daughters of her own to marry off. The sooner she could get Mary married and off her hands, the easier it would be to contrive good matches for her own children.

Robert got used to seeing Mary and her mother at all the major events he attended in Dublin. They danced several times, particularly when Lady Molesworth caught him unaware before his dance card was full.

One evening, Mary's stepmother came into her bedroom after a ball at the Castle.

"Well, girl. Do you like what you see?"

"Mama, what do you mean?"

"You've met him several times. You have danced with him too. Mr Rochfort, of course."

"He seems nice, and he is handsome, but he is a little old."

"Don't be ridiculous, girl. He is in the prime of life. You are sixteen now, and it's high time you were married."

"Married? But Mama, I don't want to be married. At least, not yet."

"You'll be married as soon as your father and I find a suitable husband for you. Do you think you would wait and let any number of matches go by? Hoity-toity, miss. You need a lesson in manners."

Lady Molesworth swept out of the room, leaving Mary lost in thought. Marriage? Her? She had dreamt of marriage since she was first able to read, but for her, it was always bound up with love. Children? She had always loved children and had played a major part in bringing up her sisters. She expected to have a family and knew she would love them.

Mary drifted off to sleep thinking of her step-mother's words.

The following Tuesday, Arthur arrived at Rochfort House. He was shocked beyond measure at his father's appearance.

"Nothing wrong with me, my boy. Nothing that the brandy bottle can't cure. I need no sawbones fussing around me."

10

At the weekend, Robert arrived and called the whole family to hear his news. "I don't know what you have heard here," he told them, "but I am to undertake some particular tasks for the Army. I am to be the Muster Master for the central counties of Ireland, and I'll be based in Athlone and at Mullingar."

"What on earth are you talking about?" asked George. "You know nothing of army matters apart from playing soldiers in the Militia."

"Well, George, you are wrong. I have spent the last six months preparing for this job at the Horse Guards. There is little about the Army in Ireland that I don't know."

Over the course of the next hour, he outlined the tasks and position he had been given. He made no mention of the enigmatic and powerful Mr Stafford or his threats. After dinner, their father retired to bed, and the three brothers sat over a glass of port. The state of his health caused them all great concern.

"How is Father? He looks worse than when I left."

"He is in a terrible way. He has been severely ill in the autumn. He still refuses to call the doctor. He says the only doctor who can serve him now is the brandy bottle."

"He does seem a lot worse," said Arthur. "I tried to persuade him to allow the doctor to come out and talk to him at least, but no. He still has a temper, though. He started shouting at me. 'I won't have a sawbones in this house', he said. 'A sawbones killed your mother, and I'll not have a murderer looking at me!' Quite untrue, of course, but there's no changing his mind."

As the weeks passed, Lord Rochfort's condition continued to deteriorate. Shortly before Christmas, he took to his bed. Early in January, he sent for Robert.

"My son, I am dying. We know this. Don't give me any flimflam. Now, when I die, you will inherit the estate. You've already got Gaulstown. I'm leaving Rochfort House to George. I cannot in all justice leave him any less. Arthur has Belfield House, and that is all he wants, but you must produce an heir!

Do you think I want the family line to be in the hands of that idiot George and his son? I need you to promise me – you find another girl, marry her and produce an heir. After that, you can do what you will with your wife. I will be dead."

This pronouncement shocked Robert to the core. He had never heard his father speak with such scorn of George.

"What is wrong with George?" he asked. "What do I need to know about him?"

"You'll find out soon enough," growled his father, in an ever-weakening voice.

Robert waited for a few moments, but his father had fallen asleep. When a servant went to wake him in the morning, the old gentleman's body was stiff and cold.

Chapter Two

THE CHANGING OF THE GUARD

The servant uttered a scream that woke the whole household, before running out of the room and downstairs to the kitchen. There, the butler grabbed hold of her, rendering her silent by the simple expedient of a slap across the face. Shocked into silence, the girl told her tale.

"It's Mr Rochfort. He's lying there, all cold and grey. He's dead, so he is."

The butler quickly went up to George's room and found him in a state of undress. He had woken up on hearing the screams.

"Sir, it's your father. Mr Rochfort has passed away in the night."

"Thank you, Danvers. We knew it would not be long. I will send messages to my brothers immediately."

By the time they had received the messages, several hours had passed.

They gathered in the manor-house library. As the oldest brother, Robert took the lead.

"Father's burial will be next weekend. I've told Danvers to arrange everything with the church in Mullingar. The parson will arrange for Father's body to be taken into town. We will go and pay our respects tomorrow. Others may come in the days before the funeral. I will write to our neighbours, here and in Dublin."

Two days later the brothers returned to Rochfort House to hear their lawyer read their father's Will. This offered no surprises. As expected, George received Rochfort House. Arthur would receive the title to the house he was living in,

Belfield House, with a small number of farms, and Robert received the title to the old family seat of Gaulstown, some four miles from Rochfort House. While Gaulstown may have been the largest of the family's properties in the neighbourhood, it was famous for being old, uncomfortable and in urgent need of repair.

Robert spoke to family and friends before they dispersed. "While I thank you for coming here today, I must advise you that there is a reason for my returning to the county. I ask you to be aware of the possible appearance of French spies. We are living in dangerous times. The French wish to recruit Catholic Irishmen into their army. This, we cannot allow."

His mostly Protestant audience looked at each other in alarm. French spies in the area would mean greater surveillance by the authorities. The landowners and contractors who supplied the garrison were particularly keen to avoid any additional scrutiny.

Over the next weeks, as winter moved into spring, life resumed its sleepy normality. There were no reports of Frenchmen in the area. The army and militia carried on with their drills and exercises. Robert's tenant farmers carried on preparing for the harvest. Flynn, his land agent, circulated among his tenants to tell them their landlord was increasing their rents and by how much.

When they complained, he told them, "Be happy your landlord is Mr Robert and not Mr George Rochfort. Mr George is putting his rents up by twice as much."

George, although in possession of few social virtues, had at least produced an heir. Robert's jealous nature seized on this. It lent urgency to his father's last instructions to produce an heir of his own, and he determined to find himself another wife.

Two months after his father's funeral, he paid a call on his brother George at Rochfort House. The soft Irish rain fell around them.

"Good God, George! What are you trying to do to the place?"

14

"I'm going to turn Rochfort into a proper manor-house. This is just the start. I need more space here, anyway."

Robert gave him a hard stare. "Why on earth do you need more space?"

"Because I so desire, and no other reason. You have Gaulstown, I have Rochfort House, and I will make it into a fine house. A house fit for a lord."

Before dinner, their nurse brought George's children into the room to meet their uncle. At their head was George's son, Gussie. A fat, whiny child of six, he seemed destined to share his father's looks and temperament. His four younger sisters all looked browbeaten and in a state of terror, as their mother told them to line up for inspection. Their nurse glowered at her charges as they made their bows and were promptly ushered out to the nursery.

Meanwhile, Arthur returned to his military duties, and shortly after found himself posted to Gibraltar. The Spanish had only recently ceded Gibraltar to Great Britain. The garrison there needed to remain ready to counter any attempt by Spain to regain the colony.

The pace of life in Mullingar was always slow. At the height of summer, Robert moved back into Gardiner Row in Dublin. While Mullingar was attractive, and his duties with the garrison made some call on his time, in general all was quiet. Robert wanted to waste as little time as possible before picking up at least some of the threads of his louche lifestyle.

When he arrived in Dublin, he found several invitations waiting for him, requesting his presence at dances, balls, and the theatre. Robert consigned several of them straight to the fire, just keeping those he thought would amuse him.

He also found it useful being able to refuse invitations on the grounds of being in mourning for his late father, but only when it suited him, of course.

Chapter Three

IN WHICH A MATCH IS MADE

The year passed. When not away on duty, Robert spent much of this time at Gaulstown, which was larger than Rochfort House but famously dilapidated. Robert started work on some of the most urgent repairs.

It also formed an excellent place to base himself. He could split his time between military duties at the Mullingar and Athlone garrisons and those at Dublin Castle.

One evening in Dublin, Kitty, a young Dublin actress and Robert's mistress, was entertaining her patron. Kitty made frequent appearances at the Theatre Royal. With a love of gossip, she knew all the locals and military men who had an interest in the theatre.

She and Robert were relaxing in Robert's bed after an energetic evening of lovemaking. Kitty could still feel the warmth and impact of Robert's hands on her body.

"Do you know a young girl called Mary?" she asked.

"I know several of that name," he replied.

"Mary Molesworth? Young, pretty and just out of the schoolroom. She is always at the theatre."

"Oh yes, I know her – and her mama."

"Well, a friend tells me that her mama is determined that her daughter marries an earl at least." Kitty stretched and purred like a kitten.

"That's hardly news," replied Robert. "Lady Molesworth's ambitions for her step-daughter are well known. She has three daughters of her own to marry off. No doubt she wants Mary off her hands so she can concentrate on finding husbands for them."

"You could do worse. The girl seems amiable, and bright. I assume you know she will come with a considerable fortune?"

"That would sweeten the pill, of course, although I'm not yet an earl. The prospect of having Lady Molesworth as my mother-in-law, or being a regular visitor to Mullingar, fills me with horror."

"Do you care? Get her with child, let her produce an heir, and then both of you can do what you like. Like your first marriage. You know Mr Tennison has died, don't you?"

Robert glanced at her, his expression hardening. He grasped her hair and pulled her head hard towards him. "Of course I do," he rasped. "What do you know about my first marriage? And what is this about Tennison?"

"Only what a few people remember – you married his daughter, and she died of the pox while carrying your child. They say her father died of a broken heart. Is there any more?"

"No," replied Robert, with a tone of finality in his voice.

Kitty made a mistake. "How did she get the pox?" she asked.

Moments later, the back of Robert's hand slammed across her face.

"Never speak of my family again! You are here to please me and for no other reason. Get out."

She staggered up from the bed and seized her clothes. She watched him with real fear in her eyes and saw the veins in his neck throbbing. Kitty had felt his ire before. As soon as she was dressed, she flung herself at Robert's feet, fearing his temper. She hoped to be of use to him, and so it proved on this occasion.

"Get up and get out," he shouted.

As she walked to the door, he added, "Be back here next Friday at midnight."

Kitty grasped the purse he held out and scuttled out of the room, down the stairs and out of the back door.

Robert was a frequent visitor to Mullingar during the

winter. His duties included making sure the regiments stationed there and at Athlone were up to strength. War with France was never far away. Early in the new year, he called his officers together in the barracks at Athlone.

"Gentlemen," he began, "you know that the natural state of affairs for Britain is to be at war with France. If we are not at war with France, it is Spain. In short, we are always either at war or about to be at war. That is why we keep an Army, and that is why it must be kept up to strength. We must be prepared. And, gentlemen, I can tell you, it will not be a long wait."

This brought Robert's mind back to the remarks of the enigmatic Mr Stafford.

"You are all to keep your eyes and ears peeled for any suggestion of the French being active in his area. I warn you to keep a close eye on the farms. A bad harvest means the destitute wandering the land, and rents remaining unpaid. It also means more people deciding they are good Protestants and joining the Army. That is good for recruiting, but if they decide that they can only be Catholics and wish to serve, they must be stopped from joining the French."

Flynn, Robert's land agent, appeared to be more amenable to the local farmers when bad weather and blight affected their crops. He believed that the tenant paying a lower amount and keeping the land in working condition was better than no rent paid and a family evicted.

George, however, was not sympathetic. "You are a fool, Robert. They all have money, and they must be squeezed. I make them pay or go."

He did indeed seem to be collecting a good amount, judging by his newly-announced plans for extending Rochfort House. To Robert, these seemed haphazard, and he decided that he needed to see less of George.

In truth, the brothers had little liking for each other. Robert still owned some land to the north of George's house, also bordering on to Lough Ennell, but was both annoyed and jealous that his youngest brother had inherited their old family house. He thought that, as the eldest son, he should have been allowed the pick of the estate. He thought the time had come to leave his own distinctive footprint on the area.

Robert started looking for the best architect and builder he could find in Ireland. He wanted someone who could design a new hunting lodge – palatial in style, suitable for a baron – on his land to the north of Rochfort House. He would call it 'Belvedere', and it would be the finest house in Westmeath.

His thoughts also turned again to the requirements of providing himself with an heir. Always a jealous man, his previous dislike of George had extended to loathing. He started to feel a sense of urgency in acquiring a suitable wife. Her dowry could go a considerable way to cover the cost of his new home.

Back in Dublin, Lady Molesworth was, unknown to Robert, keeping a sharp eye on his comings and goings. He returned to Dublin late in the spring of 1736, and an invitation to dine with the Molesworths arrived via a groom just two days later. With a need to find an heir pressing more on his mind, and, with a view to her fortune, he decided that he could do worse than Mary Molesworth.

Mary's feelings never entered his head. All he needed was for her to produce an heir. After that, she could lead any life she wanted providing she brought no scandal on his family.

On Saturday evening, his carriage stopped outside the Molesworths' house in Henrietta Street. Robert entered to find the rooms furnished in the latest style by the fashion-conscious Lady Molesworth.

"Robert Rochfort," the butler announced.

Those gathered turned to inspect the new arrival. While Robert was well-known in Dublin society, he accepted few invitations to households like this. When they went in to dine, Lady Molesworth grasped him firmly by the hand. "Please, sit by me," she purred.

Robert found himself on his hostess's right-hand-side, with Mary on his other side next to an elderly cleric. The priest showed little or no interest in conversing with her, or indeed in anything that would distract him from his dinner.

Lady Molesworth was a skilled and adroit hostess. She did all that was necessary to make sure all her guests, and particularly Robert, enjoyed their dinner. Her cook had done wonders with salmon from the Liffey and beef and pheasant from Lord Molesworth's estates.

While paying due attention to his hostess, Robert also spent some time trying to talk to Mary. At the back of his mind was the thought that he may have to devote more time to her. She was certainly decorative enough for him.

By some curious trick of memory, Robert remembered Kitty telling him that his host's daughter was keen on the theatre. This at least gave them a subject to talk about. Mary was no fool. At her father's insistence, her governess had educated her charge in line with her own modern outlook on education for young ladies. She could answer with sense on most topics, and Robert enjoyed his dinner more than he had hoped.

As the gentlemen joined the ladies, Lord Molesworth took Robert by the arm. "My wife tells me you have cast your eye over my Mary. Now, while I love her, and only wish her happiness, her ladyship insists that Mary should marry soon. Let's talk further on this another day."

"Well?" Lady Molesworth asked her husband later that night.

"Well what, Madam?"

"Don't play the dullard with me, my lord. Did you speak to Rochfort about Mary?"

"Madam, you will, I am sure, be delighted to know that I have indeed spoken to Colonel Rochfort about Mary."

"Hmm."

His reply had the effect of quietening Lady Molesworth, at least until after the guests had all left.

Robert left shortly after, remarking to himself that this was a good night's work. On arrival home, he went to his study and poured himself a large brandy. He heard movement behind him and caught a whiff of perfume in the air.

As he turned, Kitty advanced towards him wearing only a thin transparent shift. She slid into his arms and ground her lips against his with unexpected savagery. He found himself responding and led her, their arms and lips entwined, out of the study and into his bedroom. There, it took few of her wiles to bring him to a fever pitch. She tore his clothes off him and dragged him onto the bed.

"I want you now, Robert. I want you inside me!"

Robert raised himself over her, and descended on her, crushing her and entering her in one motion, both of them caught in the throes of lust and desperate for satisfaction.

Afterwards, as they lay in each other's arms, he turned to Kitty.

"How dare you present yourself to me like that? Like a common whore."

"Oh Sir, I am sorry for being so bad. You must punish me."

Robert promptly turned her over his knee and administered a dozen hard blows to her buttocks with the palm of his hand. The sight of her buttocks shining bright red, with the marks of his fingers on them, was enough to rouse him again.

Robert had no illusions about Kitty and knew she was an exceptional actress. He also knew she enjoyed his more unusual tastes.

In Henrietta Street, Mary lay awake, thinking about the man she had met. She wasn't stupid, and knew that she must marry, and please her parents. What she hoped for was to find a husband who loved her, and whom she would love.

Mary had sometimes thought she was losing her heart before. In a city, full of young officers from both the Army and the Navy, it would not be surprising if her head had been turned. She was not stupid, though, and was far too sensible to believe that any of these youthful fancies would come to anything She treated them as just that: a fancy, to enjoy and to get over.

The next day she was sitting in the drawing room when a footman announced Miss Doyle. Katherine Doyle was the same age as Mary, and had been her friend since early days in the school-room.

As soon as Katherine sat down, she started her eager questions.

"Well, what is he like?"

"What is who like?"

"The phantom colonel, of course?"

"He is very nice."

"What? Is that all? That is not a description. I think I have seen him at a levee."

"Well then, you know what he is like. He is tall with dark hair, and he looks exactly what he is, an officer in the Army."

"He was in uniform when I saw him. Can he talk?"

"Of course. I found him interesting. He was telling me of his home."

"Where is it? Is it large and magnificent?"

"I don't think so. It's old, but he plans to build a new home. A hunting lodge that's large enough for a family to live in."

"He is talking to you about a family? He must be serious."

Mary blushed. "Don't be silly. Anyway, it sounds delightful. He lives in County Westmeath, near a town called Mullingar, and he has business in the Army there, and in Athlone."

"Will there be a ballroom?"

"I don't think so. He doesn't seem the kind of man to give balls."

"How dull!"

"No, he's certainly not dull. He talks well and dances well. I like him."

"Ah, but Mary, do you love him?"

Mary felt her eyes moisten. Her voice dropped to a whisper.

"Yes, my darling Kate, I believe I do."

As Mary fell asleep that night, she dreamed of herself and Robert, of a home in the country, with her sitting in the garden in the sunshine with children at their feet.

While she slept, her dreams became more fevered. She remembered the feel of the hard muscles in his arms and chest as he held her.

Her stepmother, on the other hand, slept like the proverbial log, secure in the knowledge that her plan had started on the road to fruition.

Throughout the winter and spring, Robert continued his routine of spending as much time as possible in Dublin. He would visit Mullingar and Athlone during the week when his duties required him to attend to the garrisons.

On his rides across the county, he came across families wandering from place to place with a desperate look in their eyes. The first few times he had made enquiries as to why they were wandering, but now he no longer did so. His groom advised him that they were former tenants of his brother George. His brother's reputation for being a hard landlord was well earned, it seemed.

Robert's architect had produced plans for a new hunting lodge in the Palladian style. Workmen swarmed over the ruins of an old chapel on the site, clearing the ground and saving any dressed stone that could be reused.

Over at Rochfort House, George's improvements looked to be cast into the shade by his brother's new home. Knowing that George would be seething with annoyance, Robert smiled with satisfaction.

Lady Molesworth's plans also continued to develop. That summer, her husband received a letter from Robert, asking if he may call on him in Henrietta Street. Such a formal request could only have one meaning.

The following day, both men were sitting in Lord Molesworth's book-lined study.

"Will you join me in a glass of sherry, Colonel?"

"Thank you, my lord. I'm sure you know why I'm here. Time passes, and I must take a wife sooner rather than later. Not to beat around the bush, I would like to ask Mary to be my wife."

Lord Molesworth raised an eyebrow and gave Robert a questioning look. He refrained from saying anything, but privately, he thought it a damn strange way of declaring his love. He listened as Robert cut to the chase.

"My lord, what dowry do you intend to pass over with your daughter?"

He outlined the size and make-up of her dowry, which was still substantial.

"Her mother died in childbirth, you know. Her estate has passed to Mary as her portion. There will be a little more, but I also have three other daughters to provide for. I am now of an age where I want some peace in my life. Seeing Mary married without delay, to a man she loves, will ensure I enjoy my remaining years."

For Robert, Mary represented the best option that he had found for providing him with both an heir and a fortune. Lord Molesworth gave his consent to the match with great enthusiasm. Robert, for his part, had little doubt of his obtaining Mary's agreement.

Robert and Mary now met at balls and dinner parties with increasing regularity. One of the highlights of the season was to be a fête at Lord Molesworth's house in Henrietta Street. As the guests departed, Robert found Mary alone in one of the smaller rooms. He called her name, and she turned, and came towards him, drifting into his arms for his long-awaited embrace.

Mary lifted her lips to his. Robert was gentle at first. He kissed her and was surprised to find her respond.

She is a quick learner, he thought, and kissed her again, harder, and again found a willing respondent. He could feel her breasts straining against his coat and ran his hands up and down her back. They broke apart and gazed at each other.

"Do you love me, Mary?" he asked.

"I believe so," she replied.

"Will you do me the honour of marrying me?" he asked, confident of her answer.

"Of course." She advanced into his open arms to kiss him again, and clearly enjoyed his passionate kiss in return.

Robert strode to the door and threw it open, to reveal Lady

Molesworth standing there in a fever of anticipation. He nodded at Lord Molesworth before speaking.

"Lady Molesworth, my lord, I must inform you that Mary has done me the honour of agreeing to be my wife."

Lady Molesworth's eyes danced with delight, and she cried out, "Robert, Mary, – at last!"

Robert smiled at her. He was aware that Lady Molesworth might believe she had more influence over him than she did. He smiled. He looked forward to her discomfiture when she found out that he only did exactly what he wanted. He found it convenient to forget the influence of Mr Stafford.

Lady Molesworth fussed over Robert and Mary with an expression of delight on her face. Lord Molesworth expressed his entire satisfaction with the arrangement. Robert gave Mary a delicate kiss in public for the first time, before leaving Henrietta Street for Gardiner Row.

With a smile of satisfaction, he mulled over the events of the evening. The night had produced the added frisson of a prospective bride who showed every sign of returning his passion. He fell asleep dreaming of his bride's eyes and the swell of her breasts beneath her dress.

Chapter Four

A WEDDING AND A JOURNEY

Over the next few weeks, Lady Molesworth found her energies and talents employed to the full.

"My lord, I have written to Robert and asked him to prepare a list of guests he would wish to invite. He is dining with us on Friday, and I will tell him of my arrangements. There will be guests from London as well as Dublin who will wish to attend, I am sure."

Lady Molesworth's first call was for her dressmaker.

"Nichols! My step-daughter is to be wed. She requires a suitable wedding gown. For a reasonable sum, of course. I also will need a new dress."

"Certainly, my lady. I propose to return tomorrow with some samples and some pattern books. Will your stepdaughter be available?"

Two weeks before the wedding, Mary heard a knock on her bedroom door just after she had retired for the night. Before she could call out, her stepmother came in and sat on the bed.

"Mary, you are getting married in two weeks."

"Yes, Mother," Mary replied, rather puzzled over this late-night call.

"Mary, it has occurred to me that you may not know exactly what your duties will be as Robert's wife."

"Well, I will run his household, and accompany him to parties, and be hostess for him."

"No, Mary, I mean your duties in the marital bed."

Mary smiled to herself. She had seen animals and pets mating and giving birth to their young, and she had discussed with her school friends what she should expect from a husband when they were wed.

"Don't worry, Mother. I know what is expected of me."

"Yes, well. It will all be over very quickly, and you'll soon get used to it. I'm sure Robert won't bother you too much."

With that Lady Molesworth got up and left Mary to her dreams.

As the wedding approached, Robert gave little thought to whether he was in love himself. He had never loved anyone, let alone his first wife. He had had affairs with women as he grew up, and he had maintained a series of mistresses. Even now, he still saw Kitty at regular intervals.

The day of the wedding dawned bright and clear. The six bells of Christ Church Cathedral rang out in the clear August air, and the nave quickly filled with the great and the good of Dublin society. No one could appear more pleased than Lady Molesworth, clearly delighted to have got her stepdaughter off her hands at small expense to herself.

"Mary, you look ravishing," she exclaimed.

"Thank you, Mother. I feel wonderful." She was about to marry a man who loved her, she was young, beautiful and confident. For her, it was a perfect day. She could feel herself glowing with happiness.

The marriage service was as full of pomp and ceremony as the church could muster, with a full choir, bells, and a guard of honour from Dublin Castle. The Dean himself, Mr Delaney, conducted the wedding, and the Duke of Cavendish, the new Lord Lieutenant, was pleased to offer the use of St Patrick's Hall in the State Apartments for the wedding party.

After the bride and groom had received their guests, and their health had been drunk, the Lord Lieutenant rose to his feet.

"I have some more news for our happy couple."

He produced a large scroll from his robe and read.

"The King has been pleased by Letters Patent under the Great Seal of the Realm, dated the sixteenth of March of this year, to confer the dignity of a Barony and an Earldom of the United Kingdom upon Robert Rochfort, and the heirs male of his body lawfully begotten, by the names, styles and titles of Baron Belfield."

The guests applauded Robert's success but suddenly fell quiet. The door had opened, and a tall young infantry officer with a shock of blond hair and wearing a major's crowns on his uniform entered the room. Robert stood up with a smile on his face while Mary looked at the new arrival and then at her husband.

The newcomer came over to where they were sitting, and clasped his brother in a warm embrace.

"Mary," Robert announced, "allow me to introduce my brother Arthur."

"I apologise for this surprise arrival," Arthur replied, "but I was determined to get back for this wedding if humanly possible." He turned to Mary and raised her hand to his lips.

Mary felt the warmth of his lips on her fingers; the sensation caused her to feel a glow deep within her. She looked up and into his eyes. They seemed deep enough to drown in. To the end of her days, she would remember the first time she looked into those eyes. At once she pulled herself together and retrieved her hand. Her fingertips seemed to be on fire.

"How long are you with us, Arthur?" asked Robert.

"A few days only. I will take the packet back to Liverpool next week, and then to Gibraltar. But this is your day; it is just my good fortune to get back in time to share it with you."

Arthur looked again at Mary and seemed to gaze deep into her soul. He knew, in a heartbeat, that he had just met the only person he could ever truly love.

As evening fell, the guests escorted the couple, now Lord and Lady Belfield, to Robert's carriage. Once inside, his head groom took the reins for the short drive across the river and up to their home in Gardiner Row. There the whole household had assembled on the steps and in the entrance hall to welcome their new mistress.

"Come and enter your new home," said Robert, handing her down from the carriage and escorting her up the steps and into the house.

Mary couldn't have been happier. She loved Robert. She loved the feel of his arms holding her, the crush of his lips on hers, the feel and taste of his mouth when he kissed her. She was no shrinking violet, and she longed to feel the passion she knew she had inside her. She did, truly, love him, and hoped that he loved her.

She couldn't know that Robert saw her only as a means of giving him children and a source of funding for his new house.

That night, Mary opened her arms to her new husband, and Robert made love to his new bride. While there was a moment of pain for Mary, she was expecting this, and it was overshadowed by the feeling of completeness and pleasure she felt when Robert entered her and moved against her. She wrapped her arms around him, feeling the muscles in his shoulders and back. She felt sensations building inside her, and instinctively lowered her hands to grasp Robert to pull him deeper into her.

Afterwards, Mary thought briefly of the advice given by Lady Molesworth. She could only assume her stepmother's experience had been different from hers.

Robert, for his part, was happy to believe he loved Mary, at least as much as he was capable of loving. Her response to his kisses and embraces intrigued him. While no suggestion of wantonness could be raised, she showed eagerness to join him in his passion. She returned his kisses like someone on the verge of great new discoveries. Robert was no stranger to the passionate arts and favoured some of the more unusual ones, but bedding a virgin who responded to him was a new experience. He enjoyed playing his fingers across her nipples and seeing her expression change as they hardened and rose. He stayed with Mary through the night with her curled in his arms and made love to her again as the sun rose.

After a week in Dublin, the couple set off in glorious weather, covering the eighty miles to Gaulstown before nightfall. Robert had arranged changes of horses in advance, and the newly-built coach road made for comfortable travelling. He was a competent and capable driver and had a fine eye for his horses. Those who knew him well thought he cared more for his horses than he did for people.

"A horse won't let you down," he used to tell his friends. "If it makes a mistake, then nine times out of ten, it is the fault of the rider or driver."

Robert and his new bride were to establish themselves at Gaulstown, which, thanks to the repairs Robert had carried out, was still habitable. Even after a long coach trip from Dublin, Mary was all smiles and charm. Mrs O'Mahoney, Robert's elderly housekeeper, conducted the couple upstairs to the rooms that had been prepared for them.

"I've cooked a chicken and a fine trout from the lough for your dinner, my lord," she announced. "It'll be served in the small saloon tonight."

Later, after they had finished an excellent (if simple) meal washed down with a bottle of wine from the Gaulstown cellars, Robert cleared an area of the table to show Mary his plans for Belvedere. She saw his eyes come alight as he described the hunting lodge.

That night, Robert again came to her bed, and she welcomed his passion with a developing one of her own. This was far from the pain, indignity and awkwardness that some of her friends had described when discussing the marriage bed. Mary found she had a sensual side to her character, and she responded to Robert's caresses and demands with increasing enthusiasm.

During their first week at Gaulstown, Robert took Mary in

his carriage to meet his brother George, and his shrewish wife, Alice. Mary had met George and Alice at her wedding but had had little opportunity to talk to either of them. While this was a mere courtesy call, it distressed Mary to find that George seemed to have a mean and avaricious nature. His wife, Alice, appeared to be no different.

"I see you are still extending the house," remarked Robert.

"It has been falling down for years. God knows how much money it will take."

"It's big enough as it is, surely?"

"Not if I want to impress people. I want a proper-sized house, and by God, I mean to have one. A house that is fit for a gentleman, not this ruin."

Mary managed not to make her discomfort obvious. Robert cut short their visit as soon as good manners would allow.

As they walked back to the carriage, Mary turned to Robert.

"I found your brother – interesting."

Robert scowled. "George does not like spending a penny more than he must. Alice is like him in that regard. His tenants hate him. He demands his rents, won't allow any leeway, and won't carry out any repairs to the farms."

Robert also explained that without a son of his own, the disagreeable child Gussie would, on Robert's death, be in the direct line of succession to inherit the title and the estate.

Mary understood at once why Robert was so keen to have an heir. Having seen Gussie, she could hardly blame him.

"What of Arthur? Has he no family?"

"Arthur has never married, although he has had admirers by the score. He likes female company, but not the idea of marriage or settling down. Besides, he is enjoying life in the army too much. He is now serving in Gibraltar."

Mary thought about the relationship between the brothers. An instant dislike of George and his family spurred her thoughts to the hope of providing Robert with the son and heir that he wanted. Though at the back of her mind was the memory of Arthur's eyes and the burning sensation of his lips on her fingertips.

After two weeks, Robert departed for the garrison at Athlone. Fortunately for him, the country remained quiet, although he did notice the number of homeless and other vagrants. Some of these would look to find work for the garrisons, who remained the biggest employer in Westmeath.

The men among them could take the King's shilling and join the Army, and ensure a living for themselves and a means of support for their families. The female members of the families had a harder time. The younger, prettier girls could assure themselves of an income by selling their services to the soldiers. For the older women, though, there was little work available, apart from picking potatoes at harvest time or digging peat. It was dirty and backbreaking work, but it gave them the chance to scrape together enough coppers to tide them and any children over the winter.

Mary found this first absence a little irksome, although she knew before she married Robert that this would be a necessary part of their married life. Her natural charm and diffidence soon won over the hearts of the staff at Gaulstown. Having someone in permanent residence caused everyone to pull together and to direct their energies to clean and refurbish the older parts of the house.

"The house looks different. It smells different too," Robert remarked when he returned from his first trip. "What have you done to the place?"

"Just cleaning and some repairs. The maids have been cleaning all the rooms, one by one. A lot of the windows and sashes leak, though, and there are some leaks in the roof."

"There have been leaks in the old house for many years. I don't want to spend any great sum on the place yet, especially if I am to build Belvedere."

That night, Mary welcomed him to her bed again, and they made love several times over the next few days. Before he left for Dublin, Robert told her that he wished to leave the entire management of the house to her. Mary took him at his word and looked forward to another week of rearranging and reorganising. She knew she would have to employ more servants; for years Gaulstown had been looked after by six elderly staff, all of whom had been there for many years. Half a dozen maids and footmen were to be added to the staff in the house, while the outside staff were now to include another gardener and a boy.

In Dublin, Robert made his calls at Dublin Castle and on the Lord Lieutenant.

"Things seem to have started well for you, my lord."

"Thank you, Your Grace. It has been hard, but I believe we are keeping a lid on the area."

"I'm sure you will be pleased to know that Whitehall is also happy with your performance here. Tell me, how does your bride like her new home?"

"Very well, Your Grace. She runs Gaulstown with quiet efficiency. The servants love her, which is good. I am away a lot, of course, but she doesn't complain."

The only cloud on Robert's horizon was the increasing number of vagrants, many of whom, he realised, were former tenants of his brother George.

Now back in Dublin, Robert wasted no time summoning Kitty to his bed. Her sensuous charms and her happy acceptance of his desire to dominate her fed a dark need in him. Moral questions had never beset him before, and didn't do so now.

Kitty asked after his new bride, and Robert enjoyed telling her of the pleasures of introducing a high-born lady to the ways of the flesh.

Two months after their wedding, when Robert returned from one of his trips to Dublin, Mary met him in the drawing room. She seemed a little agitated.

"Robert, I have some news."

He looked at her, with a quizzical expression on his face.

"I believe I am with child," she whispered.

Robert professed himself delighted, but that night he did not come to her bed. The following evening, she asked him if he intended to come to her.

"But my dear, you are with child," he announced, with a satisfied tone in his voice.

While she was still able to, Robert and Mary hosted a small number of dinner parties to allow the senior officers of the garrison and the local families to get to know her better. Mary continued to charm her new acquaintances, with the sole exception of her brother-in-law George and his wife.

In the fifth month of her pregnancy, the household packed up, and decamped to Dublin, to stay in Gardiner Row until after Mary's confinement.

The months passed, and Mary settled down to await the birth of their child. Morning sickness had given way to a ravening appetite, and, as she grew larger, to an increasing but selective hunger. Robert engaged the best doctor he could find: a Dr Reardon, recommended by Lady Molesworth as 'the best Doctor in Dublin', who had assisted in the delivery of many of her friends' children.

Mary was a young and healthy woman. Childbirth was simply part of life, and she was as prepared as she could be. Several of her friends had recently given birth, and Mary thought she knew of the pain involved. She determined to accept it and to produce a beautiful son for her husband.

Robert never once came to Mary's bed during her pregnancy. The charms of Kitty were enough to satisfy him. In his eyes, this allowed Mary to concentrate on carrying and delivering his son. Never did he doubt for a moment that it would be a son. He made a point of telling his friends and acquaintances that he would shortly have a son and heir.

Mary's pregnancy also gave him ample opportunity for visiting and supervising the building of his new hunting lodge. It was soon evident that this would be a magnificent building. Mr Castel, the German architect he had engaged, was a regular visitor to Gaulstown. Robert had received assurances that Mr Castel would provide him with a hunting lodge in quite the latest Palladian style. He was determined to put Mary's dowry to good use.

Springtime approached, and Mary felt the coming of the season. All around her, life was bursting forth from the gardens of Dublin. For Mary, this was a perfect sign that augured well for the birth of her son. As April turned into May, Robert was away at Gaulstown when Mary's waters broke. The butler sent for the midwife recommended by Dr Reardon. Danvers also sent a groom with a message to tell Robert that her ladyship had gone into labour. He gave him a purse of ten guineas and instructions to change horses as often as he needed.

Twelve hours later, the door to Gardiner Row burst open and Robert entered to the sound of muffled screams coming from upstairs. Robert bounded up the stairs and was about to burst into his wife's bedroom when the door opened. The doctor and midwife came out, the midwife carrying a blanket containing a lustily crying baby.

"How is he?" asked Robert.

"Who?" asked Dr Reardon.

"How is my son?" cried the earl.

"My lord, you have a fine healthy daughter."

Robert's face went white, and in a flash, his mood darkened. He threw open the door to the room and screamed out, "How dare you!"

Mary lay there, exhausted, waiting for the midwife to return with her infant. She burst into tears, not knowing what she had done wrong.

"I must have a son," he shouted. "I need a son and heir, madam, not a daughter."

With that, he turned and strode out of the room, the servants cowering out of his sight. As he entered his study, they heard him shouting for brandy.

The entire house fell quiet, with not a sound except Mary's muffled sobs. As the baby started to cry, the midwife passed her to Mary, and the infant began to feed. As she did, Mary decided that come what may, in spite of Robert's anger and disappointment, she had done nothing wrong. She was not going to bow her head for producing a fine, healthy daughter.

Over the next few days, she had visits from both her father and stepmother.

"My first grandchild, and she is a lovely baby," said her father. "You look very happy with her."

"Oh, Father, I love her so much. I just wish that Robert could love her too."

"Well, what did you expect?" snapped Lady Molesworth, whose interest in the baby was cursory at best. "Of course he was disappointed. He expected you to give him a son. He has been telling everyone that you would have a son, and now you have made him look foolish."

Robert had gone straight back to Gaulstown the morning his daughter was born, without saying goodbye or seeing Mary or the baby. A few days later, he received a visit from his brother.

"What brings you here, George?"

"I came to ask about my new nephew?"

Robert gritted his teeth. "You have a niece."

"Oh, how nice for you. Do you have a name for the babe?"

"I neither know nor care," snarled Robert.

George looked apologetic while smiling to himself. Robert noticed how smug he looked, and his face darkened again.

"I'll leave you to your day then." George strode out to his horse.

Robert once again felt a stab of jealousy pierce his heart. George had managed to produce a son. Why hadn't he?

Two weeks later, Robert ordered his horse and rode towards Dublin. He arrived in the evening to find his wife and child in the drawing room in front of a fire. Mary had just finished feeding the baby, and the scene appeared to be one of domestic family harmony. Robert himself was tired after his ride, but spoke to Mary in gentle tones.

"Do we have a name for the babe?"

"Her name is Jane," said Mary. "One of the canons from Christ Church Cathedral came and baptised her last Sunday. We could delay it no longer."

"Thank you. I will return tomorrow, and I wish you goodnight." With that, he turned and left the room, before leaving the house for a meeting with Kitty. There, between bouts of savage lovemaking, he told her of his disappointment.

"My lord, just wait a little. You now know she is fertile and can carry a child to term. Wait a few weeks, get her with child again, and you may well have a son by this time next year."

Robert mulled over Kitty's words. In his heart of hearts, he knew that the choice of a son or daughter had purely been luck.

If he was honest with himself, he was becoming bored with Mary. She was passionate enough, but lacked the will or tastes to enter the games and practices that he enjoyed himself.

He decided to take Kitty's advice, and a few days later, picked up and held his daughter, to his wife's evident delight. Mary's face fell when he announced that he was returning to Gaulstown.

There, for the next few weeks, he divided his time between his military duties and his new hunting lodge, which, by this time, was now half completed. Work had started on terracing the small hill on which it stood. Eventually, these terraces would be turned into parterres, and a knot garden planted there, at the continuing suggestion of Mr Castel.

When Robert returned to Dublin, some two months had passed since the birth of his daughter.

"You look ill. Is there something wrong with you?" he demanded.

"I'm sorry, Robert. It is just from carrying our daughter." Mary still looked pale and tired. It was clear she was still feeling the effects of her pregnancy and a long labour. He decided to wait before seeking her bed again. He would do so when she was ready to bear another child. In the meantime, he had Kitty and her charms.

Like any young mother, Mary was the centre of attention in her circle of friends. They all came to congratulate her and to cast adoring gazes at the new baby. Robert received the congratulations of his colleagues at Dublin Castle and the garrisons and his friends.

He learned to accept these with good grace, but next time, it would have to be a son. What Robert Rochfort wanted, Robert Rochfort got – whatever the cost.

Chapter Five

DISAPPOINTMENTS AND SUCCESSES

"Robert, what do you intend for Christmas?" asked Mary, one morning in late November.

"That, my dear, depends on you. What does the doctor say?"

Like many men, Robert's knowledge of, or interest in, a woman's health was cursory at best, and regarded as a subject best avoided. Unless, that is, it interfered with anything that he might want.

"He told me I am much improved, and I do indeed feel better."

"Excellent. We will return to Gaulstown for Christmas. I'll start making arrangements, and I suggest you do the same with Nurse and the servants."

With that, he turned and left the house to go back to the Castle.

In early December, the family and assorted servants and staff assembled on Gardiner Row and mounted several carriages and carts. This time, the trip was slower, due to the size of the party, and the fact that it included a wet-nurse and the baby.

The winter weather had been wet and breezy, and it was cold. When they dismounted at Gaulstown, the butler threw open the door to the largest saloon and dining room where a large fire burned. The travelling party paused to warm their hands, and the housekeeper took Mary, the nurse and the baby up to the rooms prepared for them.

Downstairs, dinner was soon ready. Mrs O'Mahoney had brought to the table the best the estate could offer. Robert and Mary dined on trout fresh from the lough, and the estate's own lamb (cooked in the French style), and washed down their dinner with a glass of claret. Mary had drunk little in her short time as an adult, and, after the exertions of the day, she felt her head spin.

"Robert, I need your help," she cried, grasping the table.

Robert looked at her and the empty glass and gave a small cynical smile. He pushed back his chair and strode to Mary's side, picked her up with ease and carried her upstairs to her room. His years of dalliance with a succession of mistresses paid off. He found it easy to remove Mary's dress, shift and undergarments, before joining her on the bed.

Mary was still awake, but barely conscious. She felt rather than saw Robert as he bent over her to kiss her, then lowered his lips to one of her nipples as he licked and bit it. Mary squirmed and uttered a half-hearted protest while feeling her juices flow despite herself.

"Mary, I'm your husband," growled Robert; as he licked, kissed and tasted every inch of her body. Mary felt herself trying to respond in kind, kissing his chest and exploring his body with her tongue in a way she had never done before. It didn't take her long until she pulled Robert onto her and into her. Robert filled her, and she felt every nerve in her body tingle and explode.

Seconds later, Robert rolled off her and turned away before leaving her side for his own bed. By the time he reached the door, Mary was asleep.

For the next few days, Robert came to her bed every night, desperate for her to conceive again. Much to his increasing annoyance, she failed to conceive that month, or for the next few months after that. Although he was assiduous about joining her in her bed, the attractions of Mary's young body were starting to pale.

Mary had previously believed that Robert's constant lovemaking was proof that he loved her. Gradually, as the weeks went by, she began to suspect that he was only enjoying her body for her to conceive another child. Away from her bed, Robert seemed cold and indifferent.

They were back in Dublin making the most of the season's social calendar.

"Robert," she announced one morning, "I think I may be with child again."

"Are you sure?" Doubt and annoyance crossed Robert's face, followed by a slow smile.

"I think so. I am two weeks late with my monthly time."

"Good. I will arrange for a Doctor at once."

The following morning the doctor arrived.

"My lady, how long is it since his lordship joined you in your bed?"

"He comes to my bed most nights. Well, at least two or three times a week."

"My lady, it is too early to say with certainty if you are with child again. Do you have any sickness in the morning? Does the sight of anything upset your stomach?"

Mary replied no to both questions.

"I'll return next week, and we can talk again. Do let me know if you are sick in the mornings."

A few days later, when she still hadn't begun to bleed, he pronounced her to be pregnant.

Both Robert and Mary were delighted.

"This time, it will be a son. I know it," Robert announced.

"But Robert, what if it's another girl?"

"It will not be a girl, Mary. This time, you are to give me a son."

"Robert, whatever God gives us, I will love it."

Mary wondered to herself just how little Robert knew of the realities of parenthood. Once again, she felt she was being forced to accept that Robert didn't love her.

"Robert," she pleaded. "Do you know, you have never, ever told me that you loved me?"

41

Robert looked at her in astonishment. His voice showed both anger and surprise.

"Love you? What are you talking about, woman? You are my wife. Mine. That is enough."

With that, he turned on his heel and stormed out of the house.

As in Mary's first pregnancy, Robert stayed away from her bed. Once again, she suffered morning sickness and the various cravings and inconveniences of pregnancy. She hoped to find this second pregnancy easier as she now knew what to expect. Jane, her baby daughter, was now walking and seemed fit and healthy. Mary saw her every day and loved her with all her heart.

Her feelings for Robert were also changing. She eventually realised he didn't love her, beyond her ability to give him a son. At the back of her mind was the memory of a pair of dark eyes, burning into her soul, and the heated touch of a pair of lips on her fingertips.

She paid two extended visits to Gaulstown while she was pregnant. Her natural youthful and open nature continued to charm the staff.

For the last two months of her pregnancy, Mary and Robert returned to Dublin and Gardiner Row. This time, worn down by pregnancy, Mary felt tired. All she could do was hope that her unborn child was a son. Robert would have his heir. Whether he would return to her bed was a matter for later.

For Robert, being in Dublin meant access to a better doctor and midwife, plus, of course, the constant companionship of his mistress. He had no intention of ever returning to Mary's bed unless she gave him another daughter. Should the child die, they would have another, and so on, until she gave him a son. If Mary died in the process, he would find another wife.

This lack of concern for others was a trait he had evinced all his life. His only considerations were his own wishes and desires.

As the days grew shorter, Mary felt herself growing larger and slower. Her pregnancy seemed interminable this time. Eventually, she noticed a tightening of the muscles around the baby, so different from the kicks she had felt for the last months. She summoned her maid and made her way upstairs to her bed. The midwife and doctor appeared after an hour. Dr Readon examined her.

"Your baby is on its way, but you are still some hours from delivering. Call me if you need me." The midwife took up residence in an armchair in Mary's room and ensured all was ready for the baby's arrival.

Late the following evening, Mary's contractions started. Her waters broke only a little time later, and the midwife fussed around her, telling her to rest and save her strength.

The butler sent a note for Robert, who returned from Dublin Castle to find the house in an uproar with servants heating water and running around with fresh towels. Again, the midwife forbade him access to Mary's room, telling him this was woman's work. He retired to his study and ate a cold dinner washed down with a glass of brandy while he awaited the birth of his longed-for son. He was asleep in his chair when he heard movement, looked up and saw the dawn lightening the sky through the windows. He went out into the hall and heard a noise from the first floor, then voices raised in excitement. He bounded upstairs and met Dr Reardon coming out of Mary's room.

"My lord, you have a son!" he exclaimed.

Robert went into Mary's room to find her propped up in bed nursing the infant in her arms. The midwife spoke.

"My lord, her ladyship has done well. You have a perfect son."

"Be quiet, woman," he snapped. The midwife turned and fled to the shelter of her chair. He turned to Mary, who offered him a tremulous smile. While tired and sore, she was sure he was pleased with her for giving him a son and heir.

"I have a son!" He repeated it louder. "I have a son – at last!"

Robert bent and kissed her brow, and looked down at the

baby.

"Have you given thought to his name?" Mary asked.

"Not yet," replied Robert. "We will wait a few days and decide before his christening." After another long hard look at his son, as if trying to find a family likeness, he turned and stepped out of the room, making as quiet an exit as he could, and made his way to the Castle to see Lord Cavendish.

"Your Grace, I have a son," he announced.

"Excellent," replied the Lord Lieutenant. "His Majesty will hear of this without delay."

"Begging your pardon, Your Grace, but why would His Majesty be interested?"

"My lord, not only have you retained His Majesty's friendship, it seems you share more than you realised. Last year a widow named Mrs Simpson became His Majesty's latest mistress. It appears she has mentioned your name, and to good effect."

"Louisa? Yes. I remember her well." Robert had the fondest memories of a buxom blonde widow who excelled in the carnal arts.

"The political situation here in Ireland remains stable while Scotland seethes. His Majesty's forces can only cope with one rebellion in the country at once. Hence the importance of making sure that Ireland remains calm and secure. While your task has not been difficult, we can maintain the peace here. In short, you have been lucky, and His Majesty is pleased."

Robert grinned. Royal acknowledgement for his efforts was beyond his wildest dreams. Such recognition could bring real advancement.

Lord Cavendish continued, "Make no arrangements for the christening until I advise you."

This had the effect of leaving Robert puzzled. He was a man who, in the ordinary course of events, liked to see everything planned and set before him. He descended to the officers' mess, to receive their congratulations. As men, they all understood the importance of having a son and heir.

He returned home to find Mary and the baby asleep. The next morning, he held his son in his arms for the first time.

"Mary, my dear, Lord Cavendish has asked me not to make any christening arrangements until he advises me. He is advising His Majesty of our son's birth."

He told Mary of his conversation with the Lord Lieutenant, omitting all reference to his former mistress. He did mention that he appeared to be enjoying His Majesty's favour.

His next duty gave him a twinge of perverse pleasure. He wrote to his brother George, to tell him that Mary had produced a son, and Gussie would no longer inherit. He took great pleasure in imagining George's face when he read this news.

The following week, Robert was summoned to the Lord Lieutenant's office. "I have here a missive from St James," his host announced. "His Majesty has graciously agreed to be your son's godfather."

Robert was astonished.

The Lord Lieutenant continued, "The christening will take place next Sunday in Christ Church Cathedral. His Majesty will not be attending, of course, but I will be standing as his proxy."

Robert knew that a proxy for a god-father was quite usual. The thought that his son would have a royal godparent, and so could expect additional honours and rewards, only heightened his pleasure.

"He must be christened George," he announced to Mary. "Anything else would be a snub to His Grace and to His Majesty."

Invitations to the christening were sent out to all the senior officers and officials, and to Robert's brothers. George accepted the invitation. While he disliked his brother, he relished the opportunity to mix with the great and the good. He had Army contracts to renew, and fodder and meat to sell to the garrisons. Besides which, Alice had made it perfectly clear that his life would not be worth living if he refused. She could never let an opportunity like this slip from her grasp.

Arthur was, as far as Robert knew, still stationed with the garrison in Gibraltar. In one of his infrequent letters, he mentioned how the engineers there were cutting through the rock to provide cannon firing positions over the town and bay. In his last letter, he mentioned his desire to see the baby being christened if possible, though Robert knew the chance of this happening was small. Service abroad in the Army took scant notice of the personal wishes of its officers.

While Mary privately thought there were already enough Georges in the family, her views counted for nothing in the face of having a royal godparent.

At the christening, held in Christ Church Cathedral, baby George was happy and hardly cried at all. The Dean conducted the service and was mercifully brief, and the company adjourned to Dublin Castle afterwards for a luncheon. When all the guests sat down, and were busy eating and talking, the noise level in St Patrick's Hall was extreme, but it fell quiet when the doors opened, and Arthur entered the room.

He looked very much as if he had been travelling for several days, and fatigue showed around his eyes. He strode over to the Lord Lieutenant and saluted, then turned and bowed low before Mary and his brother.

Robert gestured to the footmen, who quickly made room and laid a place for Arthur.

"Brother, to what do we owe the pleasure of your appearance?" said Robert, happy to see Arthur, but curious as to how he had managed to appear in such a dramatic fashion. "This is the second time you have managed to make an entrance like this."

"My apologies. I have been travelling for ten days," replied Arthur. "I was to deliver despatches to Whitehall, and completed my business last week, then came on here as soon as I could. It was only when I came to the Castle that I realised what day this was."

Arthur pulled himself together and forced himself to continue in as natural a manner as he could. "Now, it's a few weeks leave, and I'm posted to Athlone to be adjutant there."

Mary raised her head to look at him, and suddenly they looked at each other, and for an instant, they were alone in the world. The intensity of his gaze took her straight back to their first meeting. How different was that look to any she had ever received from her husband?

In London, Arthur had called into the Horse Guards to leave despatches from the garrison in Gibraltar. While waiting there, he found himself summoned by an usher, with instructions that he was to be taken to a special meeting. Puzzled, he was shown into a large office where an elderly gentleman was sitting at a desk. He gestured for Arthur to sit, and spent two minutes completing his letter, before sanding and sealing it.

"Major Rochfort. Let me introduce myself. My name is Stafford. Allow me to congratulate you on completion of your attachment in Gibraltar. You come highly recommended."

Arthur's chest swelled with pride. Praise like this was not common in the Army.

Mr Stafford continued, "My role here is specialised. However, I work in close collaboration with the Secretary of War. We like to try to assign officers where they will best be suited. You have family associations in the centre of Ireland, and our instructions are for you to proceed there. After a period of leave, you will take up a role attached to the Garrison Commander in Athlone. Your particular responsibilities are to keep a lid on Ireland."

"In what way, sir?"

Stafford explained the position of the Irish population, who were mainly Catholic. France was always a threat, and especially so with Scotland still in an uproar after the rising by the Old Pretender. News had reached Whitehall of his son, the Young Pretender, styling himself Prince Charles Edward Stuart. He was, apparently, known to Scots loyalists as 'Bonnie Prince Charlie'. This imposter was still only a boy, but the government was afraid that sentiment for a Catholic monarch would lead to Ireland becoming involved.

Arthur's family, Stafford continued, held a large part of the

County of Westmeath as their estates. They represented the area in the Irish parliament. Arthur's task was to ensure that central Ireland stayed loyal to the Crown.

"How many years is it since you have been in Ireland?" asked Mr Stafford.

"Two, sir."

"You will find many changes at home." Mr Stafford handed him two packets of orders. "These are for his Grace the Lord Lieutenant, and these are for your commander in Athlone. You will report directly to Colonel Monroe, the Garrison Commanding Officer. Your duties are clear and separate from your brother Robert's position."

"Sir?" asked Arthur, "What is it that you are not telling me?"

Mr Stafford looked at him intently. "Major, you have been recommended to us as an unusually astute young man. I see the reports did not lie. We need eyes and ears in Ireland, and you will be those eyes and ears. You must be aware that your brother Robert is the Muster Master for the area? You know he oversees all the recruiting in the area, for the garrisons at Athlone and Mullingar?"

Arthur nodded.

"Your brother George supplies both those garrisons with fodder, beef and other items, under various contracts. Our colleagues in the Treasury advise us, however, that they have concerns both with the amount and administration of these contracts. While I realise this is your brother, we do not want you to spy on him, but we do want – how can I put this? – to regularise the situation. Your whole family exerts a great deal of political power in Westmeath. Your brothers and your father before them were or are Members of Parliament for the county. I emphasise that we must have stability. See what you can find, and we may be able to bring your brother into line. Profit on a contract is natural, but the Treasury needs to reassure itself. Also, I want you to develop contacts in all the towns and parishes. All this will help us keep Ireland at peace."

"Thank you, sir. I'll do my best."

48

"A man can do no more than that, Major. Thank you for coming to see me, and I wish you a good passage home."

Arthur bade farewell and left, taking the stage the next day for Liverpool, and onward to Dublin. Throughout his trip, he mused on Mr Stafford and his instructions.

Chapter Six

ARTHUR, HAVING ARRIVED BACK IN IRELAND, LEARNS MUCH

The day after the christening, Arthur presented himself to the Lord Lieutenant at his offices in the Castle. He passed across his packets of orders, and Lord Cavendish and the Garrison Commander read them in detail and dismissed Arthur with hopes that he would enjoy his leave.

He returned to Gardiner Row to find his brothers breakfasting.

"So, Arthur, what are you to do?" asked George.

"I am going to take some leave. I need some horses, I must put Belfield House back into repair, and I want to get some hunting and fishing in."

"And what about your new post?" asked George.

Arthur explained as much of his new posting as he could. He could hardly tell them that he was to spy on them. He knew that George was prickly at best, and would be even more so now that his son had lost the chance of inheriting the title.

As his brothers finished breakfast, Mary came and joined them. Arthur explained again what he was planning to do over the next few weeks. As he talked, he watched Mary and reflected on his feelings for her. He looked at Robert and saw how his brother's eyes held no signs of emotion or care. Arthur knew that he had to look deep into his own soul. His immediate reaction was one of horror.

He had fallen in love with a married woman. Not just any woman, but his brother's wife.

He announced that he planned to leave the next day and arranged with Robert to use some of the horses from his stables. Arthur left Dublin the next morning, on a borrowed horse, with the rain falling softly.

The poor winter weather made the coach road seem longer. Arthur arrived at Gaulstown as the sun set. Even though he had been away for so long, the housekeeper still knew him, and her face lit up when she saw who it was.

"Mr Arthur! Oh, my lord, how many years is it? Come in, sir, come in. Come to the fire and warm yourself. Sarah, make Mr Arthur's old room up for him."

"Right, Mr Arthur, you sit in the drawing room, and a glass of brandy will be with you in a moment."

Arthur chuckled and smiled. He had always been a favourite with the staff.

"Mrs O'Mahoney, you never change. I'll be here for a few days. My brother and his wife will be with us in a week or so. I'll get out of your way, but I'd much prefer it if you brought me a dish of tea."

"Oh, Mr Arthur, it's good to see you again. Sure, and you are looking grand. I'll be bringing you your tea in a moment. Dinner will be served in an hour, so you have plenty of time."

The following morning, he had a horse saddled and rode across the fields to Belfield House, just two miles from Gaulstown and part of the Belvedere demesne. This was his own small manor-house, and in need of some repairs, but was fundamentally sound, and would provide Arthur with an excellent base.

Mrs O'Mahoney arranged for a couple to start work at Belfield House as Arthur's housekeeper and groom. Mr and Mrs Murphy had worked with her before, and she knew they were looking for a position. Besides, as Patrick Murphy had been in the Army, she thought he would easily fit into Arthur's requirements.

After established himself at Belfield, Arthur rode over to Mullingar as soon as he could. He found several friends and acquaintances serving with the detachment there. More

51

importantly, he contacted the West Meath Hunt and arranged to ride out with them twice a week until he left to take up his post in Athlone, planning in the meantime to buy a decent horse at the Mullingar market. It was the work of a moment to get hold of a fishing rod and tackle. He planned to try for some of the notorious Lough Ennell trout over the coming weeks.

For the next few weeks, life continued at a slow and even pace, with hunting and fishing for Arthur and the expansion of his house for George. Robert and Mary had decided to remain in Dublin. A wet-nurse was employed again, and baby George thrived. His mother, however, was suffering from a fever caught soon after the christening. She was forced to take to her bed, and the Doctor attended her every day.

For Robert, like most men of his time and age, anything beyond holding his infant to admire and to be admired by the females of the household was beyond him. For a son, however, nothing was too much trouble.

Again, he stayed away from Mary's bed. For him, the charms of Kitty and her fellow courtesans were far more arousing. Mary's sickness after the delivery gave Robert another reason to seek his comforts elsewhere. With a wife and baby in the house, he was more discreet than he had been previously, but even so, he still managed to slip away to see Kitty or one of her friends once or twice a week.

At the end of February, the Doctor caught Robert in the hall, as he left following a visit to check on Mary's condition.

"My lord, I am happy to tell you that your good lady is now well enough to travel. There is something you should know, though. This sickness almost certainly means she will be unable to conceive another child."

Robert mulled over the import of this news, but the next day gave instructions to move his family back to Gaulstown. With two young children in the train, together with nurses and servants, the whole move took more than a week

Mary came downstairs. "Mrs O'Mahoney? We need a bigger room for the nursery now. I believe the third bedroom along on the north side will be best."

"Begging your pardon, my lady, but the windows there are a terrible fit. The draughts blow something terrible. The room across on the other side will be better. It's the same size, and the windows are better. We get less wind on the east side, too."

"Then I'm sure that will be fine."

Mary spent several hours arranging for pictures to be hung and placing furniture in the best position.

Robert made several trips to Mullingar, some for the garrison, others to expand his stable. Irish bloodstock was well-known, and he managed to buy several hunters and hacks, and a good-looking team of four greys.

He also joined Arthur for several hunting and fishing trips on Lough Ennell. On most occasions, they could rely on a good fight with one or more of the local trout. They also made a valued contribution to the menu for dinner. Fallow deer roamed the demesne as well, and a good specimen would make a beautiful trophy, apart from providing meat for the household.

One morning when Arthur was at Gaulstown after a successful morning's fishing in the lough with Robert, the nurse entered the drawing room, carrying baby George and followed by an energetic two-year-old. This was the first time that Arthur had seen Robert together with Mary and the children, and it struck him what a perfect family they looked. Two beautiful children – at least as far as he could tell. He was the first to acknowledge that this was something he knew little about, and his brother and wife appeared happy and devoted to each other. At nights Arthur mulled over his position. He couldn't explain why he felt for Mary as he did, he only knew that he had found a kindred soul. A soul who was married, and to his brother.

Two weeks later, at the end of his official leave, he headed for Athlone and his new posting. The city was a good three hours' hard ride away, but he could get a change of horses at Kilbeggan and Moate if need be. The Rochfort name was enough to ensure that any horse would be sent back to Belvedere.

Athlone was the major city in the centre of Ireland, and the barracks occupied a large plot on the bank of the Shannon. The barracks were new, having been built after the Jacobite Wars. Arthur found himself given an office and tasked with meeting progressively with soldiers and officers. These came mostly from the small Protestant communities in villages in western Westmeath and Roscommon. Gradually, he built up a picture of life in the midlands of Ireland and discovered how many recruits were joining the army. He spoke with all the parish priests and vicars as he went around, trying to identify those with Jacobite leanings or any whose loyalty to the Crown might be questioned.

Mary was establishing a pleasant routine in Gaulstown. She had her children, a large (if extremely dilapidated) house, servants, maids and gardeners, the authority to buy anything she might need, and a husband with rank and title.

The one thing she craved was love. Robert had never returned to her bed once he knew for certain she was pregnant for the second time. At night, she would dream of the nights they had spent before she conceived, especially 'that' night when she had drunk too much. Why would he not return to her? She wanted to feel his arms around her and holding her, the hairs on his chest, the muscles in his body, his knees pressing hers apart before entering her. She wanted to feel complete again.

Robert started spending more time away. He would return to Dublin every two weeks, to meet with his colleagues and superiors at Dublin Castle. These duties took little of his time and allowed him to engage the services of a succession of mistresses. Even the long-suffering Kitty found herself dismissed and replaced by another actress, Chloe – a handsome brunette widow.

Chloe had lost her husband, a major in the infantry, to fever in the West Indies. She was more than happy to live under

Robert's protection. She also found herself drawn bit by bit into his world of domination and submission. She was submissive by nature, and dependent on Robert. Only once had she dared to complain, which spurred Robert into one of his rages. His blow caught her on the side of the head and knocked her to the floor, though fortunately, she was not visibly marked.

They were both more careful after that. Chloe never complained again, and Robert always made sure never to leave any signs that would prevent her going out in public.

Unbeknown to Robert, Arthur's success in working with the local farmers and priests alike did much to ease his own military duties. The general poverty of that part of Ireland meant that there was a constant supply of recruits. The resident battalions never fell far below strength, and a poor harvest could be guaranteed to bring their numbers up.

For Mary, that first year at Gaulstown should have been idyllic. She was the woman who had everything she could wish for. Everything that is, except the love and comfort of her husband. She still loved him and was prepared to forgive him any peccadilloes – if he would only return to her bed and make love to her as he could and should. Some weeks after they had returned to Gaulstown, she went so far as to enter his room shortly after he had retired for the night. The candles were still lit as Robert finished undressing. Mary approached him and tried to embrace him, opening her arms to put them around his chest.

Robert looked at her without an ounce of warmth. "What are you doing?"

"Only what any woman who loved you would do," she replied.

"Go back to your room!" he answered with ice in his voice.

Mary looked at him and saw no feeling in his eyes. "Why, Robert, why?" she asked.

"Madam, you have done your duty, as have I. My son is asleep in his nursery. That is all I want or need from you."

"Will you never come to my bed again?" she begged.

"No, and you should not be asking me this. Do you want

people to believe you a strumpet?"

Mary recoiled with horror and fled with tears in her eyes. After reaching her bed, she sobbed herself to sleep.

Against her better judgement, she found her thoughts turning towards Arthur. She found herself making comparisons between him and Robert, in which Arthur appeared better at every turn. But every dream would end with a harsh return to reality and a blinding realisation that she had married the wrong brother.

The following morning, she rose late. After visiting the nursery, she descended for breakfast to find that Robert had had his horses put to his curricle and was on the way back to Dublin. Mary knew at once that he was angrier than she thought.

That night in Dublin, after cursory calls into Gardiner Row and to the Castle, Robert went straight round to Chloe's lodgings. Later that night, as they lay entwined in her bed, he enjoyed telling Chloe of the events of the previous evening, taking great pleasure in describing how he had humiliated Mary. He also enjoyed watching Chloe's reactions, both horror and fascination, as he told her.

A week later, Robert returned to Gaulstown and surprised Mary when he walked into the house one evening. He had sent no word of his coming, but slipped back into his routine as if he had never been away. So the weeks turned into months, and Robert's trips became as regular as clockwork. He would be at home for some days and ride over to Mullingar to attend to his duties there. He would visit Athlone and stay for one or two days in the barracks. While there he would often see Arthur and would discuss with him the current situation with the population. They would also discuss whether the country was likely to rise in support of the Jacobite cause.

While support for the Jacobites may not have been evident, it was clear that here was an increase in robbery and theft. Miscreants, when found, would face a quick trial then death or transportation. For some of them, this almost seemed preferable to being left to starve. At least they and their families would have something to eat if they were sent to the New World or the Colonies. In the main, the cause of the poverty seemed to be due to greedy landlords increasing the rents paid by the tenant farmers.

Chief among these appeared to be their brother George, who was using this practice to increase his land holdings. He was now controlling several hundred small farms, which he was busy combining into large ones and installing new, well-off tenants.

Naturally, this put Robert and Arthur in an awkward position. One day in autumn they rode together to George's house. He was at home, although evidently preparing to leave. For once, there did not seem to be any alterations or remodelling going on. George waved them into his study with an impatient air and offered them a glass of sherry. This they both declined. It didn't seem appropriate, given their reason for calling.

Robert explained their concerns. He also emphasised that those in government shared these concerns. George turned red and looked as if he would explode, while Alice, his wife, entered the room and stood beside her husband.

He waited for Robert to finish, and spoke in icy tones.

"Leave my house at once! Coming here, spying on me. Everything I do is legal and above board. Robert, you've always had a jealous streak, and that's your problem. Because I run my estates in this way, and I prosper at the expense of lazy tenants, you are jealous. Well, I tell you – leave my house now. Arthur, you can get out too. You both come over here, playing at being soldiers."

The brothers looked at each other. They had not expected a response like this. It was evident they had hit a nerve, although they had never so far suggested that George had acted outside the law. The brothers offered a short bow to Alice, who stood there with a disapproving expression on her face. They turned, and with a curt, "Your servant, sir!" left the house.

On the road back to Gaulstown, they discussed George's reaction. Arthur undertook to make some more discreet enquiries as he went around the countryside.

At Gaulstown, Mary was waiting for them with lunch. She announced that she was planning to drive across to Rochfort House in the trap to see Alice.

"No, don't do that," Robert snapped. "Today would not be right for a visit." When Mary looked puzzled, he added, "George and I have had a difference of opinion over the management of his estate."

Mary's brow furrowed, but Robert offered no further explanation. When it became apparent that he wasn't going to add anything, she bade her farewells to Arthur and left to spend some time with the children. Arthur too left and headed back to Belfield House.

Life slipped back into its routine, although both brothers continued to make some discreet enquiries. George had made extensive enlargements to his estate; that much was clear to them both. Through his land agent, and by using his political influence as Member of Parliament, he had been able to buy land as tenants had abandoned or been thrown off their farms. George had also made some judicious loans to landowners in financial trouble. By foreclosing on those loans when they failed to meet them, he had increased his land holding by a considerable amount. This meant he also controlled much of the beef, horse, peat and grain trade in the area.

Late in 1739, the temperature started to fall. A freezing wind blew from the north, and many of the areas' rivers and lakes began to freeze.

In December, the family again packed up and returned to Dublin, ready for Christmas and the forthcoming season. Before they left, Mary was sitting with her children when she suddenly realised that, apart from Robert, the servants, and the occasional visit from Arthur, she hadn't spoken to another adult for several weeks.

The move back to Dublin was managed without a hitch. While it took a long day, even with daylight at its shortest, they could leave before dawn and be sure to get to Dublin by sunset. Robert noted, though, that the condition of the roads was worse than usual for the time of year.

Christmas that year at Gardiner Row was a happy affair. Mary was the hostess at several parties and dinners. Arthur attended several of these, although George and Alice failed to make the trip to town.

That winter, George Rochfort preferred to stay home and use his new income to design and plan a house of his own. This would rival and surpass that of his brother. Even though Robert held the title, George had now managed to make a far larger fortune. Turning this wealth into cash wasn't easy, but he reckoned that he could take enough income from his land holdings to build his house over the next four or five years.

Over Christmas, Mary managed to spend time with some of her friends from her childhood.

"Izzy, my love! It is a year since I saw you."

Isobel Fairfax crossed the room and embraced Mary, before stepping back to hold her at arm's length.

"Oh, Mary, you look tired, and you are so thin."

"I am tired. Two young ones and Robert being away much of the time make for an exhausting life. The move back to Dublin was hard this time too. I seem more tired than usual. I'll be here for at least two months, I expect, so I'll be better soon."

The two, who had been friends since childhood, exchanged news of Katherine Doyle and other mutual friends.

"Mary Carmichael has sailed to the Indies with her husband. He is to be stationed in Barbados. The slaves cause great problems there, it seems, and we have lost poor Anne."

Mary was shocked. "What happened?"

"She died giving birth to baby James. He is still alive, but Lord Allen is distraught. He has taken the baby and his nurse back to his parents in England."

The two friends were glad of the opportunity to talk face to face; occasional letters could not give a full picture of their former companions. Suddenly, Mary realised how lonely she had been over the last months. While she loved her children as much as any mother, they couldn't compensate for the loss of time with her friends.

Another fact became apparent after talking with other married women. Her own and Robert's marriage was exceptional in that he never came to her bed. She missed his lovemaking more than she could say. While some older friends accepted that their husbands' attentions would flag over time, Mary had only been married for four years.

She was beautiful and young. She welcomed her husband's attentions. So what was she doing wrong?

As the seasons changed and the New Year brought spring and a season of birth and renewal, she made up her mind to speak to Robert again.

Chapter Seven

FATEFUL MEETINGS
AND A CHILL WIND

When spring was in full flow, and all the roads were passable, Robert ordered the household to return to Gaulstown. This time, with the benefit of practice, the move was carried out with speed and efficiency. Over the following months, Robert and Arthur both found themselves increasingly busy, spending regular periods away on duty in Athlone and Dublin.

Winter that year struck with a vengeance, with icy winds and temperatures plummeting to ten degrees below zero. After a poor harvest, the tenant farmers found their fields flooded, and their cattle dying. Now they were faced with starvation.

Late one afternoon in January 1740, the Lord Lieutenant spoke with Robert. "You must get the word to the garrisons in Mullingar. All units of the army are to stay in barracks unless they have specific orders to go out on patrol. Nothing can move in this weather. Your job will be to ensure the garrisons have sufficient fuel and food, and you must obtain this locally. You can expect no help from Dublin."

"I'll leave in the morning," said Robert, and he waited for the clerks to prepare a written copy of his orders before going back to Gardiner Row.

"I am leaving for the garrisons at first light," he told Mary. "There will be trouble in the country with this weather, and the garrisons need my attention."

"Why?" Mary cried, alarmed.

"The weather," he replied. "The rivers are freezing over. We are getting reports of people dying of cold." He called for his valet. "Lay out a clean uniform for me tomorrow, and pack a portmanteau. I'll take it on a spare horse."

Next morning, he rode westwards at a steady pace, stopping at the inn at Enfield to change horses.

"Stay with the horses, and bring them on tomorrow," he told his groom. "I have arranged an additional mount for you, so you will ride with a spare."

The man nodded and turned away from the wind. In the stables, the groom rubbed down and fed the horses they had used so far. Even an experienced countryman such as him, who had known Ireland from birth, had never felt cold like this. As soon as he could, he finished bedding down the horses and headed inside to keep warm in front of the fire.

Robert wrapped his cloak around him and set off again, making good progress despite the icy wind. The guards on duty at the garrison in Mullingar pulled themselves to attention when they saw him. They were all wearing greatcoats as a shelter against the wind, with woollen scarves wrapped around their faces.

Robert went straight to the garrison commander, Colonel Bryant.

"There was little traffic on the road today. Nobody is going to try to rob someone in weather like this. Especially not an armed soldier on a decent horse."

"How is the countryside?" the Colonel asked. "We have not been able to patrol to the east for several days."

"The rivers are freezing. The farmers cannot get their peat in from the stacks, and water is becoming scarce."

"What more do we need to do here?" asked the colonel.

"The garrison remains your priority, of course," answered Robert. "We can do little to help the general populace. You must secure a water supply, and bring in whatever extra supplies of peat, fodder and foodstuffs you can find."

The next morning Colonel Bryant explained these instructions to his officers. The corn-chandlers and merchants of the town were summoned and instructed to ensure all stores in the garrison were full to overflowing. The soldiers made sure the wells in the barracks were clean, and any ice removed. A rota for breaking and removing ice every morning was set up. As soon as these preparations were completed, the garrison troops were, with some exceptions, restricted to the barracks, but those with homes and families in the town could stay with them. They found themselves twice as busy making sure their homes were adequately supplied with fuel, food and water.

Nobody, not even the eldest, could remember cold like it. Out in the countryside, families were forced to burn much of their stocks of peat. Prayers were said in all the churches, both Protestant and Catholic, for an end to the freeze.

In Dublin, Mary found life quiet and subdued. Word came from the Castle that they needed Robert to stay Mullingar. He would not be returning before the end of the freeze.

Fuel was running out. Coal and wood for cooking were becoming difficult to find. Even peat was hard to get. The ruts in the road were too deep and hard for the carts to move. The Liffey itself froze, and ships could not get up to the wharves to unload.

Mary moved the children and their nurse into one room with her. The children shared her bed to help them all keep warm. During the day, they spent all their time in the kitchen. Where possible, Mary allowed the servants to go home to their families in the countryside.

"What food do we have?" she asked the housekeeper.

Mrs O'Mahoney answered, "Well, 'tis getting scarce, but we have enough flour for bread for a few weeks. There's always potatoes and such like. For sure, we'll manage."

But only two days later, disaster struck. Not only for Mary and the Dublin household, but through the city and most of Ireland. The Great Frost had spoilt the potatoes stored on the farms. The cold was so severe the local people could not get their potatoes from the store, and those they could get out were black and rotten. The cattle and pigs were starving to death. Some meat came into the city, but it was expensive and of very bad quality.

In short, the people were dying by the hundreds.

Straight away Mary put the entire household, including the children, on short rations to eke out their supply of food. Mrs O'Mahoney was a marvel at producing something edible from very little, but there was no enjoyment in the food. Even milk for the children was becoming impossible to find.

Robert, for his part, found himself working long days in Mullingar. The garrisons were also hit by the famine, even with military storehouses to fall back on. Supplies of salt pork and beef (some of it of most doubtful vintage) were dug out of the stores. Getting water for cooking and drinking was a major problem, with Dubliners melting cauldrons of ice every day.

Soon the peat for the fires started to run out. One day, when the wind had dropped, Robert rode out to Gaulstown, calling at Rochfort House on the way. He found his brother and his family with well-stocked larders and stores. The house was warm, and there seemed little sign of the famine.

Robert asked George how he had managed to ward off the effects of the famine.

"Simple, Robert. Simple," he replied with a smile. "I bought several farms last year, and I evicted their tenants. They had a choice. They could leave with their miserable possessions, or leave with the same possessions but earn a few coppers moving their stores of peat and oats to Rochfort House."

Robert shook his head and remounted his horse. On his way to Gaulstown, he saw several bodies at the side of the road, all frozen hard. Glancing over the hedges into the fields he saw the carcases of several animals. A small flock of ravens flapped from carcass to carcass, pecking lazily at the frozen remains. Even these resourceful birds found difficulty finding any nourishment here.

His family houses at Gaulstown and Belfield House were locked, barred and bolted, with their servants dispersed to their home villages. Robert carried out a cursory check of the outside, but the extreme cold was so bad that even the local criminals were staying at home and concentrating on staying warm.

The garrison received irregular dispatches from Athlone and Dublin. Athlone was in much the same state as Mullingar. If anything, the loss of life within the town was even worse. The River Shannon was frozen over. People were using the ice to make a shortcut across the river. The local population had stripped many trees and bushes of reachable foliage in a desperate attempt to find fuel. Again, here, animals were dying of starvation in the fields. Supplies of oats and corn were fast running out.

They heard from Dublin that the Lord Lieutenant had banned any vessel exporting grain from the country. Some of the local priests and bishops undertook what little relief they could.

In Dublin, Mary, her children and the small group of servants that were still there watched as the streets filled with people protesting at the lack of food.

"What do they want, ma'am?" asked the children's nurse.

"Bread, Nurse. Bread or oats," replied Mary.

The crowd headed down the street towards the river and towards the Castle, but dispersed as night fell and the temperature dropped. Mary was sure they would be back sooner or later.

One day in February, a horse drew up at the house, and a rider dismounted and entered the hall.

"Mary! Danvers! Anyone?" he shouted.

There was no sign of the usual dull hum of conversation. No sounds coming from the kitchen. No children's voices. He ran downstairs to the kitchen. In there, making bread, was Mrs O'Mahoney, with her arms floury from kneading the dough,

"Where is everyone?" cried Robert. "Where is Danvers?"

At the butler's name, Mrs O'Mahoney's face fell. "Ah, sir. Mr Danvers took and died in the frost."

Robert's face now also fell. "And Mrs Rochfort?"

"She is grand, sir. The children too."

"Where are they?" asked Robert.

"In the park, sir, walking with Nurse."

At that moment, he heard the door open, and Nurse's voice calling to the children, followed by Mary giving instructions to them all. Robert walked out into the hall and seized his son from his nurse's arms. He hugged the boy until he started to complain, and did his best to free himself from his father's grip.

Mary ran to Robert's side and took the baby from him. Soon peace was restored.

Jane, now three years old, hid behind the nurse's skirts, looking out from behind her at this strange and unfamiliar man,

"What happened to Danvers?" he asked.

"He couldn't stand the cold. Two weeks ago, he didn't wake in the morning. The housekeeper went to his room and found him lying stiff and cold in bed."

"And the rest of the staff?" asked Robert.

"All safe as far as we know. I sent most of them back to their villages. They could care for their families there, and they could get peat for their fires."

"When do they come back?" asked Robert.

"Soon, I hope. You know the state of the roads."

"Indeed. I rode in on the post road this morning. It is a morass and still frozen in places. It is almost unusable because of the ruts and holes."

After a simple lunch of bread, cheese and cold sliced beef, Robert rode across the city to the Castle and headed up to the state apartments. He was announced at once and led into the Lord Lieutenant's office.

"Welcome to Dublin, my lord. Now tell me if you will, how goes the garrison?"

"Much reduced, Your Grace. We have lost a quarter of the strength. It is the same in the countryside. When I rode here, there were bodies of men and beasts lying in the fields."

"What do you know of Athlone?"

"The same, Your Grace. The country is bare. Many have died; others have fled to the coast to take a ship."

"We have a new situation. Tell me, what, if anything, do you know of Captain Jenkins?"

"That name means nothing, Your Grace. What regiment is he from?"

"Not a regiment, but a ship. Captain Jenkins was in command of the sloop *Rebecca* and was taken by the Spaniards in the West Indies. They sliced off his ear, and he petitioned Parliament in London. Consequently, we are now at war with Spain."

"And how does that affect us here, sir?"

"You will be busy this year, my lord. The Secretary of the Army requires you to send two companies from your garrison to Maidstone. He will require the same from Athlone."

"How soon do you want them to embark, Your Grace?"

"Within a month, if possible."

"That will leave the garrison seriously undermanned, Your Grace."

"So you will need to recruit replacements. All those who enlist will at least get fed. Given the state of the country, that might be attractive."

Robert left the Castle and returned to Gardiner Row. Mary was waiting there for him with the children.

"I must leave again," he announced.

Her face fell.

"It seems the country is at war with Spain."

"When do you go?"

"Tomorrow, at dawn. The garrison is to send two companies to England. I will be sending out the recruiting men immediately."

"But the people. They are dying in the fields."

"Better they die there than the country dies. This is war. We have no choice in the matter."

"When do we return to Gaulstown?"

"In a month. You will hear from me before then."

"But what of Arthur? Have you heard from him?"

"He is alive. The garrison in Athlone has suffered as we have. They too have to send two companies of men to

England."

"But what about the servants?"

"What do you mean, the servants?"

"Danvers is dead; we still have not heard from many of them. We don't know how they have survived back in the country."

"Madam, that is your job. I have a task for the garrisons and must find and recruit a thousand men. You must find and employ some servants. Do not speak of this to me again."

With that, he turned and walked out of the house to his horse, mounted and rode west towards Enfield and Mullingar.

Mary watched him go. Her face crumpled, and tears rose to her eyes. She reached for the handkerchief in her reticule, wiped her eyes and then sat up straight and rose to her feet.

"Right! Children? Mrs O'Mahoney?"

Moments later Jane and George ran through the door and into her arms, as Nurse followed them into the room. Mrs O'Mahoney brought up the rear.

"His lordship has had to go straight back to Mullingar. Unfortunately, we are left to manage matters here ourselves. We must stay on short commons until the weather breaks."

Mary sat with the children. Could Robert not see the problems they had? There was no food in Dublin. Nothing was coming into the country. The city was filling up with rogues and vagabonds. The weak – both human and animal – had died in the Great Frost. Those that remained were those who would fight to stay alive and steal from anyone. As yet nobody had tried to steal from Gardiner Row, but reports were reaching Mary's ears of robberies and riots in the city.

At the end of April, the freeze broke. The Liffey started to flow again, and blocks of ice floated down the river to the sea. The rising temperature unfroze the wells, and the kitchen maids could again bring up water in a bucket.

Mary called for Mrs O'Mahoney. "How do I get a

replacement for dear Danvers?" she asked the housekeeper.

"Why, ma'am, I was thinking the same. 'Tis not only a butler you'll be needing but a couple of maids and footmen as well."

"How so?"

"Well, three of the maids have sent word that they are on their way. But I hear that a groom and a footman and two other maids perished in the cold, and that one of the other menservants has left for America."

"Where can we find replacements?"

"Well, I'll be making some enquiries. I do know a male relative at home who is seeking to become a butler."

"Send him to me," replied Mary.

The following week, Mrs O'Mahoney presented Mary with a middle-aged man with a friendly face.

"This is my cousin, Michael Pearce," she said. "He has been working as a gentleman's gentleman for some time now."

"Why did you leave that gentleman's service?" Mary asked him.

"Well, ma'am, the gentleman died in the frost, so he did."

Mary noted down Pearce's details. "I will give you a month's trial. If your work is satisfactory, you may have the position of butler permanently."

"Begging your pardon, ma'am, but what would you be paying me?"

Mary looked at Mrs O'Mahoney. She was only beginning to come to terms with household accounts. "One moment, please. Would you wait outside?"

Pearce left the room.

"Mrs O'Mahoney. This is the first time I have engaged a butler. What do I pay him?"

"Well, ma'am, you pay me a guinea a month. He should have the same."

Pearce was called back into the room and declared himself happy to be engaged on those terms, starting the following Monday. Between them, Pearce and Mrs O'Mahoney were soon able to engage replacements for the missing staff from their own extended families.

Life in Dublin was slow to return to normal. Meat was now scarce, as there was no grain to feed the beasts. Potatoes had rotted in the ground. At least the melting ice had allowed the watermills to work again, and grain was being milled, but the price of flour for bread was climbing higher and higher every week. A quartern loaf, which had previously cost a penny, was now costing as much as sixpence.

One day in March 1741, when it seemed spring had returned to Ireland, Mary was walking in the gardens with Nurse and the children when she heard the roar of the crowd. They turned and fled back to the house, passing groups of men, unarmed, and most looking starving. She could see little sign of any organisation among them, or of anything resembling weapons or arms. As they entered the hall, Mary was sure she heard the sound of shots from the road.

Later that day, Robert arrived back with no word of warning.

"Well, that should stop them," he said.

"Stop what?" asked Mary.

"The mob, seeking free food."

"But they are starving. Nobody can afford to eat."

Robert turned to her and scowled. His voice hardened, and his face showed not an ounce of sympathy for the starving. "Nobody can afford to riot," he snarled.

"Why are you here?" asked Mary.

"I have brought two companies of infantry to embark for England. They will board in two days' time, and march for the depot at Maidstone."

"But what of the fighting outside? We heard guns."

"You will hear no more guns today. It seems I arrived in perfect time. The mob had assembled and were moving towards the river. We marched to cut them off and stopped them at Smith Field. A few hasty fellows fired their guns, but two volleys from my men soon put a stop to them."

"But Robert, they seemed mostly unarmed."

"They are now. We arrested several and took them to the Castle. They will see how His Majesty deals with rioters."

"But what will happen to them?"

"Oh, the ringleaders will hang. The courts will sentence the others to be transported."

Seeing his eyes light up as he described their fate, Mary shivered, and not from the cold.

"I have engaged new servants," she remarked.

"I am glad to hear it. I was surprised I had to tell you to do it. I expect my wife to run my establishments."

Mary's face fell. She had hoped for some words of appreciation. It was as if she was simply part of the furniture.

"Right. We leave for Gaulstown in two days. I am off to the Castle." With that, Robert turned on his heel and walked out of the room. She neither saw nor heard anything of him until noon the next day, when he appeared in the hall and demanded breakfast.

"Where have you been?" she cried. "We were worried."

"Never ask me such questions, madam. Where I have been or where I shall go is no concern of yours. I advise you not to worry on my behalf." Robert sat down to a breakfast of bread and fried pork. "What is this?" he demanded.

"Robert, there is famine in the city. There is little food available for anyone. There is nothing left of the money that you left me."

He stood up. "Very well, be packed ready for tomorrow. I am going back to the Castle. At least I can eat well there." He strode out of the room without a backward glance.

Mary looked at the door as it closed behind him. Is this what her life had become? While she loved her children dearly, she knew there was a gaping hole in her life. When she talked with those of her friends who were still in Dublin, for them, marriage was far more than the relationship that she had with Robert. He spoke to her with less feeling than he spoke to his groom or the servants.

Robert returned to the Castle and was shown up to the Lord Lieutenant's suite. He gave Robert a broad smile and offered him a glass of wine.

"Thank you, Your Grace."

"No, we thank you, my lord. Your companies are already

on board. They seem to be reasonably fit and healthy, and they will be most welcome in Maidstone."

The two men made small talk and discussed the requirements to replace those of the infantry who had died, deserted or had been discharged. After another glass of wine, both men descended to the officers' mess for dinner. There the fare was a lot more substantial than was available at home, and Robert dined his fill on chicken, mutton and salmon. After dinner, he walked around to his mistress's house.

Chloe opened the door to him.

"You look thin," remarked Robert, brusquely.

Chloe looked at him with a puzzled expression. "My lord, all are thin in Dublin now. Bread is dear, meat also. We have had a famine here."

"The price you pay for bread is no concern of mine," he stated. "The price I pay for you is." He pulled her into his arms and devoured her lips. Chloe took his coat and shirt off, put her arms around him, and dug her nails into his back. He welcomed the pain. In the morning, his back would be marked with scars. Their clothes fell to the floor, and Robert fell on her, holding her down and entering her again and again. She was powerless to move.

Eventually, satiated, Robert rolled off her. She rose and reached for a gown, before stretching her arm out for a bottle of wine.

She poured them both glasses and turned to him. Her face might be drawn and thin and her ribs visible beneath her robe, but she clearly knew her value to Robert. She turned and bent over before him.

"Punish me, my lord. Show me how bad I have been to you."

Robert struck her hard, several times, leaving the imprint of his fingers on her buttocks. Chloe looked around with the trace of a smile on her lips, and Robert seized her by the hips and pulled her towards the bed.

In the morning, he rose at dawn, tossed a purse onto the table and left.

For Mary, it was back to a life of intense loneliness. She filled her days with her children and running the household, but after George had ordered Robert and Arthur from his house, it was impossible for her to visit Alice. Not that she wanted to; she was irritated in the extreme by Alice's incessant complaints and her railing against what she saw as the unfairness of their situation. Her and George's son Gussie could no longer inherit the title, Robert was building his hunting lodge, and, although this was unspoken, Alice seemed out of all patience with her husband, no matter how much money he was making.

Mary tried making more visits to Mullingar and to the garrison there. Yet, as the wife of the former local Member of Parliament, and the sister-in-law of another, her opportunities for friendship were limited. It was easier to be friends with the wives of officers at the garrison, but there were few of these. Most officers were unmarried or had left their families in England. There were occasional visitors from other manor-houses in the area, but Robert seemed to have lost the ability to be hospitable. He was spending more and more of his time in Dublin.

When there, Robert spent whatever time he could in the arms of his mistress.

Chloe was also showing herself to be another excellent actress, and would throw herself into most of whatever requests Robert made of her.

She freely acknowledged that her patron had a cruel streak, which seemed to grow worse as time passed. Where once a playful slap was fun, now Robert was threatening to use his belt on her. That was a step Chloe was unwilling to take.

One evening Robert asked her how she spent her time when he was away from Dublin. He expected her to reply that she spent it waiting for his return. Unfortunately, she made the mistake of telling him she would go out to the theatre, or to meet friends, or (even worse) to meet other gentlemen. There were regular performances at the Theatre Royal with farces, classics, comedies from the Restoration and musical items. The theatre was an infamous venue for gentlemen to meet women of a particular class, even when other ladies were present. For dashing widows and married women whose husbands were away, the theatre brought with it the chance of amorous dalliance. This would always bring that eternal question; would the lady welcome the gentlemen's attentions?

Chloe's admission that she would visit the theatre piqued Robert. He started to question her, and she admitted to having met several gentlemen more than once. Robert's eyed darkened, and his hand swung around with full force. It caught her on the side of the head, and she fell over into a crumpled heap on the floor.

Robert sat in a chair watching her rise to her feet and looking dizzy. At the same time, he could feel a strange warmth invading his loins. "Get up!" he ordered. There was no disobeying him when he used this tone.

"Come here!" She moved slowly towards him.

He drew back his hand and dealt her another blow on the side of the head, and she fell to the floor again.

"Remember this. I own you. I own you every hour of the day. You will never, ever entertain another man again. Tell me this. Did you entertain him here?"

"No," she replied, dragging herself up into a chair.

Robert stared at her, feeling the flush of warmth all over his body after the rush of adrenalin had made him strike out. "Drink this," he said, thrusting a glass of brandy into her hand and watching as she gulped it down.

"Come here," he commanded, grasping her wrist and pulling her towards him.

George's sale and purchase of land had an unexpected consequence. His land agent split the acreage up into small park-sized estates, which wherever possible were sold to wealthy English gentlemen who wished to purchase an estate in Ireland for hunting or fishing. At first, this was a success. Several English Protestant families moved into the area and began to build modest country houses and hunting or fishing lodges. After buying their estates, they had little enough left to use in creating anything as magnificent as Belvedere.

Gradually, more and more families moved into the area. Mary was delighted, convinced that the new neighbours would mean new friendships. She still felt lonely after seeing Robert depart for Dublin or Athlone.

Arthur was one of the most regular visitors. Although his work often took him away from the area, he would always call at Gaulstown when he returned.

One day in summer he arrived and found Mary in the drawing room, weeping into a handkerchief. He heard her muffled sobs as he opened the door, and strode to her side.

"Why, Mary. What is wrong?"

Mary shook her head, finding difficulty in speaking. She was terrified of blurting out the real reason for her unhappiness – Robert's physical coldness to her.

"Oh, Arthur. It's nothing. It is only that Robert left for Dublin two days ago, and I was feeling a little low. You must forgive me feeling sorry for myself."

Arthur put his arms around her and hugged her, before letting her go and sitting her on the sofa. His tones held purely brotherly concern, but Mary's heart beat faster in her breast, even after such a short embrace.

"Do not concern yourself, Arthur. Robert will be back soon." Mary knew in her heart that she could never be disloyal to Robert. While Robert did not seem to love her, Mary was sure that she loved him; after all, she had given him two children. She was ready to forgive him any peccadilloes if only he would take her in his arms and make love to her as she knew he could. She would remember for the rest of her life the night she had responded so wantonly to his lovemaking.

"You must stay for dinner," she said.

"Of course," replied Arthur, "You need someone to cheer you up."

When Robert returned the following week, Mary told him

of Arthur's visit. "He stayed for dinner and rode home by moonlight. We had a most amusing time."

Robert professed himself delighted. When they met a few days later, he told Arthur so.

"Please, feel free to stop and dine whenever you are free. You do me a favour. It is much more pleasant if Mary is in a good humour when I am home. There is nothing I like less than a woman with the megrims."

Chapter Eight

COLD WEATHER AND A COLDER HEART

Spring eventually arrived, and the entire household made ready to depart for Gaulstown and the summer. Robert had suddenly announced their return without any discussion or warning. At Gardiner Row, all was a cacophony of noise and movement. Robert's carriage was ready in front of the house while the servants loaded two carts with their baggage.

Robert mounted his favourite bay hunter (now thin and out of condition) then bowed his head towards the window of the carriage, where Mary, Nurse and the children were waiting.

"We shall stop for lunch at Enfield," he announced, then sat up and cantered off, his groom hurrying behind him.

The journey to Enfield seemed interminable. Traffic on the road seemed heavier than on previous occasions. They had to stop to allow some detachments of soldiers marching towards Dublin. Families were also on the road, sometimes with a handcart, but more often with their possessions on their backs.

"Where are they going?" Mary mused.

"To America, ma'am," replied Nurse. "Or to England."

"But why? This is their home."

"In America and England, they can eat. Here, in this benighted island, they can only starve."

At Enfield, the innkeeper showed the party into a private room that Robert had arranged for them. A tolerable lunch was waiting, but of Robert, himself, there was no sign. "His lordship stopped, ate a quick meal, told me to make this room ready, and left," the innkeeper told them.

"When was this?" asked Mary.

"Oh, about an hour ago," replied the innkeeper, although Mary got the impression this was his stock response to any question of time.

Another full hour passed before Mary, and the children had finished their lunch and could resume their trip. The groom advised her that the inn had not been able to offer them a change of horse, but their horses had been rested and had had a feed of oats. Like all Ireland, the inn was short of provender for both horses and men. Mary couldn't help but notice the number of beggars outside the inn. Many were children, and all appeared thin and ragged.

The party continued the journey through the afternoon, arriving at Gaulstown before nightfall. Robert had arrived two hours earlier, changed horses, and ridden on alone to the garrison.

The housekeeper welcomed them all. She'd had no warning of their impending return, but Robert's arrival earlier had allowed her some time to get rooms opened and aired. Mary and the children took up residence in their old bedrooms. These had the charm of familiarity, and it was the work of a moment to unpack. Mary's maid would arrive the next day, but she was perfectly at home looking after herself with Nurse fussing over the children. They seemed to have taken the carriage trip very much in their stride. Indeed, Jane was full of questions about the horses, and about the beggars they had seen, and the families trudging towards Dublin.

"Do you have everything you need for the children, Nurse?" Mary inquired anxiously.

"To be sure, they're grand. The carts will be here tomorrow with the rest of their baggage. They'll be asleep soon."

After a lonely dinner, Mary too went to bed. Although sleep came quickly that night, she couldn't help but reflect on Robert, his behaviour, how he seemed to regard her, and how (if possible) she could change this.

Over the coming months, they saw Robert infrequently. He called when he rode over to Athlone, but most of his time was spent at the garrison.

The tenants of all the Rochfort estates struggled to survive. While they had enough peat to warm themselves, much of their seed-corn had been eaten. When Robert went around his own estate with his land agent Flynn, they found some of the smaller farms deserted.

"Where are these people?" asked Robert at one farm close to Gaulstown. His voice betrayed his irritation. He had hoped that all his own farms would be working normally by now.

"All dead, my lord."

The land itself looked burnt by the frosts. Even where they had been sown, the corn and oats were hardly growing, and the potatoes were rotten in the potato-clamps.

"Dead also?" asked Robert, as they arrived at another deserted farm.

"No sir, gone to America from Cork."

The famine continued throughout the summer. They heard accounts of other riots in Dublin and other cities, although not put down with the same savagery exercised by Robert. Travel by road was no longer safe for the casual traveller. Brigands and thieves stood by to rob anyone they thought might have food or money – as Robert himself was soon to discover.

One night, as he was riding back from Athlone, a man jumped up from the ditch beside the highway and tried to seize his bridle. A second man followed the first one into the road. Robert calmly drew a pistol and fired at the first beggar, who screamed and let go. The second robber tried to grasp Robert and pull him from his horse. But Robert spurred his horse forward, then drew his sword, and with a cry of "There will be no highway robbery around here!" turned and slashed down at the second man, almost severing the thief's arm.

By now both men were screaming for help.

"Certainly," said Robert, and ran them through with two quick thrusts of his sword, before calmly continuing his journey home.

That night, at Gaulstown, he told Mary of the attack.

"But what did you do?" she asked.

"What do you mean, 'What did I do'? They were dead. I did nothing and came home."

Mary looked at him, silently appalled.

Reports of robberies continued through the summer. Even though the weather was good, the following harvest was poor, and hunger continued throughout the land. But it hardly affected them; Robert's land-agent made sure the rents were paid on time, and that he obtained suitable quantities of peat and grain for the house.

Arthur, meanwhile, was having the same problems as Robert. He had had to arrange for two companies of infantry to march to Dublin for the war. Hardship in Athlone was even worse than in Mullingar. Many more farms lay empty and idle, and the price of bread and other foodstuffs was exorbitantly high.

While life at Gaulstown seemed to be returning to normal, many of the neighbouring houses remained unoccupied. In several cases, the families living there had gone over to England, where conditions were not so bad.

One day, with summer in full bloom, Mary was walking in the garden. The sun was shining, and the children were playing happily with Nurse. Mary heard horses and walked around to the front of the house. There she found not Robert but Arthur. Her face burst into a smile. Arthur's arrival never failed to lighten her spirits. He was famous for being agreeable and entertaining company and had the happy knack of never outstaying his welcome.

Arthur left his horse with a groom and picked up baby George, who now was just able to walk. With the child in his arms, he walked over to her.

"Dear Mary. How are you?"

She thought for a little. "Changed," she replied. "And how are you?"

"We are all changed. Such a winter as this would alter any

man or woman. Oh, Mary, this is a benighted island indeed."

"You look thinner. Your hair seems to have a touch of grey. Are you not well?"

"Me? Never better. Compared to most people, that is. It has been a devil of a business, and I fear it is not over yet."

"How so?" she asked.

"The harvest will be terrible. The cows are not in-calf. Next year there will be no milk and little food for man or beast."

Mary was alarmed. "But what about the people? What about the farms?"

"They must do what they can. A lot of farmers have given up. Some have joined the Army. I thought we might have to send out the press gangs to replace the companies we sent to England, but it seems everyone wants to take the King's shilling and declare themselves as Protestant. That way at least they get food. The Duke of Norfolk's Regiment is fully mustered here, I am happy to say."

Mary smiled. "Come indoors. I will order tea."

Sitting in the drawing room, Arthur looked at his sister-in-law. While all had suffered in the famine, it seems Mary had suffered more than most. She was painfully thin, and she looked terribly care-worn.

He searched her face for signs of strain and lowered his eyebrows.

Mary looked at his face and saw him looking at her closely.

"You asked me how I was, and I answered that I was changed. In truth, it is much worse!" she burst out.

"Why ever not?" asked Arthur.

"I cannot confide in anyone how I feel. I honestly believed we should all die during the last winter. Now you tell me we should expect more famine this coming winter. I am worried to death about the children, and,,," She faltered.

"And what?" asked Arthur.

"It's Robert. He has forgotten me."

"What do you mean?"

"Arthur, do you know how long it is since Robert came to my bed?"

As soon as the words had left her lips, Mary could sense Arthur's embarrassment. She was at once solicitous. "No, it is wrong of me. We must never speak of this again."

"But Mary, the light has gone from your eyes. You are still young and beautiful; you have two exceptional children. He must be mad."

"No, we must not speak of this. Please go."

Arthur stood up, grasped Mary's hands with his own for an instant, then turned to leave. As he mounted his horse, he swung around to look at her.

"Please come again," she said, in a voice so quiet that he could barely make out the words.

Arthur looked away and rode off back to Belfield House, where he spent a disturbed and dream-filled night, with the picture of Mary visiting his dreams. The following day, he rode to the barracks at Mullingar to meet with his brothers in arms. There the talk was all about the new war with Spain and the prospects for service overseas. The officers of the Duke of Norfolk's Regiment detachment in Ireland were sure they would deploy into Europe. For a career infantry officer, a war represented the only real prospect of promotion or advancement.

Arthur was more sanguine about the war. As a garrison officer, he would not be posted overseas in normal circumstances. He was now as busy as he had ever been. Although the current war was with Spain, it was known that the French were recruiting again. Arthur had found that the best way of avoiding losing recruits to the French was to take them into the garrison. A couple of pints of the finest ale and they would usually sign to take the King's shilling.

That week, when the brothers were alone, Arthur cautiously brought up the subject of Mary's unhappiness.

"What do you mean, she is unhappy?" Robert snapped.

"The life has gone out of her. She is like a candle that has been blown out."

Robert paused before replying with an icy tone in his voice. "What business is it of yours?"

"None, only I remember her as full of spirits and life. That has changed."

"I would thank you for keeping your nose out of my affairs," replied Robert, sharply.

There was little Arthur could do but to consent. Interfering between a man and his wife was unthinkable.

When Robert was next at home, he remembered Arthur's words, and his face darkened. With ice in his voice, he spoke to Mary. "What have you been saying to Arthur?"

Mary went still as stone, and her face went white. She turned away from Robert so that he would not see her change of expression.

"Why, nothing. Why do you ask?"

"He tells me you are like a candle that is snuffed out or some such rubbish."

"I cannot think what he means," she whispered.

"Let me make it clear. You are my wife. You are the mother of my son. You live in my house and live wholly at my beck and call. In short, Mary, remember that you are mine in all things."

"Yes, Robert, of course!"

"Now leave me. I am in Dublin tomorrow."

She left and returned to her bedroom. Sarah, her new maid, helped her undress.

"Sarah, are you married?" she asked.

"No, ma'am!"

"But you wish to be, don't you?"

"Yes, ma'am, some day."

"Are you walking out with anyone yet?"

"Well, there is someone," the girl replied. "Simon, one of the grooms."

"I've seen him. He seems nice. Do you love him?"

"I think so," replied Sarah. "He says he loves me."

"Before you marry, make sure that you love him with all your heart. Make sure you know that he loves you. I hope you can believe what he tells you."

"I hope so too, ma'am,"

Sarah curtsied and left the room, feeling thoroughly alarmed. She had never heard Mary speak like this. She thought she did love Simon, but, in truth, she didn't know yet if he loved her in return.

Mary went to bed with a heavy heart. While she slept, she dreamed of Arthur carrying her off on his horse.

When she awoke, a gentle rain was falling: the sort of rain which can soak a man to the skin but without it appearing to be raining hard. A soft day, as the local people would say. But the clouds were a hard grey, and in her eyes, they seemed as hard as Robert's heart.

Sarah came in to help her dress, but Mary felt this was not the time to continue their conversation of the previous day.

The days passed, and her loneliness increased. Few if any visitors came to Gaulstown. Occasionally she would have the carriage harnessed and make the drive into Mullingar, but even there, the wives of the garrison officers that she had known were no longer around. Most had gone to England, with some of the companies transferred to Maidstone. One or two had died, and others had gone back to England. Their husbands considered Ireland to be a bad place for their families while the threat of famine continued. Mary's heart sank at the thought of having to make a whole set of new friends.

As August faded into September and harvest time approached, it was evident that this would be a bad year. Farmers were selling their cattle, and the price of flour was still climbing. At least this year they had a good stock of peat; this lay drying in stacks close to the back of the house.

Robert, meanwhile, continued to spend most of his time in Dublin.

Arthur rode up to Gaulstown on a morning in October. Duties in Athlone had kept him occupied through the whole of the summer. In addition to keeping the peace, his duties included ensuring the storerooms in the barracks at Athlone were full. He took the precaution of acquiring extra barrels of oats and corn. He was still hoping to buy more, but the grain-chandlers in town assured him that there was none available yet.

On arriving at Gaulstown, he could see the extent to which the land had changed. The farmers seemed far fewer in number, and such plants as there were appeared stunted and thin.

He went in, and the butler announced him to Mary. She was sitting sewing in the drawing room and rose to meet him. She looked tired and taut, like a violin string, and her eyes looked dull and leaden.

"Mary, how are you, my dear?" Never before had he called her that.

She looked at him and saw the query in his eyes. Here was someone, apart from her children, who cared about her. "I'm exhausted," she replied. "I have never been so tired."

"Oh, Mary."

She felt his arms go around her as he held her to his chest. She was sure he could feel her heart beating fiercely through her dress.

For a fleeting moment, she thought about Robert, but she shut him out of her mind. She knew that this man loved her. He loved her without rhyme or reason. She loved him – and, perhaps without realising it, had loved him for years. Arthur cared about her when it was evident to her that Robert regarded her as a mere chattel.

He was everything that Robert wasn't. He had a great capacity for love. She could feel it surround her, as she lifted her face to his.

Arthur could sense nothing except he had the woman of his dreams in his arms. He lowered his lips to hers and crushed them gently and tenderly as if this was the first kiss in time between any man and woman. He put his heart and soul into that kiss.

Mary responded to his lips. She had never felt a kiss like this. Every nerve in her body was on fire.

They clung to each other for what seemed like an age before breaking apart. "Oh, Arthur," cried Mary, with heartbreak in her voice.

"Hush now. Don't say a word," she heard him whisper. "Remember this moment."

At length, she realised where they were, and broke away from him. She saw him standing there, with love shining in his eyes, and it seemed as if the cares of the years had fallen from her shoulders. In a daze, she heard him promise to return before striding out to his horse.

After he had gone, the reality of the situation came home to her. Arthur did indeed love her. She loved him in return, but was married to his brother. The world would not accept a love like hers. Neither would her family. She was Robert's, for better or – as it now felt – for worse.

As she lay in bed that night, she remembered every touch of Arthur's lips on hers. She remembered the feel of their arms around each other and the beating of their hearts. It became the pattern of her nights. She knew; she knew that the love she had spoken of with Sarah was there between herself and Arthur.

She would fall asleep remembering that she loved Arthur and he loved her, then awaken in the morning to the grim realisation that she was still married to Robert.

After Robert's last conversation with her, she knew beyond doubt that he would never agree to a separation, least of all a divorce. Her family would not help her either. Her stepmother had almost washed her hands of her at her wedding, and her father had neither the energy or the will to annoy his wife. After her father's last letter, she knew her stepmother was already engaged in supervising her own daughters and arranging their eventual marriages. Mary knew that she would brook no interference.

Over the next two months, Mary's and Arthur's paths rarely crossed. In November, Robert announced that the family would leave for Dublin in two weeks' time. On that occasion, both Robert and Arthur were at their homes at the same time. Robert had no inkling that Mary and Arthur had feelings for each other. The possibility of such a matter arising had never occurred to him. In his eyes, his wife was his absolute property, and he naturally assumed that all men took the same position.

Although he never tried to reconcile this viewpoint with his own behaviour.

One evening, when Arthur was dining at Gaulstown, he and Robert were talking about the famine while Mary said goodnight to the children.

"Have you considered sending Mary and the children over to England for the winter?" asked Arthur. "This winter is going to be even harder than the last one. Did you not see how hard it was for Mary getting through it with you having to be away so much?"

"Do not speak of such things," Robert sneered. "The population must never hear of this. There would be more riots."

"Robert, there have already been riots this year. The harvest has failed, and men will die."

"Men always die in winter," Robert snapped. "I will hear no more of this."

Arthur looked at Mary, who appeared grateful for having the subject brought up, and then listened as Robert spoke a fateful sentence.

"Arthur, if you are in Dublin this winter, I look to you to make sure that Mary has suitable company and does not suffer any more hardship than necessary."

Arthur didn't dare to look at Mary.

Two weeks later, the family decamped for Dublin. After a few days there, enjoying Chloe's charms on most nights, Robert announced he was returning to Mullingar. He was becoming too entranced by Chloe's talents, he realised. He was sure that she was seeing other men while he was away. Someone was teaching her all manner of new kinks and twists and ways of hurting and controlling. Once again, the fire of jealousy bore into him. He was damned if anyone else was going to train the mistress he regarded as his property.

Well, she could go on and teach someone else now. Robert demanded absolute exclusivity from his courtesans, with no consideration for their lives when he was not in Dublin. On the night before he departed, as he left her apartment he dropped a heavy purse on the table.

"Oh, and Chloe, this is goodbye."

"Are you sure, my lord?" she gasped.

Robert relished her shocked reaction. "Indeed I am. I need no more tricks from you. I can find another mistress and enjoy teaching them to her."

Chloe watched him go. Inured as she was to the ways of men like Robert, she had always known this would happen. Ever the fine actress, she waved him away airily. She would never allow him to see her beg. Not unless he was paying for the privilege.

As Arthur had forecast, the famine hit hard again, and this time was worse. Although fuel was available, and extra peat had been cut all over the country, the problem lay in the availability of food. Potatoes, oats, corn, beef and milk, all were in short supply. There was less beef available as many of the cows had failed to calve, and weak cattle had died the previous winter.

Dublin households, including Gardiner Row, stocked up on what they could. The strangeness of the weather brought blizzards and snow and another freeze. This proved to be short-lived but still disastrous; the ice that formed on the Liffey broke up after a few days and floated down the river in great chunks, causing damage to both bridges and boats.

This time, though, some relief was available. The Archbishop of Dublin paid for food for the poor from his own pocket, a gesture copied by some of the other leading citizens.

Snow in November was followed in December by heavy rain, flooding and more cold weather. For Mary and the children, there was nothing to do but wait things out as best they could. This year, at least, they didn't lose any staff. Robert had left her funds to buy food, even at the prevailing prices. Again, her biggest enemy was boredom. There were a few of her old friends in Dublin, but the cold and conditions prevented visits. The theatres were closed. There were no subscription dances or concerts. Even dinners at the Castle had been curtailed.

Riots occurred again in Dublin, and the troops were called on to disperse them. Some ringleaders were hanged or deported, but those in authority knew that starving men will always become desperate.

Chapter Nine

DEEP WATERS

In early January, Arthur once again presented himself at Gardiner Row.

"Is her ladyship at home?" he asked Pearce.

"She is, sir. Lady Mary is in the drawing room. Do you wish me to announce you?"

"If you would be so kind."

Pearce threw wide the drawing room door. "Major Rochfort, your ladyship."

"Arthur, how kind of you to call. Thank you, Pearce. That will be all. I will ring the bell for tea shortly."

As soon as they were alone, Arthur swept her into his arms and held her. From the moment of Pearce announcing him, she felt as if he had lifted an enormous weight off her shoulders. She had gone from a world where she had to answer every question and to solve every problem to one where she felt protected and sheltered. For a few seconds, she could relax and enjoy the sensation.

They broke apart, and he looked at her. He could see that her entire expression had changed. Her face seemed to shine with a luminous quality. It was if a light shone from behind her eyes.

His arms went around her again, and she raised her lips to his. Again, he crushed them, and again they broke away, to enjoy the feeling of being loved.

They stood and looked at each other for some moments. Mary reached out for the bell pull and summoned the maid. By the time she arrived, they had composed themselves and relaxed, and Arthur had seated himself in another chair.

"Bring tea, if you please," ordered Mary, and the maid bobbed a curtsey before leaving the room for the kitchen.

As Mrs O'Mahoney made the tea, she listened to the maid's description of the fine young officer who was visiting her mistress.

"Ah, yes," replied the housekeeper. "He's a grand lad, is Mr Arthur. That's Lord Belfield's brother."

"I heard Lord Belfield's brother was a horrible man."

"Ah, that would be Mr George Rochfort. A very different man to Mr Arthur."

"Why, what has he done?"

"Never you mind. What Mr George does is his business and none of yours. Keep asking questions like that, and you'll find yourself at the next hiring fair. Now take this tray of tea up to her ladyship at once."

Two minutes later, the maid returned to the kitchen with the news that Mr Arthur was to be staying overnight. Mrs O'Mahoney was puzzled. But then, why should she be? Mr Arthur was his lordship's brother. The rules of society hardly applied to people like that. Besides, she had no power to turn him away.

Not that she would have done so, in any event. Mr Arthur had long been one of her favourites.

That evening, Mary and Arthur dined together. After Mrs O'Mahoney's finest efforts had been eaten and enjoyed, Mary rang for Sarah.

"I am going to bed; I will look in on the children first."

Sarah left and went up to Mary's room to help her undress. Mary climbed the stairs after her but headed towards the nursery. After looking in at the children, both providentially asleep, she carefully listened out, to hear Nurse's regular and gentle snores. She closed the door and went next door to her room where Sarah helped her to prepare for bed.

Arthur waited in the dining room, tasting and enjoying the

brandy Pearce had brought him. The fumes surrounded his taste buds. He felt intoxicated, and not from the brandy.

An hour later, Mary heard a tap at her door. She jumped out of bed, pulled a robe around her and tip-toed to the door, opening it a crack. When she saw Arthur there, in his shirt and breeches, she opened it wide.

They fell into each other's arms and kissed long and hard. This time, there was to be no breaking away, no decorum observed. Mary peeled Arthur's shirt back from his shoulders to reveal his chest, gleaming in the candlelight; his muscles firm and well-defined. Arthur reached forward for her nightdress and lifted it from her, before loosening his own belt and dropping his breeches to the floor.

She felt his mouth seeking out her nipples, his tongue flicking over them while his hands ran over her body. She had never felt like this, not even on the one night of real passion she had spent with Robert. Tonight, she would allow no comparisons. Tonight was purely for each other.

He took her hand and led her to the bed.

That night, for the first time, she knew real love. This was not the imagined kind in storybooks or plays, and not the kind of love that Robert showed.

For Arthur, it was the same. He was not inexperienced and had had lovers in the past, but this time he knew he had finally met the love of his life.

As the dawn approached, after they had spent a sleepless night in each other's arms, Arthur rose and returned to his room. There he caught a quick hour's sleep, before rising and dressing before going down to breakfast.

Mary was there before him, with the children. "Say good morning to Uncle Arthur," she said, and Arthur received a shy hello from George and Jane.

"You must excuse them; they are only young. Nurse will teach them their manners, won't she?"

Nurse took this to mean that she should take the children

back to the nursery, leaving Mary and Arthur alone over breakfast.

"My love, we must be careful. Discovery would ruin us both," said Arthur.

"I know," said Mary in a voice little more than a whisper, "but I want to shout it to the rooftops. I love you."

"I love you too, and you know it, but discretion is everything. What we do is dangerous."

"I understand that, but I ask myself if I care."

"Do not make that mistake," said Arthur. "Robert is not a kind man. If he finds out, he would be mean and vindictive. He would hurt you, and I do not want that to happen."

"So what might we do?" asked Mary.

"We must be careful. I must go to the Castle today. I will stay here tonight, and tomorrow I must go back to Athlone for my duties. I will have much to do, but I will be back. Trust me in that."

"Oh Arthur, I trust you in all things. But I am at the Music Hall tonight. Mr Handel has arrived in Dublin and is giving a concert, and I am to go as one of Lord Devonshire's party. Most of the officers from the Castle are going. It breaks my heart, but it would be best if you didn't stay here."

Arthur's face fell. He looked at Mary and saw she was about to speak. He raised his hand, palm forward.

"No, don't say anything. You know how much I want to stay, but that would be madness. I will stay at the Castle tonight."

Arthur left for the Castle, where the Lord Lieutenant and the other senior officials were keen to hear his appraisal of the countryside and the chance of another famine. The Lord Lieutenant was trying to arrange some shipments of grain from the Americas. None was available in England, and Europe was riven by war again. Rumour had it that the merchants in County Louth were hoarding several thousand barrels of oats. As this and potatoes were the main food for the population, the Lord Lieutenant had already put a ban on the export of any grain.

Mary sat at home and played with her children all day. That night, she joined the Lord Lieutenant and his party of friends for the concert. Throughout the performance her attention was cursory, as her mind was filled with thoughts of Arthur. Eventually, it was over, and her carriage returned her to Gardiner Row, and she could retire to bed.

There she dreamed of every time Arthur had touched her. Every kiss, every caress. She woke in the morning still thinking of him. It took an enormous effort of will to rouse herself and behave as if nothing had happened. To give herself something different to do, she went down to the kitchen to see Mrs O'Mahoney.

"Major Rochfort told me yesterday that the famine is coming back."

The housekeeper's face dropped. "Oh, ma'am, not again. Whatever next?"

"We need to make sure the larders are full, and we need to make sure we have enough food to last right through the rest of the winter. I want you to go to the markets and see what you can find."

Over the next week, Mrs O'Mahoney visited all the grain-chandlers and millers and managed to order a few sacks of wheat, corn and oats. She also visited the butchers and ordered a barrel of salt pork and another of salt beef. The household was now as ready as anyone could hope to be. Some fresh vegetables were still available on the market, but at a prohibitively high price.

Robert also returned to Dublin on a flying visit in January. This time, the famine in the country was much worse. On a recent trip to Athlone, he had been attacked again. He spurred his horse into a canter straight away and rode away from the single ghoulish wraith-like body that had jumped up at his horse. When he arrived at the barracks, he told Colonel Bryant, who remarked that the attack was not unusual.

"I will send a patrol to the area tomorrow, but there won't be anything. Perhaps a body. The people are dying like flies. The famine is even worse than last year."

Robert spent the night in the barracks and rode back to Gaulstown in the morning. There were still two servants there, keeping the house locked and weatherproof. A similar arrangement was in place at Belfield House, Arthur's small manor-house. The gardeners were still living in their cottages and keeping the households supplied with peat and whatever vegetables they could harvest. There were no potatoes at all, and only a limited supply of oats. With care, they had enough for the servants to last until the spring.

"How many men are we short?" Robert asked Colonel Bryant later that week.

"Altogether, one hundred and seventy. We still have not replaced those we sent to England last year. Thirty-three men are sick. For every five men engaged last year, we have lost two – either rejected through sickness, or deserted, or died. Keeping this garrison occupied and up to strength is almost beyond my strength. Last week we lost two young officers. Ensign Mitchell went out on patrol with his platoon, and ruffians attacked them near the Dublin road. He took a pistol ball through the chest."

"Damn," Robert snapped. "And the other officer?"

"Sold his commission. He received word from his London agent that his commission as lieutenant had been sold, and that he should travel to London to settle accounts. I had to let him go. We will get a replacement at some time. Replacements for both of them, I hope."

"And in the meantime?"

"More work for everyone. We need to get through this winter, and then try to rebuild and recruit in the summer. At least nobody is leaving to join the French."

"Do we need the press gang?" asked Robert.

The Colonel scoffed. "To press what? Those that are left can barely pick up a musket. No, we must leave recruiting until people have enough to eat. Then they will join of their own accord."

The next day, Robert made the long trip to Athlone. The weather was foul. Icy rain and strong wind made any progress slow. Even taking a spare horse didn't add to his speed, and it was an hour after sunset when he finally arrived in the town. After handing over his horse to a groom at the barrack stables, Robert strode towards the commanding officer's office, dripping water from his coat.

Colonel Monroe waved him to a chair. "Welcome to Athlone, my lord. A poor welcome it is too."

"How bad is it?" asked Robert, handing his sodden coat to a servant. "And, perhaps more to the point, how bad do you believe it will get?"

"Men will die, again. Some have already. Out in the fields, they are perishing in droves."

"And the garrison strength?"

"Out of a nominal roll? From four thousand men, I have, perhaps, three thousand two hundred. I should have four troops of cavalry, and I have barely two. We will lose more horses before the spring, too."

"What about new recruits?"

Colonel Monroe sighed and shook his head. "They are barely strong enough to sign their names. We have had several who joined up and then died in the first week."

Robert scowled. "We must get through this winter and rebuild in the spring. No doubt we will need to send more troops to England. The war does not go well at the moment."

"War with Spain over this man Jenkins' ear, war with France now because of the Austrians. We need good weather, and we need to replace those we have lost. Whitehall will insist we send them more troops next year. In fact, we can expect them to demand more men every year until there is peace again."

"Is my brother here, or is he out with a patrol?" Robert asked.

"Neither. He is in Dublin."

"The devil he is," exclaimed Robert. "Well, no doubt I will see him shortly."

"Yes, he left three days ago. I expect him back in another week."

The officers parted, and Robert went to his room. A servant had taken his portmanteau from his horse and unpacked it.

Later that evening in the mess the wine flowed, and the officers were all discussing the war. Without exception, the junior officers were hoping to go to the continent. War meant the possibility of promotion. The senior officers were more sanguine, especially those who had seen a battle and knew the damage and pain warfare brings.

Arthur's name was often mentioned during the evening. He was popular with all officers young and old. The senior officers all commented on his ability and efficiency, while the younger ones spoke of his affability and friendliness.

Robert mentioned that he had hoped to see him there. "Does anyone know why he went to Dublin?" he asked the mess.

"I heard he had an urgent appointment," said one of the younger lieutenants.

No one could add any more than that.

Robert looked puzzled, and his face darkened. He swore under his breath before turning abruptly and leaving the mess.

Chapter Ten

HUNGER STALKS THE LAND

It was, as forecast, a terrible harvest that year.

The farmers gathered what they could, but everything was scarce, and prices rose inexorably.

One night in late autumn, Arthur and Mary were locked in each other's arms. He had arrived in Dublin that afternoon and called at the Castle, purely to let the authorities know he was there and would also be there the next day. He planned to go back to Athlone the day after that.

"Major Arthur, my lady," Pearce announced. As soon as the door had closed behind the butler, Mary flew into Arthur's arms.

"You are all right, you are safe?" she breathed.

"Of course, my love. Why would I not be?"

"But what are you doing here?"

"This time, I came to see you."

Her heart leapt again. She now knew what it was to be loved for her own sake and not only as the means of producing an heir.

"When must you leave again?"

"The day after tomorrow. I will ride back to Athlone, and I plan to be there inside a day. It is over eighty miles, but with a decent change of horse, I should be fine. I left a horse at the inn in Kilbeggan."

"Oh, Arthur my love, do take care! I couldn't bear it if anything happened to you."

"Don't worry," he replied. "Nothing ever happens to me."

They dined together, then spent the night in one long whirl

of passionate and tender lovemaking, abandoning all thoughts of sleep.

Next morning, the household was already stirring when Arthur roused himself from Mary's bed. After placing a kiss on her sleeping forehead, he tiptoed back to his own room to shave and dress.

At breakfast, he restored himself with coffee, bread and bacon, and then left. For once it wasn't raining, so he decided to walk the mile to the River Liffey before crossing to the Castle.

"Arthur! What are you doing in Dublin?" asked one of his fellow-officers when he appeared in the mess.

"Oh, checking on our situation with the war, and with recruitment, and seeing how many troops we will need to send to England," he replied. As an excuse to be in Dublin, it would suffice. His comrades seemed satisfied, and he spent a useful day at the Castle before leaving to walk back to Gardiner Row in the afternoon.

When he arrived, Mary was out with Nurse and the children. He went down to the kitchen where he would be sure of a warm welcome from Mrs O'Mahoney.

A few minutes later he was sitting at the table with a cup of tea, watching the housekeeper preparing dinner for the evening.

They chatted about the house, and the older servants, and his parents, whom she had known when she had joined the staff as a young girl. As he finished his tea and stood up to leave, Mrs O'Mahoney turned to him.

"Mr Arthur, do be careful!"

"Careful about what? What do you mean?"

"Don't take me for a fool, Mr Arthur. I have seen how her eyes light up when you arrive. She is a different person when you are here."

"Oh, Mrs O'Mahoney," he whispered. "I love her."

"I know, sir, I know. But if this ever reaches the ears of Lord Robert, well I don't know what he will do. I'm not so much worried about you, it's what he might do to her ladyship that concerns me."

"Oh, Mrs O'Mahoney, what am I to do?"

"To be sure, I don't know. You had better get a posting to the Indies. Somewhere far away. That way at least you would both be safe."

"I would do anything to keep her safe."

"I'm sure you would, but this can only end one way, you know that, don't you?"

"I will be careful, Mrs O'Mahoney. I promise."

"You make sure you are, now," said the housekeeper as he moved towards the door.

Mary, Nurse and the children arrived back at four in the afternoon. While Nurse took her charges up to the nursery, and Mary consulted with the housekeeper, Arthur was left to his own devices.

While waiting for her, Arthur visited the nursery and spent some time playing with the children. George was five years old and happy to chatter to anyone who would listen. Jane was a bright girl of six and was full of questions for her uncle.

Mary went up to say goodnight to the children and found Arthur sitting on the floor, playing with them. Jane was balancing on his knees while George was curled up on his chest, giggling away at being tickled.

Mary took one look at this scene of domestic bliss and went fussing to Nurse in mock alarm.

"Oh, Nurse, how could you? How will we get them to sleep?"

The nurse looked up apologetically. "There was nothing I could do, your ladyship. Mr Arthur demanded that he be allowed to play with them."

"*Mea culpa*," said Arthur, laughing. "Nurse, I will leave them to your tender mercies."

"Hmmph. Thank you indeed, sir," replied Nurse. "We'll get them to sleep eventually, I dare say."

Arthur went and stood by the door with Mary, watching the children. "They were delightful," he said. "I've had a lovely half–hour."

"And now we have to get them calmed down and off to sleep. Thank you indeed," replied Mary, doing her best to sound cross.

As Nurse fussed around the children, Arthur and Mary slipped away and went downstairs to dinner.

Mrs O'Mahoney had produced her best dinner with what was available, sacrificing one of her prize chickens. She cooked this in a sauce of wine and salt pork, with some mushrooms. Potatoes were still unobtainable, but they had some bread, and wine to lift their spirits.

When dinner was over, they stayed talking in the drawing room until the household had gone to bed. They talked about everything: of Mary's marriage, and how Robert had treated her, of her life at Gaulstown, of Arthur's childhood and growing up with his brothers. When all was quiet, they tiptoed upstairs and into Mary's room.

Tonight, Arthur made love to her as slowly, gently and tenderly as he could. She responded to him by melting into him. They slept, woke, loved some more, again and again until they heard the first sounds of movement from the kitchen.

Arthur and Mary kissed as if it was their last ever kiss before he crept back to his own room.

After a quick breakfast, Arthur went down to the kitchen to say goodbye to Mrs O'Mahoney. As he did so, he begged her to take good care of Mary.

"I always do, Mr Arthur. Please make sure you do the same."

He went out to his horses, with a groom standing by to give him the halter for a second horse. With his portmanteau tied on behind the saddle, he headed out at a steady canter on a road almost empty of traffic.

After a long day, with a short break at Kilbeggan for some bread and cheese and a change of horse, he arrived in Athlone as the sun was setting. It was a hard ride of eighty miles, and he was stiff and sore in every muscle as he dismounted. He passed the reins of his horses to a groom and limped into the officers' mess. The first person he saw there was Robert.

"Welcome to Athlone, Arthur."

"Thank you; it is good to get here at last. A tough day in the saddle."

"And how is Dublin?"

"Starving again, but it will pass."

"And Lady Belfield?"

"She was fine when I saw her, the children also. They grow fit and strong. She has given you a fine pair of young ones."

"I'm sure they are. I demand no less. Did you stay at Gardiner Row?" asked Robert.

"I did. It's more comfortable than the mess and gives me a chance to see Lady Belfield and Mrs O'Mahoney."

"Is all well?" asked Robert,

"It seems so. Although, all is not well at the Castle. The war has ground to a halt. The War Office requires more and more men. It seems we must send several companies to England."

Robert mulled over this reply, although it was hardly news. "We can do nothing until the spring, in any event. We are almost one thousand men short from the roll here, and nobody in the town or countryside is fit to take the shilling. They look like scarecrows. They would be worse than useless in a battle with the Prussians. What do you intend to do here?"

"On Monday, I will be working my way through all the towns and villages south to the border of Westmeath. I need to find out how many have died and try to find out what food is required by those left alive."

"Find out what they are hiding," cried Robert. "We need that food here."

Arthur gave him a strange look. "The people need it. They will die without."

"Your duty is to the garrison. I tell you now: if you find any food in store, make sure they deliver it to the barracks here as soon as possible. The Army needs our men, and it needs them fed."

Arthur knew Robert could be a hard and cruel man, but he was shocked to hear him condemn the starving to death.

"But Robert, we will need the people alive. We need recruits every year, and we need the land worked, or there is no food and no forage."

"Arthur, you are a weak and sentimental fool. Get out and carry on with your instructions. I will hear no more from you."

There was nothing left for the brothers to say to each other. Ashen-faced, Arthur turned and went to his quarters. There, his dreams were not of Robert or the starving people, but everywhere he saw Mary. In his heart of hearts, he knew there was no clear solution to their quandary.

He was equally sure that Robert must never know, and must never ever suspect.

The following Monday, Arthur left with a cavalry troop, heading eastwards towards Kilbeggan. Wherever possible, he followed the border to King's County, but everywhere they went, they saw death stalking the land. Bodies lay unburied in the fields. Every so often they would see a small group of men with a horse and cart, collecting bodies for burial. Arthur made sure the troop didn't disturb them. It was clear that the winter would be hard for everyone in Ireland, whether a landowner, farmer or soldier.

The patrol stayed overnight in Kilbeggan. Luckily, they were carrying some rations, which the innkeeper was happy to use to concoct a stew of sorts. They were all carrying some feed for the horses as well. In the morning, they left the main highway and headed north to Newels Bridge before skirting Lough Ennell round to Rochfort House.

George gave them a grudging welcome. The soldiers could bivouac in the stables, and he condescended to allow his brother to join him at dinner.

George and Alice kept a lavish table, considering the famine gripping the country. They even had potatoes. The cook produced a rabbit and a chicken with some vegetables, and Arthur ate as well as he had in the country for many weeks.

"What brings you up here?" asked George.

"We need to see the state of the countryside, and how the people are coping. How are the beasts and horses?"

"I can tell you that. The people are lazy. They have enough

103

food, but they insist on hiding it. In the spring, they will all appear from their hovels again."

"The crops are not growing," replied Arthur. "All farmers will have difficulty paying their rent next year."

"They pay their rent or leave," George thundered. "The choice is theirs. There's no reason I should suffer because of their idleness."

Arthur stared at him, horrified.

The next morning, Arthur took his patrol over for a routine check on Gaulstown and Belfield House before continuing to Mullingar. Both were weathering the winter as well as he could expect. The servants kept the houses clean and dry, and with care they had enough food and fuel to last until spring.

They arrived in Mullingar barracks as night fell. As the men settled into their accommodation, Arthur reported to Colonel Bryant.

"It's a frozen hell out there. God help any tenant this year. More so if his landlord is my brother George, and those like him. We will see many deaths in the next weeks."

That year, winter was hard for the garrisons. Little concession could be made to the season. Robert had gone back to Dublin, and George rarely left Rochfort House in winter, so Arthur was the only member of his family working over the festive season. Luckily, he found plenty of company in the officers' mess. There were even a few invitations for dinner from the well-off merchants in the town, particularly those with daughters of marriageable age. The weather and the events in the countryside were enough to prevent any dances or parties.

As soon as possible, Arthur completed his patrols of the countryside. January started with more hard frosts. The frost slowed the patrols. They could not risk the horses at speed on the frozen ground. No farmstead, hamlet or parish had escaped without death among the people or animals.

Early February saw Arthur back in Dublin. Again, Robert was away, and he and Mary made use of every waking night-time moment.

On the day before he departed, disaster struck.

Arthur was arranging to leave the next morning when Robert arrived on a mud-spattered horse, accompanied by a groom.

He dismounted and strode up the steps to the front door while the groom took their horses to the stable. Inside the drawing room were Arthur and Mary, sitting on the sofa, making the sort of conversations that can only be interesting to two lovers. They started, and Arthur jumped up.

"Robert! What a surprise," he cried out.

"So I see," snapped Robert, with a face like thunder.

"Mary and I were talking."

"Evidently."

Mary intervened, in an attempt to placate her husband. "How are you, Robert? How was the journey? You must be cold and tired."

"As good as any journey in February in Ireland. Long, cold and wet. Now let me get dry and warm in front of a fire."

Mary stood up, trying to look full of concern, and Arthur put some more coal on the fire.

"I was packing. I am riding back to Athlone in the morning," said Arthur, trying to make conversation.

"Please feel free to continue," replied Robert. Arthur took the hint and left the room to pack for his return trip.

Robert sat down and asked Mary to ring for some tea and some brandy. Mary looked at him with one eyebrow raised.

"Goddamit, woman. It is cold; I will have brandy. Do not dare to criticise me in my own house."

Mary allowed a mask to slide over her face and hardened her expression. She could not afford to give Robert the slightest cause for alarm. Her expression and her voice had to remain neutral.

"I'm sorry," she murmured. "I meant no criticism."

At this moment, the maid entered, and Mary ordered her to bring up a tray of tea and a bottle of brandy. "Quickly, please. His lordship is cold and wet."

How true, she thought. Robert was cold, at least to her.

"How long has Arthur been here?" Robert demanded.

"Two days," she replied.

"Staying here?"

"Of course."

"I would have thought he might have preferred the officers' mess at the Castle."

"I cannot say. He is at the Castle during the day when he is here."

"How many times has he stayed here?"

"Oh, three or four. You told him to make sure I was all right during the famine, didn't you?"

Robert scowled at her. "Well, yes," he grunted and strode out of the room.

The next day, Arthur left in the early morning. Robert's sudden presence had denied the lovers a final night of passion.

At eight, Robert rose and dressed. After breakfast, with no sign of Mary, he called for his horse and left for the Castle. On arrival, he was immediately shown into the Lord Lieutenant's suite of offices.

"Good morning, my lord," said Lord Cavendish. "How goes the road?"

"Terrible, Your Grace," replied Robert. "Ruts, holes and water. I made a foul trip. It was good to arrive last night and get warm and dry."

For the next two hours, the two men discussed the progress of the war. This seemed to be extremely complicated, and Lord Cavendish freely admitted he barely understood it, beyond the fact that they were, as usual, at war with France.

"It seems that the matter of Captain Jenkins' ear is to be forgotten, and our cause now is to make sure the right person succeeds to the throne of Austria."

"Does this affect us here?" asked Robert.

"Yes," replied Lord Cavendish. "Four companies of the Cheshire Regiment will transfer this spring to England. They can then journey on to Prussia. For us, the replacement of these troops is of vital importance. I pray every day for a mild spring and a good harvest."

"It is bad in the country. People are still dying. Rents will go uncollected. My brother will foreclose on as many tenants as he can, and expand his estate."

"Ah, yes. Your brother. Word of George has also reached us. We cannot offend him, of course. As a Member of Parliament, he wields too much influence – but sadly, influence he does not use altogether in our interests. We know he is trying to corner the market in the supply of beef and grain in the area. We will be watching him."

"What of Arthur, Your Grace?" asked Robert.

"What of him?" replied Lord Cavendish.

"He was here yesterday. I thought he would have made himself known, or that you had requested his presence."

"Was he, by God? No, indeed. He has been doing an excellent job in Athlone and Westmeath, but I haven't seen him here for several weeks."

Robert was surprised. He determined to take the matter up in the officers' mess that night. When he did, several officers confirmed that Arthur had indeed been there. They had all seen and spoken with him during the day, but he hadn't stayed in the barracks at night.

At dinner that night, Robert asked Mary if she knew why Arthur was in Dublin.

"He had business at the Castle, of course," she replied.

"It seems not. He was there, but nobody appears to know why," said Robert.

"I can't imagine him coming all the way in this awful weather without having good cause," she replied, in a placatory tone.

The matter was dropped, but this didn't stop Robert mulling these strange events over in his mind. After two days, he too left Dublin and returned to Mullingar, where he could brief Colonel Bryant on the progress of the war and the pending transfer of the Cheshire Regiment.

As February drifted into March, and the days grew noticeably longer, Robert found his duties taking him to Athlone. When he arrived, he was shown into Colonel Monroe's office, and, as in Mullingar, they discussed the war and the requirements for recruiting over the summer. Both officers had noticed the sprouting of the grass and oats in the fields as February came to an end. A warm spring was helping the farmers, and, if they were lucky, would feed the cattle and horses they would need for the troops.

"Is Arthur in Athlone?" asked Robert as they came to the end of their discussions.

"Why yes. He should be in the mess or in his quarters," replied Colonel Monroe.

"I will walk across and find him. Oh, by the way. Why was he sent to Dublin?"

"He wasn't, as far as I know. Why do you ask?"

"When I arrived at my house in Dublin last week, Arthur was there. He had been there for two days, and he came back to Athlone the next day. His brother officers all saw him at the Castle, but nobody knows why he was there."

"Then you must ask him yourself. I understood him to be at his house near Mullingar, to make sure all was well after the weather," added the Colonel. "He has been over there several times."

"I will." Robert got to his feet, turned, and went in search of Arthur.

He found him in his quarters. He was sitting at a small desk, writing his military diary, and looked up as Robert knocked, then entered.

"Good evening, Robert. Welcome back to Athlone."

"Good evening to you also, brother. I trust you managed all you hoped in Dublin." Robert turned and sat on a small stool. This had the benefit of lowering him to the same level as his brother so he could look at his face.

"I did indeed," replied Arthur, speaking slowly and carefully. He felt nervous seeing his brother like this.

"I trust you found Mary well."

"She seemed well to me, as did the children. You are lucky to have two such delightful children. So much nicer than George's brood."

"Ah, yes," replied Robert, evidently pleased to hear such a comment about his children. "Arthur, a question, if you please. What was it exactly that took you to Dublin? At the Castle,

108

nobody knew the reason for your trip."

Arthur looked slightly shamefaced. "I have to say, I had an appointment with a lady."

"Oh, who?" asked Robert.

"I cannot say. But rest assured – you don't know her."

Arthur knew of Robert's predilection for ladies-of-the-night, even if he didn't know of his more unusual tastes.

"And was your trip worthwhile?" Robert continued.

"Oh, yes! I managed to get to know this particular lady remarkably well."

"Colonel Monroe thinks you were at Belfield House."

"I didn't feel it necessary to disabuse him. I was most careful not to be specific about exactly where I was going."

Robert looked sharply at his brother. His eyes narrowed, and the tone of his voice became threatening. "Hmmm. I wouldn't play that particular card again."

"Thank you for the advice. I won't. Have you dined yet?"

"No, so if you haven't I suggest we do so in the mess," said Robert. "I don't know what the cooks have conjured up, but we can live in hope."

The pair of them got up from their chairs and headed over to the officers' mess to dine. Robert's hopes proved false. Dinner turned out to be salt beef, bread and turnips. There was, at least, some porter available to wash it down.

Their dinner proved to be a convivial occasion. Some of the other officers were present, and the conversation was fast and witty. Arthur's natural gift for making himself agreeable to all came to the fore, and everyone went off to bed in a joyous mood.

Everyone, that is, except Robert. Something was nagging at his mind. Something that he couldn't put his finger on. After tossing and turning for an hour, he fell into a fitful sleep.

Once spring arrived, both Robert and Arthur were busy from dawn to dusk. The crops were growing well, the weather was kind, and the tenant farmers could look forward to a reasonable harvest. Potatoes for seed had to be imported from

England. Those that were planted did not grow well, but other vegetables did grow, and the grain harvest looked better than they had hoped.

George Rochfort had, in his own eyes at least, had a "good" winter. Rarely leaving the immediate area of Rochfort House, except for occasional trips into Mullingar by carriage, he had engaged a new land agent: a hard man by the name of Miller, who would accept no excuses from tenants when quarter-day arrived. He would, however, offer them a loan, at high interest, secured by their livestock or harvest. He also provided this facility to tenants on farms belonging to other owners. All this with George's full knowledge and support.

When the tenants could not pay the exorbitant rates of interest, they were flung off their farms. If George held the mortgage or loan, he would foreclose and add the acres to his estate.

"It's been a good spring and looks like being a good summer," he remarked to Alice. "More farms, all with some sort of crop on them. Wait a year or two until the beasts are grown again, and we can build a new house here. A house suitable for a Rochfort. This place is more than old, it's decrepit."

"Indeed it is," replied Alice. "You need a house that you and young Gussie can be proud of."

Discreet enquiries showed that Mr Castel was still in Ireland, and had recently completed some work at Trinity College. Through his land agent, George arranged for him to come to Mullingar as soon as the roads were clear. When he eventually arrived, George's brief to him was short and precise.

"I want a house that makes that look like a hovel!" he exclaimed. They were standing outside George's existing house. He gestured to the north, to where Belvedere could be seen on a slight elevation. The winter sun, coming fitfully between the clouds, reflected faintly from the windows.

Mr Castel looked long and hard at Rochfort House and its

hotch-potch of alterations and amendments. He looked over to Belvedere, and then he looked at George, before answering slowly in his heavy German accent.

"This can be done, but it will cost a great deal of money."

George looked hard at him as if daring him to suggest that he couldn't afford it. "Money," he replied icily, "is not your concern."

"Very well, I will begin at Easter," said Castel. "Everything is clear, yes?"

George answered in the affirmative. Mr Castel left, mounted his horse and made his way back to the inn at Mullingar.

The order duly arrived for the Cheshire Regiment to join the Army on the continent. They were required to march, not to Dublin, but to Cork, where they would board a ship for the Low Countries. From there they would march to the Rhine Valley to join the rest of the Army.

In both Athlone and Mullingar, the town came out in force to see the regiment depart. Fully half the available garrisons had been sent to the war. These would have to be replaced, and the recruiting officers would be active throughout all the midland counties.

Arthur and Robert found themselves travelling beyond the confines of Westmeath, to every town where recruits might be found. The sons of farmers who had been turned off their land joined up in droves. Some refused to declare themselves Protestant and enlist, preferring to move with their families to America or England if they could raise the funds for the passage. Many became bonded servants, bound to an unknown master in the Carolinas, but even this was better than staying in Ireland to starve. The harvest may be good, but if it was all to go to the landlords, how would they feed themselves and their families?

Some weeks later, Robert brought his family back from Dublin into the country. Shortly after their arrival, Arthur called at his own Belfield House. His own small estate was in fair condition, and he took the precaution of reducing the rent and making sure all his tenants had supplies to last them until harvest.

One evening, both Robert and Arthur were in the barracks in Athlone.

"What do you do next week?" asked Robert.

"Nothing here. I am going to Belfield House to speak to my agent."

"Dine with us on Friday at Gaulstown. Mary would enjoy it."

Arthur was suspicious. He had never known Robert to give any consideration to what Mary would or wouldn't enjoy. But he could hardly refuse such a handsome invitation, and it would allow him to see Mary, if only briefly.

"I'd be delighted. Tell Mary I am looking forward to seeing her."

Chapter Eleven

WALKING ON DANGEROUS GROUND

The following week both brothers returned to their homes.

At Gaulstown, Robert said, "I've invited Arthur to dinner on Friday. He has accepted, and asked me to give you his regards."

Mary was on her guard at once. This was most unexpected. Did Robert know anything? Did he suspect? Nothing in his looks or demeanour led her to think that he did. She made her mind up to enjoy the evening when it came, but to be careful. She was sure that Arthur would do the same.

Aloud, she said brightly, "That will be delightful. I will make sure we give him something suitable. We can make a feast of it."

On Friday, Robert announced that he had invited George and Alice to dinner as well. This was so unusual as to make Mary even more worried. She knew Robert detested George, and would never normally invite him to dinner. She did at least have a chance to warn Mrs O'Mahoney so extra food could be cooked.

When Friday night came, Mary was on tenterhooks as she and Robert sat in the drawing room listening out for the sound of horses' hooves on the gravel. While Robert seemed intent on the book he was reading, Mary could not concentrate on her sewing. She was desperate to make sure Robert didn't notice anything amiss.

At the stroke of seven Arthur arrived. He had been telling himself that he must, for Mary's sake, act purely as a loving brother-in-law. No trace of familiarity could pass between them, or Robert would be sure to suspect. Ten minutes later, George and Alice arrived in their carriage, and the company made small talk before going in for dinner.

Arthur felt the tension in the air throughout, He spent much of dinner covertly watching Robert, and noticed that Mary was doing the same.

The food at dinner was excellent. Venison, a duck, two large trout from the lough, and fine bottles of claret and champagne.

Robert looked at Mary and Arthur and noticed their apparent lack of appetite. "Come now. Do try the venison and the trout. I caught the fish this morning on the lough."

Obediently, Arthur and Mary cut themselves a small portion of each course as the footman presented them, and forced it down. George, meanwhile, had already filled his plate and was busy enjoying his dinner.

Arthur and Mary hardly noticed what they were eating. They certainly didn't taste anything. All their thoughts were concentrated on each other. Several times, when Robert spoke, Mary was slow to respond and seem to lose her train of thought.

"Have you seen young George today?"

"I'm sorry Robert. What was it you asked?"

Robert's response came in a tone of annoyance.

"Madam, I asked you if you had seen our son today."

"Well, of course, I've seen him. I put him to bed not three hours ago. He continues to grow, and he will be a fine young man, eventually."

Belatedly, Mary noted that, once again, Robert had never asked after their daughter.

George was also watching events. He thought, quietly, "So lies the wind in that quarter?" He watched Arthur and Mary trying to hide their feelings for each other. As was his way, he said nothing but stored the information away for future use.

114

Finally, dinner was over. Mary and Alice left the three brothers at the table with a brandy and went to sit in the drawing room.

After an hour, the brothers joined them. Robert seemed at ease and to be enjoying the evening. Arthur was unnaturally quiet, although this was of no concern with George being there. George liked the sound of his own voice and was happy to keep any conversation going.

"Was the venison from one of your own deer, Robert?"

"It's one I shot at the north end of the demesne, last week. A hind of two years. An easy shot, as it happened." The estate possessed a small but growing herd of red deer; a valuable source of meat for the house.

Robert had been observing his guests throughout the evening. While he didn't suspect either his wife or his brother of anything, even he eventually realised that there was a fragility to the pair of them. Both seemed to be treading on eggshells and showing more than usual deference to himself and their guests.

At ten o'clock, George rose from his chair, followed closely by Alice. "Time we were off home. I've some farms to see tomorrow, with a view to purchasing."

"More farms, George?" Robert asked.

"You can never have a large enough estate, especially considering the plans I have for the house. Thank you for a capital dinner. Arthur, your servant!" and he nodded at his brothers and sister-in-law.

"I must be off too," said Arthur. "The moon is still up and the night is clear, so it should be an easy ride back to Belfield. Can I thank you both for a delicious dinner?" So saying, he bowed low over Mary's hand and raised it to his lips.

Mary withdrew her hand almost as if he had burnt it. She could feel the warmth from his lips affecting the blood flowing through her limbs, and she watched him stride out of the room. Exhausted with the tensions of the evening, she announced to Robert that she was going to bed.

When Mary had gone up to her bedroom, Robert sat over another brandy in his study and mulled over the events of the evening. Deep within his brain a seed of an idea germinated. The jealousy that had always been his abiding characteristic watered the seed, and gradually it began to grow.

As he rode out of the gate at Gaulstown, Arthur relaxed visibly in the saddle.

He spent the following day at Belfield House. The day was warm, and he wore just shirt and breeches as he sat in a chair in the garden reading a novel. But his thoughts kept returning to Mary. Nothing he could think of would manage to change their situation. She was his brother's wife – and his brother's ownership of her was absolute.

The sun streamed through the leaves and branches of an old beech tree, and the gentle murmuring sound was enough to make him doze.

He leapt back to full wakefulness when two hands placed themselves over his eyes. He jumped to his feet and turned around to find himself looking straight into Mary's eyes.

"Are you alone, my love?" he asked.

"Yes, for now. I rode over with a groom, but his horse threw a shoe, so I sent him back to Gaulstown. What about you?"

"The house is empty apart from me. The housekeeper and groom have gone into Mullingar with a waggon for supplies."

"My darling, do you realise this is the first time we have been alone since we were in Dublin?"

"How could I forget? I relive that last night together every night."

"Oh, Arthur. What are we to do?"

"There's nothing we can do, except grasp stolen moments like this, and make sure that Robert never finds out. Where is he today?"

"He was riding to see some of his farms with his land agent. He will be home for dinner."

"How much time do we have?"

"An hour. If the groom changes horses and returns, we

have that long at least."

They clasped hands and clutched each other, lips seeking lips, tongues entwined, and kissed with a passion for several minutes. Eventually they broke apart, and, still hand in hand, walked into the house and up the stairs to Arthur's bedroom.

Arthur quickly shed his shirt and breeches and pulled Mary's riding habit over her shoulders. Beneath her dress, she was wearing only a petticoat and shift. As their passion rose, they fell onto the bed and into each other's arms, determined to make the best use of the short time they had available.

Twenty minutes later, they lay in each other's arms in a haze of satisfaction. They dimly remained conscious of the passage of time and rose from the bed, feeling unsteady on their feet.

"Help me get dressed, my darling," she begged him.

"Of course. You'll find me clumsy, though. This is not an area in which I have any practice."

Mary laughed. "Quite the opposite, I dare say." She giggled. "Now quickly, I must start back soon."

Arthur gave silent thanks that Mary wasn't wearing anything more complicated. They checked each other's clothes and went downstairs to the hall. There they kissed again and walked out to her horse, patiently grazing on the lawn. Arthur untethered it and put a hand under Mary's boot to lift her into the saddle. Finally, he kissed the tips of her fingers, as she scooped up the reins and kicked the horse into a trot.

Half a mile away, Robert, riding back to Gaulstown, saw her horse leave Belfield House. She came out onto the highway in front of him, and she rode towards Gaulstown at a gentle canter, never once looking behind her.

That night, at dinner, Robert quizzed her gently. "How was your day?" he asked.

"I rode over to Belfield House this afternoon. It was a lovely day to ride."

"I saw you on the way back here, but you were alone."

Mary started, alert at once. "I took my groom, but his horse threw a shoe, and he had to go back."

117

"And you thought it acceptable to go on alone?" asked Robert.

"Of course. I was only going to Belfield House."

"Was Arthur at home?"

"Yes, we had a pleasant sit in his garden before I returned." Robert fell silent.

Mary asked to be excused. "I have a headache. Now, if you forgive me, I'll retire to bed."

Robert, always prone to jealousy, sat with a large brandy and considered his courses of action. What up to now had been a mild suspicion, now burned with the heat of raging certainty. He now knew, beyond any doubt, that she had betrayed him with Arthur. His own brother!

In the morning, he sat in his study, deep in thought, and made his plans. For now, he determined to let the couple think he suspected nothing. In the afternoon, he rode into Mullingar with a portmanteau tied behind his saddle, and told Colonel Bryant he would need permanent quarters at the barracks.

He took the opportunity to speak to Flynn.

"Flynn, how many years have you worked as my agent?"

"Five years for you, my lord, and another five for your father, God rest his soul."

"Do you like your job, Flynn?"

"What kind of question is that, my lord? Of course, I do. It's a grand job."

"I have an additional task for you. Now, I wouldn't generally ask you to do this, but it is important to me, and I wanted to make sure you understand that your continued employment depends on you carrying it out."

Flynn's face went white. "My lord! I have always worked in your interests. I trust I will be allowed to continue to do so."

"As long as that is firmly understood. What I need you to do is to watch Mr Arthur. You know him, and he knows you. He trusts you, and it's important that he continues to trust you. I will shortly be leaving Gaulstown for Athlone for two weeks. You will continue to watch his movements. You will also watch Lady Belfield. Should the two of them meet, you will tell me. I will call upon you on my return, and you will report your findings. Now, is that clear?"

Flynn shook and scratched his head. "My lord, it seems I have little choice in the matter. I must do as you ask, even though my heart is not in this."

"I see we understand one another," said Robert, and dismissed him with a wave of his hand.

The next day, Robert left for Athlone. Arthur was there, and about to lead another troop of horse out on patrol. Recruiting was good, and the garrison strength was returning to normal. The weather was fine and sunny, and the harvest was shaping up well.

When dining in the mess that night, Robert made sure that Arthur knew he would be in Athlone for at least a week. He also knew that, given the opportunity, Arthur would try to take at least one day off at Belfield House. Now Robert must wait.

Chapter Twelve

AN EMPTY LAND

"How many men are we still short of?" Robert asked Colonel Monroe the next morning, as they went over manpower returns and sick lists.

"We still need two hundred and seven men to bring us back to full strength. We have eighteen still sick from the famine."

"If they are still sick now, they are no use to us. Discharge them today. Are there any others who are due for release?"

"Forty-eight, between now and the end of the year."

"Good men?" asked Robert.

"Oh, yes, sir. Experienced men, several corporals and sergeants."

"Tell them all their discharge has been deferred until next year. If they query it, and it's certain some will, then tell them it's because of the war. We need experienced men to lick the new recruits into shape."

Colonel Monroe shook his head. "Do you know how people are referring to the last few years? They call them the 'Years of Slaughter', and you can see why. If you go out into the countryside, it is empty. Farms abandoned. Crops rotting in the fields and peat left uncut. But you will have seen all this yourself."

"Colonel, please note I do not want to hear you telling me that you 'cannot' find more people. I want you to tell me how you are going to find those people. On second thoughts, I don't even wish to hear that. I only want you to do it. Do I make myself clear?"

"Abundantly, my lord, but this war does not help. We know

we will have another draft transferred to the Army in England."

"Then I suggest you begin at once and give it your best efforts." Robert stood up (effectively closing the conversation), turned on his heel and left the room.

Robert spent the next two weeks riding out to the local towns when he knew the recruiting officers would be there. At the back of his mind was the thought of what Arthur might be doing with Mary. His mood went blacker and blacker. He simply could not imagine how his brother and his wife could betray him.

One morning he was at Moate, a large village where the recruiting officer had set up a table in an alehouse. But there were pitifully few men of age to enlist. Eventually, a pair of possible recruits approached the table, and the officer launched into his well-worn recruiting speech.

"Good morning, gentlemen! You look like two likely lads. The Army can use fine men like you. Do you want regular food, a uniform, and a whole shilling a day? His Majesty will pay a special Bounty to such excellent men as you. One more question and we are done. You are both members of the Church of England, aren't you? Because if you say you are, I can sign you up, and you can get that Bounty, and food for your families."

The two men looked at each other. They appeared to be in their early twenties, but both looked tired and gaunt. The attractions of food and shelter evidently outweighed any reservations they may have had to swearing loyalty to a faith different from their own.

"Come along now. Make your mark, and I'll give you your first shilling. What's more, I'll buy you a pint of beer to seal the bargain."

The men looked at each other again, and one of them stepped forward.

"I'll sign, sir."

"Good man! Name?"

"Daniel Lynch, sir."

"Age?"

"Twenty-one, sir."

"That's excellent. Now, Daniel, you make your mark here." He pushed a quill into the man's hand. Daniel signed an X where he was shown and looked at the recruiting officer, his eyes full of expectation.

"Right, my man. Here's your shilling. Hold tight to it for now, and if you see the inn-keeper inside, he'll give you a pint of beer. Now, what about your friend? Doesn't he want to sign?"

"I think so, sir. Joseph, will you sign?" he called out to the other man.

"Good man, you will be glad you have. Name?"

"Joseph Lynch, sir, He's my brother." He gestured towards Daniel.

"And how old are you, Daniel?"

The other man looked at the officer and stammered his answer.

"N-n-nineteen, sir."

"Right, make your mark, as your brother did," Joseph stepped forward and executed a clumsy X below his brother's mark.

"Here's your shilling. Now you go inside and enjoy your beer."

The two brothers disappeared inside the inn as Robert walked over to the table.

"How goes it today? Are recruits hard to find?"

"Indeed they are, sir. The country is nearly empty. Almost everyone who was able has gone to England or America. These two couldn't afford to go. They didn't insist they were Catholics so we can recruit them. The Army needs them, and they need the money for their families."

"How many more do you think you'll get today?"

"If we are lucky, we'll get another six. Not more."

"What will you do with them?"

"We will take them all before the magistrate. They'll be sworn in, and they'll be the King's men. We will march them back to Athlone tomorrow. There's a barn outside the town where they can sleep tonight. They won't get their Bounty till we get them to Athlone. We don't want them disappearing."

"We will need a lot more than eight to replace our losses," Robert said sourly.

"How many do we need, sir?"

"Several hundred."

"Can we use the press gang, sir?"

"If we need to. The magistrates will issue the orders if we ask. Get these men back to Athlone, and we will send out the recruiting officers to every hamlet and town in Westmeath."

The officer went outside, but the street was almost deserted. Some local women were heading to the market for food, and one or two elderly farmers were driving a thin-looking beast to the market or the butchers. But there was no sign of any young men of the right age; not even any youths who could enlist as drummer boys. With a sigh, the officer returned to the recruiting table and reached into his satchel for some bread and cheese for his lunch.

Robert went into the inn, where the two new recruits were sitting at a table, sipping their beer. The two infantrymen were keeping half an eye on them. Robert knew that it was their job to make sure they didn't change their mind.

The landlord brought him a plate of bread and cold meat, with a jug of beer and a pewter tankard. He ate slowly, jotting calculations in his notebook, trying to work out the best places to send the press gangs, and on what days. News that they were using the press would circulate within hours of their appearance so the operation would need to be swift and forceful.

The bed at the inn was hard, and he was up early the following morning and on his way towards Athlone by nine o'clock. He was back in the barracks by eleven and went straight in to see Colonel Monroe.

"We will need the press," he stated as soon as they were alone and seated.

"Why do you say that?" asked the Colonel.

"The land looks empty, but there are still farms being worked, there are still beasts coming to market. The men are out there, but they are not showing themselves. The only way we can meet the losses from the famine and the war is by using the press. I know we aren't supposed to press men needed for harvest, but we need men now."

"Very well, my lord. We will plan and prepare this week, and begin next Monday, working through the towns on market day. I will have the adjutant draft a schedule. Will you see the magistrate?"

"We will press in Westmeath first, and then in the neighbouring counties. There are over thirty towns in this county. That should be enough to give us more than one thousand alone. I am hoping the threat of the press will help them to volunteer."

Colonel Monroe agreed and sent for his adjutant to formulate a detailed plan and schedule. Robert returned to his quarters. There he gave his thoughts over to his other significant problem: his wife and his brother.

"Hush, my love. We have a week," Arthur whispered to Mary as he held her in his arms.

"Oh, Arthur, I'm worried that he suspects."

"We must be careful. We know that, and we are careful." Arthur kissed her as he moved out of her bed. "The household is all asleep. Mrs O'Mahoney would never give us away, anyway."

"Oh, my darling. If only I could believe you!"

"You can. You must! Now I am off before people start moving." With that, Arthur put on his breeches, shirt and boots, then turned to her. "Ride over to Belfield House tomorrow afternoon. Mr and Mrs Murphy will be in Mullingar. It's market day, and they need to go anyway. We should have at least two hours alone."

With that, he crept out of the door and down the stairs, walking the mile and a half back to Belfield House across the fields.

The next day Arthur saw his housekeeper and gardener off in the trap to Mullingar. Sure enough, within the hour he heard a horse arriving. He got up and turned around to see Mary turning into the drive. He ran over to her and lifted her from the saddle, and held her to his breast as soon as her feet were on the ground.

"How much time do we have?" asked Mary, with a look of pure passion.

"We have two hours at least," replied Arthur, taking her horse and fastening the reins to a ring in the wall.

"Let's not waste it," said Mary, and led him by the hand into the house. They went upstairs, pulling their outer garments off as they went and arrived at the door to his room with Mary wearing only a shift and Arthur wearing only his breeches. They kissed and, still in an embrace, headed over to his bed. Mary pushed him back until he fell back onto the sheets.

Arthur tried to raise himself to look at her, but she pushed him down again. She reached to unfasten the buckle on his belt, grasping his waistband and pulling his breeches down and off his feet. This time, he stayed there, drinking in every inch of her body as she pulled her shift over her head. She stood in front of him, and held her breasts as if offering them to him, then knelt in front of him and kissed the inside of his knees, working her way up his limbs until reaching his manhood. She had no hesitation in kissing the end, opening her mouth to taste him at length.

Arthur closed his eyes and felt every nerve in his body tingle and burn. He endured this as long as he could before he reached down to pull her up and into his embrace.

An hour later, they lay in each other's arms, almost drifting in and out of sleep. "You know, I have never been so happy in my life," murmured Mary.

"I feel the same," replied Arthur, raising himself on his elbow and turning to plant a series of kisses on her lips, her cheeks, her neck, and her breast. "You know I do."

"What time is it?"

Arthur turned to the table and looked at the clock there. "Half past three," he murmured.

"I must go. The children will be expecting me. Besides, your people will be back from the market shortly."

"You are right," replied Arthur. "Tomorrow I will pay a

proper call at Gaulstown, and see the children again. I'll come by in the afternoon. We will try for another meeting alone soon. I must be back to my duties at Athlone next week, anyway. And let's not forget, Robert is due back then."

"I dread his return," said Mary, with a shiver.

"I have heard that he has sent out the press in Athlone and the villages. I expect we will get them around here too, although Lord knows the pickings will be thin indeed."

"At least we have four more days," answered Mary." Here, help me on with my dress and coat."

Ten minutes later, he was lifting her back onto her horse, her leg cocked elegantly on the side-saddle.

As she left Belfield House and passed through its gates, she turned her horse for home without noticing the stationary rider some fifty yards behind her. If she had seen him, she would have recognised the corpulent and solid figure of Mr Flynn, her husband's land agent.

She didn't see that gentleman take a notebook from his pocket. After consulting his pocket watch, he carefully made an entry in the notebook before restoring it to his pocket, patting it, and continuing his journey.

Chapter Thirteen

SHOTS AND DEPARTURES

On the following Monday morning, Mr Flynn was sitting in his tiny office in Mullingar when the door opened without a knock. Flynn looked up. He was about to protest but thought better of it when he saw the formidable figure of his principal employer.

"Come in, my lord," he cried. "Come in. Do sit yourself down. Can I offer your lordship any tea?"

"No, you cannot," Robert growled. He flung himself into a chair, clearly in a foul temper. "I have only one question. Do you have any information for me?"

"Well, my lord. I do. Although if it's information you want to hear, I cannot tell."

"That is not your concern. Get on with it, man!"

Flynn reached into his pocket and produced a large, well-thumbed notebook.

"My lord, you asked me to watch her ladyship, and I have, as much as I could within reason. I haven't seen her leave Gaulstown at any time, but three days ago, I had been out with one of your tenants at Milltownpass. I was riding back when I saw her ladyship, on her horse, come out from the gates at Belfield House and head towards home." He consulted his notebook. "That would be just before a quarter to four, my lord."

"Is that all?" demanded Robert.

"Well, yes, but I can tell you that Mr Arthur and her ladyship have been out riding together. I know he has been late over to Gaulstown on at least one occasion."

"What do you mean, man?"

"Well, I was watching outside Gaulstown one evening, and I saw Mr Arthur arrive about dinner time. I stayed where I was, and I never saw him leave. That happened twice last week."

"Thank you, Flynn," Robert replied. "Although, as you said, I am not sure that this is information that I wished to hear. No, it is no matter. You have done what I asked. You will never speak of this again, save in a court of law."

"Of course, my lord," cried Flynn, indignant at the suggestion.

Robert got up and left the office, putting his hat on as he went. Flynn visibly relaxed once Robert had gone. While Robert may hold his life in his hands, all the same, he couldn't help his feelings of distaste for the task he had undertaken.

As Robert walked back to the barracks a wave of fury overtook him. What was nothing more than suspicion had now been magnified into raging certainty. The quality or quantity of evidence from Mr Flynn never entered his head. He strode into his office and seized a pair of pistols. These he loaded and primed with all the care he could muster, then tucked them into his pockets and strode outside to his horse.

Thirty minutes later, he stormed into Gaulstown.

"Where is she?" he shouted. "Where are you, *your ladyship*?" The last two words were loaded with scorn and derision.

The house fell still. He heard his children playing in their nursery, and noises coming up from the kitchen. "Where is she?" he shouted again.

Mrs O'Mahoney emerged from the kitchen, clearly frightened. "My lord, what is it?"

"My wife. Where is she?" Robert demanded. "Call all the staff."

Two minutes later a gaggle of chambermaids and servants, accompanied by the butler, gathered in the hall. By this time Robert's foul temper had increased even more.

"I want someone to tell me where my wife is," he shouted

again.

There was silence. At length, one of the maids stuttered, "She is out, my lord. She told me she would be out for the afternoon."

Robert stared at them, watching them quail under his gaze. Without another word, he walked out of the house and round to the stables. "Saddle that horse, and fast!" he barked at the first groom he found. He stood tapping the handle of his whip on the stable door while the groom saddled the nearest hunter. As soon as the groom led it out of the stable, Robert grabbed the reins and leapt into the saddle, kicking the horse furiously into a gallop.

Belfield House was only two miles away, and with a fresh horse, Robert was there in less than ten minutes. He threw himself from his horse, marched up the steps and through the front door. In the drawing room, he saw Arthur and Mary sitting close, side by side, with their heads together. When he entered, they jumped up, startled, and sprang apart.

"Robert! It isn't what you think," protested Arthur.

"It isn't? And exactly what do I think it is?" demanded Robert.

Mary rushed to Arthur's side, seeking his protection. Robert instantly had his suspicions confirmed. She had looked to Arthur for support, rather than to him, her husband.

"You bastard. You black-hearted rogue!" Robert spat. "And you! You're my wife!"

"Robert, I love him!"

"You what?"

"I love him, and he loves me!"

"What does that have to do with anything? You, madam, are my wife! You belong to me, body and soul. You are my property."

Arthur spoke up. "Robert, wait. She is innocent in all this."

"You bastard!" cried Robert, reaching into his pocket and pulling out a pistol. As he moved to cock it with his other hand, Arthur dived at him and tried to grasp the gun. There was an explosion, and Arthur fell to the floor, bleeding from the shoulder.

With a scream, Mary threw herself on his body. "You've killed him!"

"I think not," said Robert, as Arthur began to move. "But I will." He drew the second pistol from his other pocket.

"Robert, no!" screamed Mary.

"You, madam, be silent. This is between my brother and me." As he raised the pistol, Mary threw herself at him and knocked his arm, deflecting his aim. The gun discharged, and the ball went into the wall.

"Come with me, madam," he said in icy tones. "I will return to finish this business later."

He grasped her upper arm and dragged her out to his horse, mounting and pulling her up over the saddle in front of him. She struggled, but he held her with one hand while he took the horse's reins and left Belfield House at a canter.

Back at Gaulstown, he pulled her down from the horse and dragged her into the house. The entire household was waiting in the hall.

"This is my wife," he snarled. "This is her home, and here she will stay." He marched her up the stairs and into her room, threw her through the door, slammed it shut and locked it.

"My wife is in her room," he announced to the staff from the top of the stairs. "She is to stay here. Do you understand?"

Twenty heads nodded agreement.

"If I find that she has been let out, by anyone, that person will lose their post immediately. Which of you is her maid?"

Sarah put her hand up.

"You are dismissed without notice. Pack your belongings and be out of this house in ten minutes."

"But my lord!" she cried.

"Nine minutes."

The maid burst into tears and scuttled away to her room to collect her belongings.

"Remember what I have said," he shouted to the rest of the staff, before returning to his study and slamming the door.

Mrs Murphy, terrified at the sound of the shots and the screams, had hidden herself away in the kitchen. Once she was sure Robert had gone, she braced herself to go into the drawing room. Seeing Arthur lying bleeding on the floor, she ran back to the kitchen to fetch some cloths and a basin of water. She came back and carefully pulled his shirt away from the wound. Feeling around, she found the ball had cut a groove across the top of his shoulder but had, by some miracle, missed the bone. Arthur groaned, and Mrs Murphy rolled a piece of cloth into a pad and put it into his mouth.

"Here, sir. Bite on this. It will help."

She pulled him into a sitting position and lifted his shirt off him. Then she took a bottle of brandy and poured a liberal amount into the wound. Arthur screamed at the pain, but the housekeeper knew the spirit would clean the wound and help stop it getting infected. She looked for any scraps of fabric from the shirt and picked them away with a delicate touch. She also allowed Arthur to take one large swallow of the brandy.

The bleeding had almost stopped. She made some pads and bound them into place with a bandage made from a torn sheet.

"Right, sir. We have to get you away from here."

"Where can I go?" Arthur mumbled.

"Don't worry, sir. I'll look after you."

Mrs Murphy left him for a moment and went out to the stables. "Patrick, you lazy, idle man. Come here, and help look after Mr Arthur."

Her husband, the groom, came forward. "We need to hide him for a few hours and get him away. Where can we put him for now?"

"We'll put him in the peat diggings."

The two of them helped Arthur walk the fifty yards to a shed in the garden. There was a small stack of peat there that they used to help Arthur mount his horse. It only took five minutes more to walk the horse carrying Arthur into the diggings and out of sight. There they eased him off the horse and seated him as comfortable as they could with a flask of water and a hunk of bread.

Arthur felt like death; his shoulder was well bandaged, and he couldn't tell if the bleeding had stopped. Mrs Murphy's unexpected skill with bandages could well have saved his life.

He lay there on a peat bank, feeling waves of nausea come over him, followed by pain like he had never known before. He was too tired to move and could feel himself slipping into unconsciousness.

Mrs Murphy walked back to the house with her husband and discussed their best course of action. They knew they had to get Arthur away to somewhere he could heal. While they knew of his affair with Lady Belfield, she was a lady of great popularity. They saw no reason to bring her any distress, but for the time being their duty lay with Arthur.

Mrs Murphy ran up to Arthur's room and packed up enough small clothes, shirts and breeches to form a bundle that could be carried if necessary. She also grabbed a sheet to use for fresh bandages and returned to the kitchen to pack some bread, cold meat, cheese and brandy.

"What are we going to do with him?" asked Patrick.

"Whatever it is, we'll have to be quick about it. His lordship will be back soon, and we have no time to lose."

"He can't do anything to us here?"

"Don't be an idiot, man. He is a lord. He rules here now, and he will be back soon. We've got to be well away from here before he gets back."

They found Arthur sitting on the peat bank, out of the wind and as comfortable as he could make himself.

They told him what they were planning. Arthur began to protest but was cut short by Mrs Murphy.

"You are in no condition to do anything, sir. You've got a hole in your shoulder, and you have to get that fixed and healed."

Arthur nodded.

"We need money if we are to get away from here," he said in a faint voice. "Go back to the house, and look in my room. You know my trunk? Well, there is a small box in there with money. Bring it, if you can. My sword and a pair of pistols from my study may be useful."

Mrs Murphy nodded and went quickly back into the house by the kitchen door, returning a few minutes later with three leather purses, some loose coins, three blankets from her store, and Arthur's sword and pistols from the study.

"So where do we go, sir?" asked Patrick.

"I don't know, but we must move quickly. The press gang is out all over Westmeath. Eventually, I will go to Dublin; I have friends near there where I can rest and heal. But what about you two?"

"Don't be worrying about us, sir. Dublin will be grand for us. We will try to go to America. Many others from around here have gone there, especially since your brother started throwing people off their farms."

"And tonight? We must move now. Let's head for Rochfortbridge, and cross the river into King's County. There is no press there yet."

"No, sir. That way is too close to Gaulstown. Better we cross the highway near to Milltownpass. That way is only about seven miles."

"What about shelter?"

"Have you seen how many empty farms there are, sir? We'll find us a byre or cottage for tonight. To be sure, there are plenty of abandoned farms towards Rathconnel."

The three of them stepped out at a slow pace, with their bundles tied behind the saddle, and the Murphys walking on either side of Arthur to keep him from falling. By Arthur's pocket watch, they reckoned they had about three hours until dark. That should be enough time to get out of Westmeath, with care. Arthur was sweating with pain, as the shock of his wound took effect. Mrs Murphy knew they had to get him under cover and to let him rest.

"Tell me, Mrs Murphy, where did you learn to bandage gunshot wounds like that? I am blessed that you were on hand to strap me up."

"You be quiet now and save your strength, sir. Patrick will tell you as we walk."

"Well, sir, you know that Elizabeth – Mrs Murphy – and I have been married for a good age now. Well, before we came to Belfield House, you know I was a soldier? Elizabeth here followed the drum for many years. I rose to be sergeant myself and served in America and in Scotland. She helped many surgeons tying up soldiers' wounds. This is not a skill you forget."

Arthur nodded his thanks and gritted his teeth. After an hour, they stopped for ten minutes to rest, and Arthur eased himself from the saddle and sat down. Mrs Murphy cast an experienced eye over his bandages and tutted to herself.

"The bleeding seems to have stopped, but I need to change the dressing. I am going to put another strip from the sheet over this one, to hold it in place till we find somewhere."

With much difficulty, they got Arthur back in the saddle and set out, always heading south-west. The press being out, and the deaths in the Year of Slaughter, meant few people were travelling anyway. All they had to do was avoid any groups of soldiers.

Luck was with them. They crossed the Mongagh River at a ford, and with it, the county border. Dusk was falling when they started to look around for a deserted farm or cottage. It took almost until dark, but they eventually found one deserted two-room building. There was still a bed-frame there and a pair of broken chairs. A pair of pottery cups and a plate added to their treasure trove. Between them, they got Arthur off his horse, into the cottage and onto the bed-frame. There was still some dry peat on the peat-stack, and it was a moment's work to get a small fire going on the hearth.

Their supper that night was bread and cheese, but it was enough. There was a stream where they could get water, and before they lay down to sleep, they all had a small drink from the brandy bottle.

Arthur's sleep was fitful, and he started to toss and turn. Mrs Murphy got up to attend to him several times, but they had no light apart from the stars and the moon and a glow from the peat fire.

Daylight came, and they made a quick and cheerless breakfast. Mrs Murphy set about the laborious task of re-bandaging Arthur's shoulder, then they packed up their meagre possessions and tied them all on the horse. This time, Arthur tried walking. With his arm now in a sling and his good arm hanging on to the horse's saddle, he could make good progress, at least for the first couple of hours.

By noon, they had covered the ten miles to Coolestown and stopped at the inn there. Patrick went in and brought out three tankards of ale, and they sat to eat and regain their strength. They still had to keep a look out for soldiers, but after a rest and some food, Mrs Murphy called at one of the shops and bought more bread, some tea and a kettle. Loading their shopping on the horse, they headed east out of Coolestown, en route to Dublin.

Chapter Fourteen

THE CONSEQUENCES OF LOVE,
OR LACK OF IT

"Where is he?" screamed Robert, as Mary cowered in her bed. "You heard me, where is he?"

"I don't know," she sobbed. "Is he alive?"

"Yes, curse him. He was gone when I went back."

"Thank God."

"How dare you? How dare you thank God for him? How dare you thank the Lord for the adulterer who stole my property?"

"I am not your property, Robert. I am your wife."

"And the law says you are my property. I told you this before. I will never surrender you to an adulterer. Why? How could you do this? And with my brother, of all people?"

"Because he loved me. He loved me as you should have loved me. And I love him."

"What are you talking about? He 'loved' you? I have never heard the like. He 'loved you!' No, Madam, he was rutting with you, like the beasts in the field."

"He loves me more than you ever did. To you, I am only a woman to give you an heir. Beyond that, you have no interest in me at all. I am your wife, but you have never, ever treated me like one. But with him, I felt loved and wanted. I felt as if I was the most important woman in the world. I felt complete. He brought me passion. He cared for me, and he cared about me as a woman. He thought about me. All the things that you have never, ever done."

"Madam, this conversation is over. I bid you goodnight."

Robert went out of her room, slammed the door and locked it behind him, then stomped down the stairs and into his study. There he poured a full glass of brandy and sat in silence.

After half an hour, there was a timid knock at the door. Mrs O'Mahoney poked her head into the room. "Would your lordship be wanting any dinner?"

"No. Get out, woman. No, wait, send my valet to me."

A minute later, Steele knocked and entered his study, and stood by the door, waiting. He coughed, and Robert looked up.

"Lay out a fresh uniform and linen. I will be moving into the barracks, at least for a few days. Pack me a portmanteau. You will come with me. There will be space made for you in there. I will not spend more nights here than I have to. And bring me something to eat."

Steele strode quietly out of the study and reappeared a few minutes later carrying a plate piled with cold chicken, potatoes and some bread. He put the plate on the table then left the room, closing the door behind him.

Robert took a mouthful of brandy and chewed listlessly at his dinner. An hour later, the glass empty, he climbed the stairs to his room where Steele stood waiting for him to prepare for bed. Twenty minutes later, he was asleep.

In the morning, he found that Steele had made all ready, and after a solitary breakfast, he left Gaulstown, leaving Steele to follow with his baggage.

An hour later, he was entering the gates of Rochfort House. His temper was still vile but had subsided onto icy coldness.

He dismounted, and George's butler showed him into the house. George was about to go out, but took off his coat and showed Robert into his study.

"What brings you here, Robert? It's a few months since we saw you. Still pressing men?"

Robert looked at him from under his lowered eyebrows. "I could never believe such conduct from my own brother!" he rasped out.

George's face grew pale. "Why, Robert, what are you accusing me of?"

"Not you, you idiot. Arthur. He has been deceiving me with

my wife. My wife, do you hear?"

George bridled at Robert calling him an idiot. He was relieved when he realised that he wasn't the target of his brother's anger. "Surely not," he replied.

"She has admitted it. She had the gall to accuse me of 'not loving her', whatever that may mean. She is an earl's wife. She bears my name."

George looked at him sharply. "What will you do?"

"I have already done it. I found them together at Belfield House, and I shot him."

"You… You what?"

"I shot him. Are you deaf as well as stupid?"

"Did you kill him?"

"Alas, no. We fought, and I shot him in the shoulder."

"What about Mary?"

"I brought her back to Gaulstown, and there she will stay."

"And Arthur?"

"Gone. Fled the scene on horseback. I went back to Belfield House, and he had flown the coop. He obviously had help. The servants had both vanished too. The house will revert to me now."

"What about Arthur?"

"What about him? He is gone, and that is all that matters. If he shows his face here again, you are to tell me at once. Do you understand?"

"Yes, of course. But what of Mary?"

"She will stay at Gaulstown. I have Belvedere, and I will extend it and use it as my home. I wish never to spend a night under the same roof as her again."

"What about the children?"

"They will live with me at Belvedere. I will not leave them to be brought up by such as her."

George was alarmed in many ways by this unexpected news, not least by Robert's announcing his intention to live at Belvedere. He had no wish to have Robert poking his nose into his business. For the moment, he wanted time to think how he could turn this situation to his advantage. Robert's high-handed (and possibly questionable) taking of Belfield House was something for consideration later. There was no doubt that Robert had acted outside the law, but no Irish judge or magistrate would find against him.

"Robert," mused George, "You have patrols at your disposal. It may be to your advantage to send one out to sweep along the county border. A wounded man might be easy to find. Anyway, what will you do when you find him?"

Robert thought for a moment. "I will kill him. Nobody insults me like this. He may be my brother, but no matter."

"So, a duel? We haven't had one in the family for two generations, and the last one did not end well. You may want to think again, even though you are the injured party."

"I have time. He has a pistol ball in him, and I will find him. Now, I'm off to Mullingar." With that, Robert turned on his heel and walked out to his horse.

An hour later, Robert was repeating his news to Colonel Bryant in the barracks, and arranging quarters for his valet.

"I agree with your brother," said Colonel Bryant. "If we are to find him without setting the country in an uproar, I can send out a patrol. They will have instructions to keep their eyes out for a man with a gunshot wound. I will also alert the magistrates."

"Thank you. This will be a long task, but sooner or later, I will find him."

Over the next two weeks, patrols concentrated on the county border area. A general warning was passed to the magistrates and watchmen, but without results. Robert refused to escalate the search and make it public. An insult like this was not to be borne. It was Arthur that he wanted, and Arthur alone.

That particular individual was, by now, just outside Dublin. Arthur and his unlikely companions were sheltering in an inn in Rathmines, a village south of the city. Arthur's shoulder was starting to heal, and the three of them were discussing their predicament and trying to find a suitable course of action.

"Why are you doing this?" asked Arthur, as they sat in the inn, eating a plate of beef and potatoes.

"Well, sir. You see, we know you, and your brothers. We also understand how you manage your tenants and staff. We've seen how your brothers harass theirs, with rents increased, and families thrown off their land. That's not your way, sir. You have been good to us, and the least we can do is return the favour. Besides, two of your farms are held by cousins of ours. As an old soldier, I'm no friend of the watch, or of magistrates."

"What will you do?"

"America is looking best for us. They need good workers, and there's always work for a housekeeper and groom."

"How will you find a ship?"

"Oh, there's plenty of ships going over to America. There's many Irish over there too, so we'll not be feeling lonely. We are only a couple of miles from the River Liffey here, sir, and I'm planning to start looking tomorrow."

"What will it cost?"

"Never your mind that, sir. We'll manage. We have something put by too."

"No, tell me. I want to help you. If you hadn't got me away from Belfield House, I'd be dead. That's without the care you have given me over the last two weeks."

"Passage would be five pounds for the two of us, sir."

"Let no more be said. You go and find a ship, and I'll happily stand you the fares."

Mrs Murphy started to weep. "But sir, what about you?"

"I'll be all right. I'm going to cross to England and head for London. I need to make enquiries of some friends there."

"What about the horse?" asked Patrick.

"I'll sell her. She's a beautiful mare, and the Irish know their horses. I won't get all I want, but I should get something decent for her."

"Begging your pardon sir, you have a wounded shoulder. It's healing well, so it is, but you can't go humping a portmanteau around. So, first thing tomorrow, let's find a buyer for your horse, a boat for yourself, and then one for Mrs Murphy and me."

Arthur smiled gratefully. "That sounds an excellent idea."

The following day, the three of them headed north to the horse market at Smithfield. It wasn't long before a swarthy, unshaven elderly horse-coper expressed an interest.

"Twenty guineas and dat's me final offer," was the best they could get from him. Arthur knew that was cheap, but he needed to sell her, and she was too good a horse to end up in the shafts of a cart. With luck, she would be bought within a week by a gentleman looking for a useful hunter.

After concluding this transaction, they walked down to the river wharves. There, they found a hive of activity, but at the seaward end of the north wall, there was a section of boats all with posters and boards displayed, touting for custom. There was one due to sail the next day for Bristol, and, for the sum of a guinea, Arthur could secure passage on her.

More enquiries identified a ship that was sailing in two days for Boston. She was still discharging the last of a cargo of timber, and the master was happy to take two passengers who could pay a whole five pounds in cash. For a sum like that, he was more than happy to allow them to board straight away.

The trio said their farewells on the wharf before Arthur's boat sailed for Bristol.

"What will you do when you get there?" asked Elizabeth.

"I'll go to London. I need to see my man-of-business and lawyer. I also want to see a certain Mr Stafford. He is a man of power, and his advice will be useful."

Mary awoke with the first shards of daylight piercing her window. Nothing was stirring. It was too early for anyone else to be awake. She could not blot out the events of the previous day: the deafening crack of the pistol, the sight of Arthur falling to the floor with blood spouting from his shoulder, and throwing herself at Robert in desperation. The moments after Robert seizing her arm and throwing her over his horse's pommel were blank. She remembered being in the hall at Gaulstown, and then nothing.

She tried moving, and every muscle hurt. She had to get up to ease her bladder, and her stomach and breast were black and blue with bruising from being carried on Robert's horse.

A dark cloud of despair washed over her. The only man she had ever truly loved had been shot in front of her, and, for all she knew, could now be dead from blood loss or another shot from Robert. The despair overwhelmed her, and she subsided onto the bed and drifted in and out of an uneasy sleep.

When she awoke, a worried-looking Mrs O'Mahoney was placing a tray with tea and breakfast on a small table in her room.

"My lady, are you all right?"

"Oh, Mrs O'Mahoney. What have I done? What has happened?"

"No one rightly knows, ma'am. Mr Arthur has disappeared, wounded or not. So have the groom and housekeeper. His lordship left with his valet and groom early this morning."

"My children?"

"Downstairs with Nurse. I will send them up to you in an hour. I will come back in a little while and help you dress today. We'll have to turn one of the housemaids into a new maid for you. His lordship turned Sarah off without notice yesterday."

The housekeeper left Mary to her breakfast. She had no appetite, but managed to drink some tea, and ate a boiled egg.

"Do you want me to dress you, ma'am?" asked Mrs O'Mahoney. "I've brought Bridget up with me. She is a bright girl, and she can learn to look after you." Bridget, a young woman with flashing dark eyes and a red tinge to her hair, stepped forward for Mary's approval.

"Bridget will do very well, Mrs O'Mahoney, I'm sure."

The two of them helped Mary to dress. Bridget seemed a bright girl, and at length, Mrs O'Mahoney pronounced herself satisfied. They left Mary ready to go downstairs and greet her children. Fortunately, they were too young to understand what had happened, and in any case, Robert was an infrequent visitor to the nursery.

On Friday of the following week, the butler came to her in the drawing room and surprised her. "You have a visitor, ma'am. 'Tis Mr Flynn."

Mr Flynn entered and approached her. "Your ladyship. I am Joseph Flynn, his lordship's land agent."

"I'm delighted to meet you, Mr Flynn," replied Mary. This was true. Any new face, any contact with the outside world, was welcome. She had seen no one apart from the staff at Gaulstown since that fateful day. She felt starved of news. She loved her children dearly, but they were not the same as adult company.

"Ma'am. His lordship has bid me call on you to restate his instructions. These are that you stay here, within the confines of Gaulstown. He will permit no visitors or communications. There will be no letters sent or delivered. The number of servants is to be cut immediately. He tells me you are to have the housekeeper, a groom, your new maid and a gardener. The butler is to move to Belvedere, where he will be butler for his lordship. The other staff are to be dismissed."

"And the children?"

"Ma'am, I am to take the children and their nurse back to Belvedere with me today."

Mary dissolved into tears and let out a cry of anguish. She collapsed into a chair.

"Not my children! Mr Flynn, why are you doing this?"

"Ma'am, I must protest. I do nothing, except relay these instructions from his lordship. It is not for me to argue them or to change them." Mr Flynn rang for a maid and ordered tea for Mary. She glanced at him with an expression of mute thanks as she fought to regain control of herself.

Mary suddenly sat up straight and stiffened herself. "Let him do his worst. He will not break me. He will NEVER break me! I am his wife and the mother of his children."

"Ma'am, I will do what I can to help you, and to break the monotony of your stay, but my hands are tied. You know there is no arguing with his lordship on this matter. I will also make sure you have sufficient funds to live as you should."

Mary dragged herself to her feet, still feeling stunned by

the news about the children. She summoned all the staff to the entrance hall and gave them the fateful news. Four of them were to lose their positions. She told Nurse to pack both her own and the children's possessions. For the rest, she told all of them that they were welcome to stay at Gaulstown until they could obtain another position. She assured them all that they would leave with a good character and her best wishes.

An hour later, Mr Flynn was anxious to get on his way. He wanted to get back to Mullingar before nightfall. Nurse came down with a maid, carrying a portmanteau which was placed in the carriage.

Mary called the children and held them fast. She hardly trusted herself to speak, but clung to them until George started to cry. Pulling herself together, she planted a final kiss on the children's cheeks.

"Right, Nurse. Off you go now. Look after them for me."

Mr Flynn and Nurse saw how fragile Mary was, and whisked the children out of the front door and into the carriage. Mary followed them to the door and saw the carriage pass out through the gates. In her heart, she wondered when and if she would ever see them again.

Over the next week, the staff who were to lose their positions all packed their belongings and left. A subdued Mary spoke to each of them before they went and wished them good fortune.

At the end of the week, she summoned the staff that were left. She explained that she intended to make the best of things; to keep Gaulstown in as good a state as she could. There could be no lowering of standards.

The following Monday, she called for Mrs O'Mahoney. "Let us close all the unused rooms in the house. If we try to use fewer rooms, they will be easier to clean. It will also save us on peat for the fires."

The two of them went through the house, closing windows and curtains, covering furniture and locking the doors. By the end of the day, they had closed over half of the house, and the two of them were sitting in the kitchen.

"Well, Mrs O'Mahoney, I believe we should be able to manage the rooms we have left to us."

The housekeeper nodded and smiled as she poured two cups of tea.

With a sense of unease, the household settled into its new routines. Mary had, at least, access to the library, and so could be sure of finding escape in a book. Her easiest escape, though, was to sit and dream of being held in a passionate embrace by the only man who had ever shown her real love, and who was, she knew now, the only man she herself had truly loved.

At night, her memories were more intense, more personal, and she would let her hands roam over her body, remembering how his hands had done the same, before falling asleep and dreaming she was still in his arms.

Chapter Fifteen

IN WHICH WE WELCOME
A NEW REALITY

"I wish to see the Lord Lieutenant," demanded Robert. He had journeyed to Dublin the week after the fracas with Arthur. There were things he needed to clarify.

He was shown into an anteroom, and there he waited. After thirty minutes, his temper was rising, and his stock of patience was exhausted. A flunkey went past him, and Robert stopped him. "Does the Lord Lieutenant know I'm here?" he thundered.

The flunkey stopped. "I will inquire, my lord," he said and moved silently into the inner office.

He re-emerged some minutes later bearing a sheaf of papers. "The Lord Lieutenant's compliments and he will be with you in some thirty minutes. He expresses his regrets, but advises that he is busy with affairs of state."

This did nothing to calm Robert. It was another forty minutes before the Lord Lieutenant finally emerged smiling and extending his hand.

"My lord, my deepest regrets at keeping you waiting. To what do we owe this pleasure?"

In the face of the Lord Lieutenant's friendly manner, Robert's temper and irritability gave way to acute embarrassment.

"Your Grace, I have a personal matter I need to discuss."

"Of course. Come into my office. A glass of sherry?" The Duke showed Robert to a chair, closed the door and resumed his seat at his desk.

"Your Grace, I don't know what you have heard…" stuttered Robert.

"In respect of what, my lord? All I know is there was an incident involving gunfire and yourself. I see you are unharmed, so let us be thankful your attacker missed his shot."

"Your Grace, I must explain. I discovered that my brother, my own brother, has formed an attraction for my wife. I accosted him and ended up wounding him. My brother took a ball in his shoulder."

"My lord! I am appalled that a member of your family could do this. But, no matter, I can see why you challenged him. I will need to speak to your and his seconds, of course, but quite unofficially."

"Unfortunately, there were no seconds, your Grace. I didn't challenge my brother. There was no duel."

"No duel? This is most irregular. What do you intend to do now?"

"If my brother is still in Ireland, I want him arrested, and I want him to feel the full force of the law!"

"I believe you have a problem. Your brother has committed no offence in law. You, as the aggrieved party, had the perfect right to challenge him to a duel. However, by attacking and wounding him, you yourself are guilty of assault."

Robert went white. It seemed the law was not on his side, after all.

"Well, I'll bid you a good day, my lord," said the Lord Lieutenant, showing Robert to the door. "Do come back and see me tomorrow, and we can talk with the garrison commander here on matters military."

In fact, the Lord Lieutenant knew much more about the incident than he would admit. As deputy to the crown in Ireland, he was always kept very well informed on the activities of landowners and Members of Parliament. He had always known that Robert was likely to behave unconventionally, although shooting his brother was far beyond his expectations.

Robert walked back to Gardiner Row in a state of shock. He had been so sure that he had all the advantages of the law. He also suspected that the Lord Lieutenant had been toying with him.

A night with his new mistress did little to quell his worry. Emily was solicitous and did her best to put him at his ease, but was so upset that he could only manage to have sex with her once, and that of a most conventional sort.

The following day Robert returned to the Castle and spent the morning closeted with the Lord Lieutenant and his military council. Plaudits came his way for his recruiting activities. The war was continuing, but the ceaseless demands for more troops were being held in check for the moment.

The following morning, he called for his horse and headed west to Belvedere. His heart was filled with bitterness, and he felt himself to be the victim of a terrible wrong.

In his absence, various matters had piled up and required his attention. The final stages of the alterations had to be put in train. Soon Belvedere would be a remarkable gentleman's residence.

From there, he returned to the barracks at Mullingar to check on the recruiting numbers. These were still sparse, but there was a trickle coming in. When he journeyed to Athlone, he found the garrison almost up to strength. There was still some sickness after the famine of the previous two years, but a good harvest was now reaping dividends. Milk, potatoes and oats were again feeding the population.

The first subject for him to address when he spoke with Colonel Monroe was his brother Arthur. "He will not be returning to duty here," Robert stated.

"Why, where is he?" asked the Colonel.

"He has, unfortunately, received a gunshot wound." Robert could not and would not, under any circumstances, discuss his private affairs, especially with a fellow officer.

Colonel Monroe took one look at his face and decided not to follow this line of enquiry. He went on to discuss the military position and recruitment, and Robert returned to his room in barracks. He resumed his regular routine of military duties, trips to Dublin and settling into Belvedere. But inwardly, he was seething. Bitterness and jealousy started to eat away at him, and brandy brought him solace.

Arthur dismounted from the stage at the Saracen's Head in Whitehall and stretched his long legs to remove the stiffness from being cooped up in the stage for three hours. Two weeks had passed since he arrived in Bristol, and he had made his way slowly towards London. His wounded shoulder was taking some time to heal after the effects of the sea crossing, and he still found it painful.

At the inn, he asked for and obtained a bed for a week. As soon as he had some clean clothes, he paid a call on some old friends to see if any of them had news of Robert or Westmeath. None of them had heard anything. When they asked why he was favouring his left arm, he told them that he had taken a fall out hunting and damaged his shoulder.

As soon as his new clothes were ready, he dressed in his finest and headed to the War Office. He had no appointment, so had to do what any unexpected visitor would do. He asked to see Mr Stafford and sent his card up. The clerk who met him at the door gave him a searching look, but he accepted Arthur's card. On it, Arthur scribbled a note asking to see Mr Stafford on an important personal matter.

After ten minutes, the clerk returned and called Arthur over.

"Mr Stafford can see you but asks that you wait. He may be some time. The footman will take you up to Mr Stafford's anteroom."

The long-case clock in the ante-room ticked its way around, chiming the hour. Shortly after eleven o'clock, the door opened, and Mr Stafford himself came out.

"Mr Rochfort. What a pleasure," he cried, extending his hand.

Arthur rose and gingerly extended his hand in return. The pain in his shoulder flared, and his face went white.

"Tell me, how is your injury? I do apologise. It is

149

obviously still causing you great pain."

Arthur started. He had told nobody in London about his injury. "What do you know about my injury, sir?" he asked.

"I know that your brother shot you, over a supposed affair you were having with Lady Belfield. I know that you were treated by your house-servants, and by a doctor in Bristol."

Arthur's jaw dropped. How did Mr Stafford know? His puzzlement apparently showed in his face.

"Mr Rochfort, it is my job to know such things. These and much more. There is little concerned with the running of this realm that I do not know. Now, you may rest assured, your house-servants have sailed for the Americas."

"Sir, I don't know what to say," said Arthur, amazed that this gentleman appeared to know his every movement. When he looked at Mr Stafford's face, he saw the power in those eyes.

"Mr Rochfort, you will understand that my business is affairs of state, rather than affairs of the heart. The matter of yourself and your brother, and indeed Lady Belfield, is of little concern to me, save how it affects the realm."

Mr Stafford got up and walked over to a map of Great Britain and Ireland.

"Our problem is not Ireland, but Scotland. Scotland is ablaze. We know the French seek to assist the Young Pretender to the throne. We also know he has the support of the Catholic population in Scotland. Ireland is quiet and must remain so. That being the case, I cannot and will not take any action that may change this. You understand my position?"

"Indeed, sir. I only have one question. What do you wish me to do?"

"I need time, as does Lord Belfield, both to sort out his personal affairs and to keep Ireland secure. I want you to return to Gibraltar and resume your duties there. *HMS Viper* sails from Portsmouth in ten days' time. That is plenty of time for you to establish your outfit and make yourself ready. Also, some time for your shoulder to finish healing."

"Sir, I need to see my man-of-business, and, also I need to send a message to Lady Belfield."

"I can at least assist you in this. You and your brother have done an exceptional job of recruiting in the most difficult of circumstances. In Gibraltar, there is much for you to do, and you have the advantage of knowing the garrison. I will ensure that Colonel Monroe and Dublin Castle are suitably advised."

Arthur's brain was whirling. Gibraltar seemed a lifetime away, although he had friends there. At least he could get a letter to Mary, and Mr Stafford would ensure it was delivered.

"There is something else," Mr Stafford went on, "which makes my position even more delicate. You, sir, have committed no crime. Far from it. But your brother, by assaulting and injuring you, is himself guilty of a grave offence. However, I am simply not able to bring him to justice. I hope that, eventually, his temper will cool, and you can come back to Ireland. There I hope you will be able to make your peace with him."

"Sir, I don't know what to say!"

"Then say nothing, sir. If you leave your letter with my clerk tomorrow, it will be delivered. My clerk will also have your orders in writing."

"Sir, I can only thank you." With that, Arthur rose to his feet and shook hands with Mr Stafford, before the footman showed him out and back on to Whitehall.

"Mrs O'Mahoney?" called out Mary, one morning in November 1744. "Do we need provisions?"

"We do, ma'am. I'll be going into the market in Mullingar first thing tomorrow with the trap. We need flour, bacon and some calico."

Mary sighed. "I so wish I was going with you." The confinement of the last few months was taking its toll.

"I am sorry, ma'am. Mr Flynn checks every time I see him that you haven't left Gaulstown. There are too many people around that might see you, and if you ask me it's a risk not worth taking."

Mary sighed. She knew Mrs O'Mahoney was right, but it was so hard to be confined. Worst of all was the agony of not knowing if Arthur was even still alive.

The following day, Mrs O'Mahoney and the gardener, Cahill, made the seven-mile trip into Mullingar for provisions. The streets were lined with stalls selling all manner of items, with some tradesmen setting up their barrows and carts. Farmers' wives were having cooking pots repaired by the tinkers, and the smell of lead solder hung in the air. Knives, sickles and scythes were being sharpened. Wicker crates of chickens and ducks were for sale, with the stall-holder happy to dispatch the bird for the buyer. Mrs O'Mahoney enjoyed two hours of going from stall to stall, purchasing everything required for the small household. She was completing her last purchases when an urchin tugged at her skirts. She looked down and saw a child of about ten, looking up at her.

"Begging your pardon, missus, but would you be the Mrs O'Mahoney from Gaulstown?"

"And if I was, young man, what business is it of yours?" she said, looking at him sharply.

"Mr Flynn told me to give you a message."

"Well, go on then."

"Mr Flynn said would you pass by his office before you go back to Gaulstown," the urchin recited.

"Indeed, I will," replied Mrs O'Mahoney. With that, the child vanished.

Ten minutes later the trap was packed with supplies, and Cahill was getting eager to depart if they were to make it back home in time to put everything away and to cook supper.

"One minute, if you please, Mr Cahill. I have a short call to make." Mrs O'Mahoney made her way the short distance to Mr Flynn's office.

She knocked at the door and went in. Mr Flynn was sitting at his desk, alone in the room. As she entered, he rose and, to her slight surprise, shook her hand.

"Mrs O'Mahoney? Please, sit for a moment. I have a task for you."

Mrs O'Mahoney's interest was piqued.

"I know you to be a loyal and faithful servant to your mistress. Am I right in this?" he asked.

"Indeed, sir, I am. In every way."

"I have a letter for her ladyship. It is sealed and is to be placed into her hands only. You are to advise her to read it, and destroy it."

"I'll do that, sir," she replied, puzzled.

"Under no circumstances is it to be allowed to fall into his lordship's hands. This would spell disaster, for you, for her ladyship, and for myself. I may be his lordship's land agent, but ultimately my loyalty is to the Crown. Do you understand?"

"I do indeed. Now, before I leave you, may I have use of your privy?" asked Mrs O'Mahoney.

"But, of course," replied Mr Flynn. "It is a long ride home in the cart. You'll find it outside in the yard."

"Thank you, sir." Mrs O'Mahoney, she hurried out to the yard, and while otherwise engaged, secreted the letter in her petticoat.

Minutes later, she re-entered the office and left by the front door, after thanking Mr Flynn for his help.

They arrived at Gaulstown in the late afternoon. Mrs O'Mahoney hurried inside and extracted the letter from its hiding place.

She found Mary in the drawing room. "Ma'am, I have something for you. I was given it by Mr Flynn."

Mary looked up, puzzled. "Why, what is it?"

"A letter, ma'am. I am instructed to give it to you personally, and under no circumstances are you to let anyone else see it or find it." She produced the letter and handed it to Mary with as dramatic an air as she could manage.

Mary seized it. The outside, in an unknown hand, merely stated *Lady Belfield*.

She broke the wax seal and opened it. As soon as she started to read the letter, she burst into tears.

"Oh, Mrs O'Mahoney. He is alive. Alive and well."

"Well, that's grand, my lady. He's a fine young gentleman." Mrs O'Mahoney decided that Mary needed a little peace and quiet to read, and quietly left the room.

Alone, at last, Mary devoured the letter line by line,

examining every word, feeling it, smelling the notepaper, anything to regain an impression of the man she loved.

My Darling!
I am alive and well, and loving you. By the time you receive this letter, which is coming to you through the assistance of friends, I will be overseas. I cannot tell you where, but you must believe me, my darling, that I am well and in good spirits. Good spirits that is, apart from missing you. I spend every spare hour remembering our brief times together and the touch and feel of your hands. I remember the taste of your lips as I kissed you, and the shape and feel of your body as I held you.
You must believe I will return to you, my love. It will not be for some time, at least for two years, but I will come back to you, and I will find you and hold you in my arms again. Be strong and have faith. When all else fails, read this letter and remember our time together. Do not lose hope, and please believe me when I say,
I will always love you.
Your ever-loving Arthur.

The words brought her comfort and despair in equal measure: comfort from him being alive and well, but despair at being parted from him. She read it and re-read his letter many times in the following thirty minutes before coming to a decision.

She was not going to let Robert break her. She would survive, and survive well. She still had a household to run. Well, that is exactly what she would do. Confinement and boredom were easy to manage if there was hope in the end.

When Robert next arrived at the Athlone garrison, he called upon Colonel Monroe, and they discussed recruitment.

The colonel added, "Oh, I have been advised by Dublin Castle that your brother has been transferred overseas. We are promoting one of the subalterns in his place to take over his liaison work. I'm sure you will get along. Lieutenant Philips of the Ninth. He's an officer of great promise."

Robert took this news with equanimity. Service overseas frequently meant war with the French in Canada, or in the West Indies where there would be every chance of Arthur dying from the fever.

Chapter Sixteen

A WANDERER RETURNS

"Begging your pardon, sir, but they want you in the Governor's office."

Arthur raised his eyebrows. The community of officers was small in the Colony of Gibraltar, and he knew the Governor, General Hargrave, well. Even so, it was unusual to receive a summons to his office. Under normal circumstances, orders or instructions would come to him down the general military line of command. He expected to receive his orders from his own colonel. He nodded to the orderly and rose from his desk.

A clerk admitted him straight away, and he found both the Governor and his colonel examining some papers.

They both looked up and smiled at him.

The governor was the first to speak. "Good morning, Major. It seems we are to lose you."

Arthur's heart leapt. At last! "How so, Sir?"

"Yes," he went on, "you are going back to Ireland for your next posting. You are to return home on the sloop that arrived today."

Home! Arthur had not allowed himself to dream of home for many months. The idea was almost foreign to him.

A year and a half had passed since he left London. A year and a half without sight of, or word from, the woman he loved.

Before he met Mary, he had never even thought himself in love. He had never been given to introspection. He had assumed that he would, eventually meet a young girl, fall in love with her and marry her. He had a little property, and his commission. He loved his work as a major. He expected to continue to serve for a few years after marrying, before settling down at Belfield to life as a country gentleman.

And then he had met Mary. When he had looked at her, and kissed her fingertips, he had almost been overcome by her effect on him. At that stage, he could not have known if he had the same effect on her.

And, as if to give one hammer-blow after another, it turns out that not only was she married, but married to his brother.

The question of whether Mary still loved him never entered his mind. He knew, with blind certainty, that each had found in the other that one person whom they could, and would, love to the end of their days.

Over the next week, Arthur sorted through his clothes, uniforms and effects. Some he gave away; the rest he packed into his trunk. At the weekend, his orderly took this down to the *Drake* for him and placed it on board.

Arthur made his goodbyes and joined the ship with a packet of reports and documents for Whitehall. Slowly the sloop clawed her way out into Gibraltar Bay. Once clear of the land, she started to beat her way to the south-west past Tarifa Point, and into the prevailing winds. After two days, they were far enough out into the Atlantic for the captain set a northerly course for Finisterre, Ushant and the Needles.

They had a trouble-free passage. They had the advantage of speed, and even though at war, few ships would waste their fire-power pursuing or trying to chase a sloop-of-war. The weather was kind, and eight days after leaving Gibraltar, the *Drake* eased her way into Portsmouth harbour. There she dropped anchor and lay to await her next orders.

On board the *Drake*, the crew launched a cutter and took the captain and Arthur to the Hard, where they parted. The captain went to report to the flag officer, and Arthur to the stage to London.

The next night saw him dining alone at the Saracen's Head in Whitehall. The inn had changed little since he was there three years earlier. It was still a hive of bustle and noise.

His first stop the next morning was to deliver his packet of papers to the Navy Office, after which he made his way to Mr

Stafford's office. After a short wait, he was, once again, shown in.

"Major Rochfort! Come in, sit down," exclaimed Mr Stafford, coming forward to shake Arthur's hand. Arthur gave him an envelope from General Hargrave, then settled himself into a chair. Mr Stafford opened the envelope and read its contents in silence.

"Thank you for bringing this with you. The General remarks that he is sorry to lose you and commends you for your work in the colony."

"Thank you, sir."

"But now to matters of more import, at least for you. I'm sure you wish to return to Ireland, and that is, indeed, where we need you. Athlone, again. For obvious reasons, I would caution you against upsetting your brother. In your absence, His Majesty has created him Earl of Belvedere. This is a mark of the Government's satisfaction with the stability of Ireland, and for his support in the House of Lords."

"I understand, sir. Do you know anything about my other brother, George?"

"Indeed, we do. Your brother's management of his estates, and the stranglehold he currently has on trade, give us grave cause for concern. Again, he has extensive political influence in the area. So please watch, report and wait."

"What of Lady Belfield? Or should I call her Lady Belvedere now?"

"Your brother continues to keep her confined at Gaulstown. As far as I am aware, she is well, but she never leaves the estate. Her husband imposes this 'state of confinement' upon her, and in this, unfortunately, our hands are tied. She is his wife."

Arthur nodded. "What do you wish me to do in Athlone, sir?"

"You are to take over as adjutant to the Garrison Commander. Colonel Monroe still commands there. You know each other, and I have written to him to tell him of your appointment."

"Thank you, sir. This all seems to be good news."

"Let us hope so. Now, if you will go with my clerk, he will see you supplied with written orders. Your appointment starts one month from today, so that should leave you time to make your way over to Ireland and to take some leave after your Gibraltar posting. Finally, may I add, two years have now passed since the unfortunate incident with your brother. I hope he has decided to let the past lie. Scotland is in an uproar, and we cannot manage turmoil in Ireland as well."

Two weeks later, Arthur landed in Dublin. After landing his effects, he set off for Athlone. Colonel Monroe rejoiced on seeing him. He knew Arthur's competence as an officer, and, apart from that, valued his friendship.

As adjutant, Arthur was almost always working with Colonel Monroe and so had less opportunity to ride out and visit in the surrounding countryside, but he still hoped to get in one or two days hunting a week in the winter with the local foxhounds.

Arthur had had no word from Mary. He didn't even know if his letter had reached her, but for the moment he had the discretion to wait. In a few weeks, he would be able to get away from Athlone. All he wanted to do was to see her, and to let her know that he still loved her, and to find out if her feelings for him had remained the same.

One Friday in June, he left Athlone in the early morning. The roads were dry, and he made good progress, turning north towards Gaulstown at Rochfortbridge.

He was sensible enough to avoid going anywhere near his brothers' residences. He was helped in no small measure by his brother George's policy of emptying the farms that he bought in the area. Although the last two harvests had been better, the number of people in the area was still affected by the Year of Slaughter. He approached Gaulstown without seeing anyone except a small number of tenant farmers, none of whom were close enough to recognise him.

He first rode towards the rear of the house, close to the kitchen. Still mounted on his horse, he looked over the hedge and down into the garden, then walked his horse forward, peering over the boundary hedge. As he reached the entrance gates, out of the corner of his eye he saw a flicker of movement near the house. He turned his head and was disappointed when he saw it wasn't Mary.

He could tell, by the movement, that it was a woman. She walked towards him, showing no sign of alarm. Arthur stilled his horse and stayed as still as he could, sheltered by some trees. As the woman came closer, he recognised her: Mrs O'Mahoney.

His horse snickered, and she looked up, startled.

"Mr Arthur! What in the devil's name are you doing here?"

"Mrs O'Mahoney. For pity's sake, tell me. How is Mary?"

"She suffers, Mr Arthur, she suffers terribly. Sometimes I fear for her."

"How so? What is wrong with her?"

"She is fading away, sir. She does not eat. She cannot leave Gaulstown, by his lordship's express orders."

"Does he come here?"

"Rarely, sir. He has his fine new house and his fine new title. You've heard he is the Earl of Belvedere now?"

"I had heard. I hope he is enjoying it. Does he ever speak of me?"

"Never, sir. I've never heard him mention your name from that day to this."

"Can you tell Mary I am here? I'll not risk coming inside."

"I'll do that, sir, but you had best go back round to the back of the house. I'll tell her ladyship to come out into the kitchen garden. You are less likely to be seen or heard there."

At a slow pace, Arthur walked his horse back to the wall surrounding the kitchen garden. He stopped his horse and quietened it, and settled down to wait. It only took a few minutes until the kitchen door opened, and Mary came out. She looked, suddenly caught sight of Arthur's face above the wall, and ran towards him.

Arthur gazed down at the face and figure of the woman he loved. The remains of her delicate beauty were still evident, but her face was pale and wan, and her arms and body seemed stick-thin.

"My darling, what have they done to you?" he whispered, in a voice just loud enough for her to hear him.

"Oh, my love. I am dying, bit by bit. I am like a bird in a cage. I cannot leave this place. I have not set one foot outside Gaulstown since that terrible night."

"Oh, Mary. This is such a shock, for us both. We must be careful, and much more careful than before."

"But your arm, my darling. What happened?"

"The housekeeper and groom rescued me. They found me, dressed my wound and helped me get to Dublin."

"What happened to them?"

"I was able to buy them passage to America. They thought it best to find a country where they can live and work in peace. I owe them my life."

"But where have you been? You look to be fully recovered."

"I am. I've been in Gibraltar again. The garrison needed strengthening with the wars going on, and they sent me there as I knew the place. I am back now, though, and based in Athlone."

"Oh, Arthur – do be careful. Robert is not a kind man, as I know to my cost. Sometimes he visits me here, to gloat over what he has done."

"Mary, my love, I have to go back. Something must change, so let me investigate and make some plans. There has to be a way out of this, at least for you."

"Be careful, my darling. I know now you are safe and well. That is enough. I couldn't bear to lose you again now, and I know Robert's temper."

"Don't worry, I won't do anything stupid or in haste. I can't reach you to kiss you, but seeing you is enough. It has to be enough for now. Keep believing, my love."

With that, he blew her a delicate kiss and turned his horse back towards the road to Rochfortbridge. After a lonely night in the inn there, he made his way back to Athlone.

Arthur's heart lifted over the next few weeks. If he was careful, he would be able to ride over and see Mary again, even if only across a wall. He also knew that even more than before, the way was beset with traps for them both.

Mary almost danced as she made her way back to the kitchen. Arthur was alive – and he still loved her.

"We have orders to go to Dublin," announced Colonel Monroe one July morning. "Some celebrations are in order. Our army under the Duke of Cumberland has thrown back the Scottish Pretender. We have crushed their rebellion, and there is to be a parade, and a ball in Dublin Castle."

"That will be excellent," answered Arthur. While Athlone might be a pleasant and peaceful little town, the prospects for enjoyment were few and far between.

Arthur spent the next week organising his troops' visit. On the following Monday, they left Athlone, with Arthur and Colonel Monroe riding, and a half-company of infantrymen accompanying them. At a marching pace, they could expect to cover thirty miles a day, depending on the roads. Progress was good. They spent the first night at Rochfortbridge, with the officers staying in the inn and the half-company in a pair of barns outside the town. The second night they spent in the small village of Kilcock where they pressed another pair of farm-buildings into service. They could march into Dublin by a short stage on the following day.

An outrider from the Castle met them as they approached the city, and directed them to Phoenix Park, some two miles from the Castle. Each detachment had an assigned camping area and tents for their accommodation. These were up and ready for them and for all the other detachments.

As Adjutant, Arthur was busy from dawn to dusk. Arrangements for food and sleeping quarters for his men, digging latrines and dealing with the commissary all fell to him.

On the Friday of the ball, all officers received invitations to the Castle for dinner beforehand. As they waited to go in to dine, the Lord Lieutenant and the rest of the leading officials in Dublin and their wives circulated among the visitors. The local ladies were all hanging on to the latest London gossip from those guests who had come over from the capital for the event.

Suddenly Arthur saw Robert, standing in front of him with a face as dark as thunder.

"You! How dare you show your face here?" demanded Robert.

Arthur was prepared to be conciliatory, as he knew he must. This attack was not something he expected, but he responded in a placatory tone.

"Robert, I am here because I have been invited. This is not the time or place for remarks like that."

"I'll talk to you in any way I damn well choose."

At that moment, the Lord Lieutenant and his Duchess approached them and interrupted, as they made their way among the guests.

"Good evening, gentlemen," the Lord Lieutenant greeted them. "I trust you are both well and enjoying all that Dublin has to offer? Lord Belvedere, we have not seen your lovely wife for far too long. You must bring her to the Castle soon."

Arthur spoke first, and in a tone of icy bitterness. "Your Grace, unfortunately, my brother has imprisoned his lovely wife back in Westmeath and refuses to allow her to leave."

"You bastard!" exclaimed Robert, heedless of the social conventions. "You seducer!" Robert stepped towards Arthur with his fists raised as if to strike him. He reeked of brandy and was weaving slightly from its effects.

"Gentlemen!" cried out the Lord Lieutenant. "Please. This is not the time or place." By now all eyes in the room were on the two brothers. He dropped his voice. "Lord Belvedere, you might wish to ask for satisfaction."

Arthur promptly cut in. "He can't, your Grace. He has already shot me!"

"You will both withdraw at once. My Lord Belvedere, I will see you in my office tomorrow at nine."

Arthur stood to attention, and turned and left the room, collected his horse from a castle groom and rode out to Phoenix Park. Once there, he poured himself a glass of brandy

163

and sat for a while over his drink, before going to bed.

Robert stared at Arthur's retreating back. His face looked as if it was about to explode.

"Wait for a moment, my lord," proffered the Duchess, tactfully allowing Arthur some seconds to leave the castle.

Robert left as soon as he could escape the Duchess's eye and was back at Gardiner Row in less than thirty minutes. He too took to the brandy bottle and later sat drunk in his library, before rousing himself and staggering up the stairs to bed.

"You idiot!" snapped Colonel Monroe from his seat behind his desk.

Arthur stood in front of him with a downcast head, although the look on his face was distinctly mutinous.

"I know, Colonel, and I apologise for embarrassing you. Unfortunately, Robert's behaviour has been impossible."

"Arthur, I know a little of this story, and you have been discretion itself since you returned. It is time, perhaps, to tell me the full tale."

Arthur sat down and told his colonel the basics of the story. While he didn't go into details, he did admit his love for Mary and her professions of love for him. He also told him about the gunshot wound he had received from Robert.

"I knew he had shot you, but not the circumstances. I and many of us assumed he had called you out."

"Alas, no. The worst thing is that Mary is slowly dying. He keeps her locked up at Gaulstown. It is the devil of a thing to do to a woman, let alone to your wife."

"You, sir, have hit the nail on its head. She is, unfortunately, his wife. The law is firmly on his side in this."

Arthur had no alternative than to agree. For the next two weeks he found himself run ragged, as his colonel decided to keep him as busy as possible until the parade was over.

Over at the Castle, Robert appeared to see the Lord Lieutenant that same morning. He was late and looked terrible. He found himself sitting in an anteroom awaiting his lordship's pleasure. Eventually a clerk brought him before Lord Cavendish, His Majesty's Representative in Ireland. He kept Robert standing in front of his desk while he read and absorbed several documents in silence.

Eventually, he looked up. When he spoke, his voice dripped icy scorn. "You, my lord, are an ill-mannered lout. You have the manners of a tradesman. You disturb our peace with your verbal attacks on your brother."

"Your Grace, he has cuckolded me! He makes me a laughing stock."

"I think you will find, my lord, that you have done that very successfully yourself. This affair was well on the way to being forgotten. Now you have made it the talk of Dublin, and, no doubt, London. You, my lord, have not behaved as an honourable man. Now leave me."

Ashen-faced, Robert found himself dismissed and shown out of the Lord Lieutenant's apartments. He made his way back to Gardiner Row and commanded his groom to have the horses harnessed. Thirty minutes later he was on his way to Mullingar, riding as fast as the road would allow.

In Dublin, Arthur's days of activity ended with the parade through the city. His half-company behaved themselves, as he had warned them about the evils of drinking before the event. Having been promised a few hours free after, with a chance for them to spend time in the stews of Dublin, the event passed off without incident. By noon the next day, all the troops had returned to Phoenix Park and prepared to leave. By the time they reached their barracks in Athlone three days later, not a man in the half-company was showing any sign of their night of excess.

While Arthur settled back into his military duties, Robert remained alone, brooding at Belvedere. His hatred of his brother, and of his wife, grew and ate into his soul. He called at Gaulstown and screamed his hatred at her. He was incapable of seeing the changes her imprisonment had made in her.

165

Chapter Seventeen

DESPERATE MEASURES

When Arthur could arrange to get away from Athlone and his military duties, he returned to Gaulstown. Once again, Mrs O'Mahoney came out into the garden, and again, Arthur attracted her attention. Ten minutes later, he was again talking with Mary across the hedge.

"Robert was here last week. He screamed at me. He told me you had appeared at a ball in Dublin. I've rarely seen him so angry. He had been drinking again, as well."

"How do you know?" asked Arthur.

"He reeked of brandy. I was terrified. I thought he would strike me."

She still looked terrified. Arthur decided then and there that he must take her in his arms and comfort her, and wipe the tears from her eyes. He told her to wait, and rode down the boundary a few yards to a walled section. There, he used the wall to drop down into the garden. In a moment, Mary was in his arms, and Arthur was wiping the tears from her eyes.

They stood there for several minutes. They didn't speak – there was no need. The words from a thousand lost days and nights were condensed into that embrace.

At length, Mary broke away. "My love. I have an idea. A possible means of ending this. I can appeal to my father. Surely he will not be so inhuman as to send me away."

Arthur considered this for a few seconds.

"It may serve. I will return in two weeks' time, and I will take you to Dublin. Can you ride a horse? Do you feel strong enough?"

"For you, my love, for this, I can and will be strong." They exchanged a brief kiss, and Arthur returned to the walled section of the garden. He found a ladder there that allowed him to get up to the top. Once over, he called his farewells and headed back to Rochfortbridge at a steady canter.

Two weeks later, as promised, Arthur arrived back at Gaulstown early on a Friday morning. After checking to see if there were any carriages or extra horses visible, he rode through the gates and up to the front entrance. Mary appeared in the doorway and ran to greet him.

"My love, I promised to come back, and here I am. I have a horse for you," Arthur told her. "Now get your things and say farewell to Mrs O'Mahoney."

Mary turned and ran upstairs to pack, and Mrs O'Mahoney came forward from the kitchen door.

"Oh, sir, do take care."

"Of course, I will. I would guard her with my life! I am planning to take her somewhere she will be safe."

"As long as you do, sir. Now don't tell me where, then I can't tell anyone else. Your brother will know sooner or later that she's gone."

"I know that, and there's no saying what he may do. Will you be all right yourself?"

"I'll be grand, sir. I have family in England and a few guineas saved."

"Then add these to them and make sure the staff here all have something. My brother is not a kind man." With that, he handed her a leather purse. Mrs O'Mahoney tucked it away inside her dress.

Mary came downstairs, with her maid behind her carrying a valise. Arthur took this and tied it on his spare horse. She bade farewell to Mrs O'Mahoney, and Arthur lifted her onto her saddle. A moment later, he mounted his horse, and the pair of them walked their horses out of the grounds and towards the road to Milltownpass. By staying on the highway, they could travel at an easy canter, stopping every hour to rest the horses.

They arrived in Enfield before sunset and managed to get a

167

room in the inn. The innkeeper's wife brought up a surprisingly good dinner and a bottle of wine. After their meal, they retired to bed and made gentle and tender love, well aware that this might be their last night together.

The next evening, they arrived at Lord Molesworth's Henrietta Street house in Dublin. Arthur helped Mary from her horse and lent her his arm as they mounted the stairs to the front door. A footman opened the door but did not appear to recognise the visitors.

Mary asked him to take her to Lord Molesworth. At that moment the butler arrived in the hall.

"My lady. We have not seen you here for many years. How may I help?"

"Is my father in?" asked Mary.

"Indeed, ma'am. I will show you both into the library and tell his lordship you are here."

They took their seats in the library. From the furnishings and décor, this was evidently Lord Molesworth's domain. Books on military themes and the classics of the day lined two walls. The other walls were covered with paintings of horses and dogs, and a large picture of the Duke of Marlborough, Lord Molesworth's former comrade-in-arms.

After a few nail-biting minutes, the door opened to admit Lord Molesworth. Father and daughter embraced. He held her at arm's length and took a long hard look at her. After taking in her paleness and loss of weight from her face and arms and the dark circles under her eyes, he took her into his arms and hugged her. He looked at Arthur and turned back to Mary.

"What has that monster done to you?"

"He has imprisoned her for the last two years, my lord."

"So I heard. Letters I wrote to her were returned. I wrote to Lord Belvedere, but he failed to reply. I even went to see him and tried to visit you at Gaulstown, my dear, but to no avail. You look as if you have suffered terrible treatment."

"And so she has, my lord. She was barely strong enough to ride here with me today."

Suddenly a shrill voice burst forward from the doorway.

"What is SHE doing here?"

There in the doorway stood Lady Molesworth, looking neither pleased nor amused. "She cannot stay here. She should not even be here!" Her voice cut through the air in the room.

"My dear, this is neither the time nor the place to discuss the future. Our daughter needs our help. Mary must and will stay here for the moment while we see what to do."

"Thank you, Papa. I knew I could rely on you."

"Major, can you take Mary through for dinner? We were about to go in. I just need a word with his lordship," said Mary's stepmother. The look she gave Lord Molesworth did not suggest that this was a conversation he would enjoy.

Arthur and Mary left the room, and Lady Molesworth turned to her husband. When she spoke, her tone was furious.

"My lord, are you mad? Should I have you placed in protection? Get her out of here."

After years of acquiescing to his wife's demands, Lord Molesworth had reached the end of his tether. His voice was calm and his tone was like ice.

"No, I will not get her out of here. She is my daughter, and if anyone should give her shelter, I should."

Lady Molesworth stared at her husband in astonishment, and tried one last appeal. "My lord, in case you have failed to notice, she is married. She is here, not with her husband, but with her lover. She must go."

"Madam. She will stay at least for a few days. I will give her what help I can. This will not end well for her, I know, but I will try to ease her suffering."

Lady Molesworth's passions rose again and the pitch of her voice rose higher and higher. "You, my lord, are an idiot. We have a daughter about to enter the marriage market. We cannot afford one single whiff of scandal, or she will never, and I do mean never, make a brilliant marriage."

"Madam, the girl is only fifteen. She is not going to be marrying for several years."

Lady Molesworth spat back at him. "That, my lord, is beside the point. Our household is still tainted because of

Mary's actions. We cannot afford any more scandal. Now do I make myself clear?"

His lordship had drawn his line in the sand. He was determined to do what he could, and the finality in his tone brooked no argument.

"You do, madam. Abundantly clear. Now let us join them at dinner. We will talk more on this in the morning."

Dinner was an awkward meal. Mary was exhausted, and Lady Molesworth looked disapproving throughout. As it ended Arthur rose to take his leave. He collected both horses as he went, and rode over to Gardiner Row for the night.

In the morning, he retraced his steps to Henrietta Street and asked to see Lord Molesworth. His lordship received him in his library, and the two of them sat down to discuss Mary and her state of health, before moving on to the subject of the hour.

"Major Rochfort, I have asked my lawyer to join us here to advise on the legal niceties involved. He should be here shortly. I am appalled by Mary's state of health, and by her treatment. You must know I am under a barrage of complaints from Lady Molesworth about Mary's return."

"Indeed, my lord. She made it plain that she was unhappy to see Mary here, and in these circumstances."

"Major, exactly what are 'these circumstances'? I feel you should explain how we have arrived at this situation."

"My lord, this was never planned. We never intended for this to happen. If I were to point to any one reason, I might point to my brother and his inability to treat Mary as a husband should treat a wife. He, my lord, has a vilely cruel streak in him."

"So I am aware. But you are his brother, so how is it you are here with Mary?"

"I became close to her some years ago when Robert had been neglecting her. At the end of that summer, we both realised that we loved each other. In all honesty, I believe that we could not help ourselves. I kept telling myself that this was wrong, and perhaps it is, but I couldn't stand by and see her destroyed by my brother."

"My poor boy, I fear that I can bring you little hope or joy. This does not look good."

At that moment, the butler knocked, opened the door to the library and announced Lord Molesworth's lawyer, Mr Meagher.

Mr Meagher was an elderly gentleman who looked shrunk and desiccated by a lifetime in the courts of Dublin. He advanced into the room and shook their hands, and the three of them sat around a small table.

Mr Meagher opened the discussion. "Major Rochfort, while I am delighted to make your acquaintance, I fear I can bring you little good news."

Arthur's face fell, although he was half-expecting this.

"Lord Belvedere holds all the rights in this matter. He is the lady's husband. I have no doubt that he will seek her out. From what I hear of his character, I doubt if he is the sort of man who would let this lie."

"Is a divorce possible for Lady Belvedere?"

"I doubt it. It would require her husband's agreement, which he would never give. Also, it would cost a fortune in money and time. Her ladyship has given her husband two children, so you would need a private bill in Parliament."

"So what do we do?"

"You, sir, do nothing. There is nothing you can do. As I said before, all the rights in this matter lie with Lord Belvedere."

"But he shot me!" Arthur gave Lord Molesworth and his lawyer the bare facts of that incident. "Does the fact that he shot me count for nought?"

"I am afraid so. He could easily claim that this was an accident. I understand that Lady Belvedere witnessed the assault, but as his wife, she cannot give evidence against her husband. In law, a husband and wife are regarded as one person."

Lord Molesworth spoke up. "Mr Meagher, what course of action would you recommend?"

"My lord, I am afraid that the best counsel I can give you is to send your daughter back to her husband."

"Never," cried Arthur.

"Major, this is, unfortunately, nothing to do with you. You have no standing in this matter."

Arthur held his head in his hands.

"I'm going to allow Mary to stay here for a few days. You, sir, must leave immediately. I strongly suggest you return to Athlone with all speed."

"Very well, my lord, although this is a course of action that tears me in two."

The three of them rose to their feet, and Lord Molesworth rang the bell. The butler appeared and showed Mr Meagher to the door.

Arthur turned to Lord Molesworth. "I must see her, if only to tell her this myself."

"I will send for her, and you may tell her about today's meeting, here in the library."

He left to summon his daughter. After a few minutes, the door opened without a sound, and Mary entered, closed the door and flew into Arthur's arms.

"Father told me! What can we do? Can we do anything?"

"Your father has no choice in the matter. The law is on Robert's side. I do have an idea, however. It is the only plan I have. How well do you know your coachman?"

"Very well indeed, John taught me to ride as a child. I was forever playing in the stables."

"Tell your father you will return to Gaulstown. He will have John drive you. When you stop to change horses, tell him to deliver you to my estate. You can tell him to take you to "Lord Belvedere's brother's house." He will bring you to Belfield House, and we can, at least review the situation. We could go to Galway and take a ship to the Americas. There is a whole world over there, and we will be free of Robert."

"But what about the children?" asked Mary.

"At least the children are safe, and Robert will never harm them. But first, we have to find a place where we can be safe and together."

"It will be hard, but I will try, my love. No, it's more than hard. It is tearing me apart."

"Thank you, my darling. Now, dry your eyes and wait a few minutes before you see your father and agree to go back to Gaulstown."

"What about you?"

"I will leave for Athlone, but, in fact, I will go to Belfield House and wait for you."

"It seems strange that it is only two days since we left Gaulstown. Oh, how the time flies?"

"And I must fly too, my love. If you leave tomorrow morning, you should arrive at Belfield House tomorrow night." With that, Arthur kissed her, left the library and bade farewell to Lord Molesworth.

"I am taking your advice, and returning to Athlone, my lord. There seems little other option for us."

"I think that is wise. It is hard. I know what it is like to lose the woman you love. For me, it was Mary's mother. Do you know what Mary intends?"

"My Lord, Mary needs a little time to compose herself. She is still making her decision. I am sure you will advise her for the best."

Lord Molesworth noted the distress on his face. "I will let you get on your way. I suppose I must thank you for bringing Mary here. To be frank, I wish that this whole episode had never happened."

With that, Arthur left and returned to Gardiner Row. There he packed his valise and started back west, leading the horse that Mary had used.

Monday dawned dry and bright in Dublin. Lord Molesworth's house was a hive of activity. The coachman and a groom were harnessing a pair of greys to a carriage. A maid was to go with Mary to act as a chaperone. Lady Molesworth was still mortified that her stepdaughter had fled to Dublin unaccompanied by any other female.

"My lord, how you could allow that philanderer – that seducer – into this house, I do not know. Mary must leave as soon as possible. I insist."

173

Lord Molesworth took Mary out to the coach and addressed her in fatherly tones.

"My dear, I can only hope that Robert's heart softens with time. This is a terrible state of affairs, and I only wish there was a way out for you both." With that, her father embraced her tenderly and handed her up into the coach.

"Make the best time you can," he said to the coachman. "You can get a change of horses at Enfield."

The coach moved away and headed west to the main highway.

After lunch, on leaving Enfield, Mary turned to the coachman. "John, I want you to take me to Lord Belvedere's brother's house."

"Are you sure, my lady?"

"Certainly," she replied. "You had best ask directions to the house; we will be arriving at sunset."

John got down from the carriage, went to check directions with the landlord. Five minutes later, he returned, and they resumed their journey.

The day ended with them still some miles from their destination. Mary, exhausted, fell asleep against the cushions, even with the shaking of the carriage on the road.

Eventually, it came to a halt, and John dismounted, going to knock at the door. A butler appeared, and John reported his arrival to him. Mary meanwhile was still dozing in the carriage.

A man came out and walked over to the carriage.

"Lady Belvedere," he called, trying to wake her. Mary stirred, opened her eyes and screamed.

"George! Why are we here? What are you doing?" She turned to John.

"We have arrived, my lady."

Mary looked around her and saw George's face set in a most unpleasant expression.

"Indeed you have my dear. Please come inside."

The maid dismounted and helped Mary alight. She was still desperately weak and close to fainting.

She escorted Mary into the house, taking her arm to support her. Inside, the butler showed them into the drawing room.

Meanwhile, George went into his study, searched for notepaper and a pen, and dashed off a note to Robert, telling him that he was looking after Mary at Rochfort House. He sent a groom over to Belvedere with instructions to deliver the note immediately. He called his wife.

"Alice, we have an unexpected visitor."

"Good God. What is she doing here?"

"I have no idea. I've sent a note to Robert. He can do with her what he wishes."

Alice called for a maid. "Take her ladyship upstairs and put her in the small bedroom. Take some bread and milk up for her when she is in bed."

Mary had a feverish night's sleep and awoke the next morning with a feeling of dread. A maid came in with a tray with her breakfast on and left without speaking. Mary hardly noticed but got out of bed feeling dizzy and faint. She sat at a small table for her meal, and ate a little bread and drank some tea.

She spent many minutes worrying and wondering. What was she doing there? Why was she at George's house? Where was Arthur? All these questions ran through her brain again and again.

She was sitting on the side of the bed, about to try and dress, when she heard footsteps. Without ceremony, the door swung open, and Robert stood there. There was no expression at all on his face.

He stepped into the room and spoke in heartless tones. "Get dressed, you whore. You return to Gaulstown, now."

Her face, already pale with fatigue, drained. She felt faint and giddy, and she grasped the back of her chair. She would not faint and give Robert that satisfaction. She made herself rise to her full height and looked him straight in the eyes.

"Get out of my room. I will be down when I have dressed."

Robert stepped towards her as if to strike her. He lifted his hand and drew his arm back, but Mary spoke out to him. "Go on, strike a defenceless woman. Is that all you are capable of?"

Robert stopped and lowered his arm. "I will return in thirty minutes, madam," He left the room, slamming the door behind him.

Two minutes later there was a timid knock at the door, and Mary walked over to open it. Outside she found one of the maids, who bobbed her a curtsey.

Mary let her in, and the girl helped her into her dress. She was happy to help, but it was clear she had never done that kind of work before. Thirty minutes later Robert returned and entered unannounced again. Fortunately, Mary was dressed and ready to leave.

Robert pointed to the door, and Mary went through and down the stairs, followed by the maid carrying Mary's small valise. Mary went outside followed by Robert. There was no sign of John, or her father's carriage. A gig was standing by the door, and Robert gestured to her to get up into it. The maid put her valise under the seat.

Once Mary had sat down, Robert instructed his groom. "To Gaulstown." Without uttering another word, he mounted his horse and rode out following the gig.

The journey to Gaulstown took less than an hour. It was a silent ride, with the groom never uttering a word. Mary was feeling so ill and subdued, that she barely noticed.

Robert's silence continued until they were inside the drawing room at Gaulstown.

"Madam, it seems that your previous conditions here were not robust enough to contain you. You are back here, and here you will stay. I was far too lenient in my treatment of you, so we will change that. From now on, madam, you may no longer go outside the house unless it is in my company. All the staff here are dismissed. If they cannot follow simple instructions, they can have no place working for me. I am also employing guards to make sure that your confinement is as I require. Do you understand?"

She stood there, dumbfounded.

"Why, Robert? Why are you doing this?"

"Because I can, madam, because I can. You are my wife. The law cannot help you here."

"What about the children?

"What about them? They will stay at Belvedere. You will never see them again."

With that, he turned and left her standing there, and Mary collapsed into a chair, sobbing uncontrollably.

When Arthur arrived at Belfield House, he opened up the house and lit a fire in the kitchen. He went through the house and lit some lamps, drew some water from the well and checked the cupboards for any food. The only thing available was tea, but he had the foresight to bring some bread, cheese and cold meat with him. He even remembered to go upstairs and throw back the coverlet on his bed. There was a layer of dust everywhere, but it would suffice for the night. He planned to take Mary on to Galway and a ship to the Americas.

While he waited, he went over the events of the last three days. He could not have come up with a better plan, or even any alternative.

The sun had set, and still, he waited. He waited, sometimes pacing the floor, going outside to scan the road to the house, or sitting impatiently. Every so often he would look at his pocket watch, sometimes holding it to his ear to make sure it was still ticking. He would go outside and listen, in case he should hear their approach.

Still, no one came.

At midnight, he went up to bed but found sleep impossible. All he could do was worry about what had happened to them.

In the morning, as soon as it was light enough, he rode the short distance to Gaulstown. As he approached, he saw the place was in an uproar, with people coming and going, horses and carriages going in and out.

Arthur retreated to some cover in the road heading south to Rochfortbridge. The high hedges would allow him to see over them and observe the comings and goings from the house. After an hour, a pair of figures left the building and started to make their way south to the main road. Both were carrying bundles on their shoulders.

As they approached, Arthur recognised one of them. "Mrs O'Mahoney. Where are you going? What has happened to you?"

"Sir, we are turned off without a character. His lordship found out what had happened and has dismissed all the servants."

"All of them?"

"Every man jack of us, sir."

Arthur looked stunned. "Why?"

"Sure, I don't know, sir. You know Lord Robert better than us."

"I thought I did, but it's clear I know little of him. Have you heard any news of her ladyship?"

"Lord Robert has her, sir. He sent a man over to tell us to pack and leave this morning, and he told us that Lady Mary had arrived late last night at Rochfort House, and Lord Robert arrived there this morning."

The colour drained from Arthur's face. "Oh, no! Did you see your mistress? How was she?"

"Lord Robert brought her in a carriage and dragged her to her room. He then came downstairs, called the servants together, and dismissed us all."

"But where will you go?"

"We are heading to Dublin, sir. We hope to go to America. We hear the harvest is bad again, and we will leave while we still can."

Arthur fumbled in his pockets and gave Mrs O'Mahoney a guinea.

"Bless you, sir, that's grand of you."

Mrs O'Mahoney and her two companions headed south to the main road. Arthur watched them go and wished them well, under his breath. He would never see them again. He waited another hour but saw no possibility of learning anything more, so turned his horse away and started on the road to Athlone.

He arrived at the barracks in the late afternoon to find that Colonel Monroe was extremely annoyed that he had been missing, and didn't hesitate to tell him so. Arthur apologised and left to eat in the mess before retiring to his quarters. The last thing he wanted was company that night.

Over the next few days, he resumed his busy schedule of work as adjutant. While the days left little time for dwelling on Mary and her plight, the nights were different.

In Dublin, Lord Molesworth interviewed John on his return home. John told him what had happened, and that Mary had asked him to take her to Lord Belvedere's brother's house.

"I asked in the inn at Enfield, and they gave me directions. We got there about sunset, and a large, stout gentleman came out to greet us. I asked him. I said, 'Begging your pardon, sir but are you Lord Belvedere's brother?' and he said yes. He brought a maid out, and she and the gentleman took her ladyship into the house. I waited a little, and he came out again and told me to go, so I drove a short way back the way we had come. We slept in the carriage overnight and came back here."

Lord Molesworth knew George vaguely by sight and description. From what the coachman told him, he was satisfied he had met his responsibility to return his daughter to her husband in full. Hopefully, this would forestall any further criticism from his wife.

The weeks passed, and it was not long before Arthur felt he had little choice but to see if he could find out if Mary were alive and well. He left early one morning with a spare horse and made good time to Gaulstown. Arthur had no plan at all. He wasn't even sure if she was still at Gaulstown, but his concern made him blind to any alternative.

Three hours later, he rode his horse through the gate at Gaulstown and up to the door. He dismounted, expecting the door to open and to be greeted by a butler or servant. He ended by going up to the massive wooden door and banging on it with the handle of his whip.

The door opened a crack, and an unshaven bleary face looked out. "Be off with you. No visitors allowed."

Arthur was taken aback. "But I am the earl's brother."

"Don't care who you are. Be off with you." The door

slammed shut in Arthur's face.

Arthur waited a few minutes and knocked again, with no reply. When he hammered on the door for the third time, it opened to reveal a pair of ruffians, both armed with cudgels.

"We told you, no visitors," the first one shouted. "Now get out of here."

There was little Arthur could do but retreat. He mounted his horse and rode out of the gate, and turned towards the road. On a whim, he turned east on a farm track and headed to Belfield House. He wanted, at least, to see how his property stood. When he arrived, it was deserted. Nobody had been there since the fateful night he had spent waiting for Mary.

At a loss, he rode over to Rochfort House. When he arrived there, George came into the hall to see who it was. A look of astonishment crossed his face.

"You? What the devil are you doing here?" he asked.

"I must find out how Mary is," replied Arthur.

"You idiot! How Mary does is no concern of yours. Can you not understand this?"

"George, I thought that you as my brother might at least try to understand."

"Arthur, go back to Athlone. Go now. You can do nothing for Mary here."

"When the coach brought her here, why did you give her straight back to Robert?"

"Can you not understand; she is his? She is his wife, his property, and his to do with as he wishes. That, Arthur, is the law."

"She will die, you know."

"*You* will die if Robert finds you here!"

"But have you seen her? Have you seen those ruffians at Gaulstown? She is a countess and your sister-in-law."

"Those ruffians work for our brother. They are there to make sure you don't carry out anymore hare-brained rescue schemes. Did you never think what might happen to her if your attempt to save her failed? No, *when* it failed. There was never a chance of success."

Arthur's head dropped. He shook his head and walked out

of the door. The footman handed him the reins of his horse, and he swung himself into the saddle and started the lonely ride back to Athlone.

His visit to Gaulstown did not go unnoticed. Robert's two watchmen reported it through Mr Flynn, and George wasted little time before writing a note to his brother.

Robert rode over the following day, and George told him everything Arthur had said. Robert looked even more determined. With his jaw set in a thin line, he left and rode over to Gaulstown.

When he arrived, he went into the drawing room. Mary was sitting reading. When he entered, she closed the book and put it down, being careful to mark the page with what looked like an old letter. One of his ruffians stood by the door, as if to protect him should Mary attack him.

"It seems I was wise to employ my watchmen. They stopped an intruder yesterday. Most persistent, but he won't be coming back!"

"Arthur was here?"

"So it would seem," replied Robert. "But I repeat, he will not be coming back! I have plans to deal with Arthur."

"Why, Robert? Why are you doing this to me?"

"I told you, madam. Because I can! Because I have the law on my side. I can do anything I wish with you, short of shooting you or running you through. I will never, and I repeat, never forgive you."

Mary drew herself up to her full height and looked him straight in the eye. "Then do your worst, sir. You will not beat me! You will not break me!"

Robert looked at her with a sneering expression. "I have time, madam. I have all the time in the world." With that, he turned and walked out of the room.

"Wait, Robert," she called. Robert stopped, turned around and looked at her. "What of our children?"

"They are, I believe, entirely happy. Their nurse looks after them. I see them only rarely. Now good day, madam."

She stood, and watched him walk out. The front door

closed, and the light in the hall died.

She went down to the kitchen, to see the cook. Mrs Clohessy was a large woman with a sour expression and an air of permanent dissatisfaction. She was not the sort of person to chat.

"What do we have for dinner, Cook?"

"Stew," came the reply.

"Stew, ma'am, if you please," Mary prompted.

"It's stew."

"And with the stew, Cook?"

"Just stew."

Mary walked over to the range and poured water from the kettle on the hob into a small teapot. After making some tea, she left and took it back to the drawing room. There, she sat and re-read Arthur's letter, as she had done hundreds of times before.

Chapter Eighteen

THE FORCES OF THE LAW

Some weeks later, Arthur was sitting in his company office dealing with the regimental records when a packet arrived.

A packet was a rare event. He had heard nothing from Robert or George, and no information on Mary's fate. He only knew she remained at Gaulstown under guard.

The package had come from Dublin Castle. Apart from the usual regimental correspondence, it contained a letter to Arthur, bearing the crown seal.

Arthur opened it with interest. In normal times, letters that carried the Crown seal presaged good news, such as a promotion. His face soon fell as he read it. Inside the letter was a summons to appear at the Court of the King's Bench, in Dublin. It seemed that Robert was suing him for damages, for Criminal Conversation with Mary.

Arthur knew what criminal conversation was. Cases of "crim-con" were frequently reported on in the broadsheets and the *Gentleman's Magazine*. He took the letter to Colonel Monroe, who read it slowly and with care.

"My boy, this needs careful consideration. The case has been set for two months from now, and there is no doubt at all that you must attend. In the meantime, I suggest you consult one of the local lawyers here. They may be able to tell you a little more. Do you have a man in Dublin?"

"We have a family lawyer, but I fear Robert may have engaged him already. I will see a local man here, first."

"Right. You must do that without delay, so clear your desk and get yourself to a lawyer."

Arthur thanked him. An hour later he walked out of the barracks and along the quay to an office with a polished brass plate on the door announcing: *Peter Doonan, Lawyer*.

He knocked and a clerk came out, inquired his business and took his card before showing him to a chair in the corner of the front room. After five minutes, an elderly gentleman with white hair came out and greeted him.

"Peter Doonan, lawyer of this town. How can I help you, Major?"

"I hope you can help me with this, at least to tell me what it means and what I may do." Arthur gave him his letter.

Mr Doonan glanced at it and showed Arthur through to his inner office. This room was small and was lined floor to ceiling with books and bundles of papers. A tiny window looked out to the rear of the property. Once Arthur was seated, Mr Doonan produced a pair of pince-nez and perched them on his nose. He read Arthur's letter of summons through several times with great care.

"Right, sir. I'm not going to insult your intelligence, but as you can see, this is a summons to appear at the King's Bench Court in Dublin. However, it relates to a charge of Criminal Conversation. This, sir, is challenging and unusual. Do you know what Criminal Conversation is?"

"Only what I have seen in the broadsheets, sir."

"Well, it is not a crime, it's a claim for damages. It is a claim for damages because you had physical knowledge of Mary, Countess Belvedere. There are some dates given from over three months ago, to some from two years ago. Now, with a charge of Criminal Conversation, you don't get to take the stand. You cannot plead in your defence. Equally, neither can the plaintiff or the lady concerned. There will need to be some evidence or other witnesses. Also, sir, there is a jury, but the judge can direct them."

"Thank you for that, sir, but I need to know exactly what I should do."

"I can do little for you here. You need a Dublin man for this. You need a lawyer who knows the game there. And, sir, believe me, it is a game."

"Mr Doonan, thank you very much. You have been a great help. It seems that I must go to Dublin immediately."

"That, sir, is a course of action I can only recommend," replied the lawyer, bowing Arthur out of his office.

Colonel Monroe had seen the court summons, so had no compunction about letting Arthur go.

"You must go, and go soon. Come back when you have your legal case sorted out, but for now, you need to be there!"

The next evening, Arthur rode into Dublin and up to Robert's house on Gardiner Row. Much to his disgust, he was refused entrance. The butler there was apologetic, but firm in his refusal.

"I'm sorry, sir, but Lord Robert was most explicit in his instructions. You are not to be permitted to enter."

Arthur withdrew, and rode to the Castle. He knew his rank would get him a bed in the castle barracks.

The next morning, he called on the lawyer his family used. As he thought, that gentleman refused to see him and asked that he leave, citing a conflict of interest. Arthur returned to the barracks and enquired if anyone could recommend a good lawyer.

"Why do you need one, Arthur?" asked the adjutant.

Arthur could do little but tell them. It would be all over Dublin in a matter of days.

"My brother is suing me for damages, for Criminal Conversation."

"Your brother? I'm appalled. What man would sue his brother?"

"You don't know Robert," replied Arthur.

"So what's behind his claim?"

"I made a mistake, and the mistake I made was to fall in love with his wife. Robert took umbrage, not unnaturally, but instead of being a gentleman, he shot me in a brawl. While I was in Gibraltar, he imprisoned Mary in the old manor-house."

"Well, I'll be damned. If he wanted satisfaction, why didn't he call you out?"

"Oh, he knew I would win a duel; he is a terrible shot with

185

a pistol."

"So now he does this? It won't go down well at the Castle. It's not the sort of thing they like to hear about the local peers."

"Robert is unlikely to care. He seems supremely unconcerned with the views or opinions of anyone else but himself."

"I would recommend John McBride, on St Stephen's Green. He is reliable and honest, and that's a rarity among lawyers."

"Thank you, Cyril. I'll try him tomorrow morning. In the meantime, I'll see you in the mess this evening."

The next day saw Arthur searching out Mr McBride's office. A servant answered his knock on the door, and Arthur gave him his card. The lawyer himself was away in court, but, according to the clerk, would be in his chambers that afternoon. He advised Arthur to return at three o'clock. This was Arthur's first experience of the delays that often seemed to go with any dealings with the law.

When he returned, Mr McBride received him in his inner office. This was all polished dark wood, a large desk and piles of bundles with documents, all bound up with red linen tape.

"Mr McBride, I have need of the services of a lawyer, and you have been recommended to be as being both a good lawyer and an honest one."

"I try to be both, sir. Now how may I be of service?"

Arthur told Mr McBride all he felt that he could say about his circumstances. The lawyer listened intently. When Arthur had finished, he sat, thinking about the issue for some minutes. At length, he lifted his head.

"Major, you have told me much, but you have not told me all. That is good. I must advise you, so do not tell me if you are guilty or not guilty. The matter as it stands depends on upon two things. As you know, neither you, your brother nor the lady concerned will be allowed to take the stand. The issue of Criminal Conversation is always strange. It depends wholly on what other evidence your brother has, if any. He, as plaintiff, will seek a sum in damages. Should the court award

186

damages, these may be substantial. It depends on the judge hearing the case and the plaintiff's claim. Some judges are notoriously venal; some take a moral view, while others regard this a trifling matter. We shall have to wait and see. There will be a jury, but they will normally act as directed by the judge. Do you know which lawyer is representing your brother?"

"Our family lawyer, Michael Molloy, of Chequer Lane."

"I know him, of course. He is good, but more for family matters than cases like this. Without knowing the evidence that they have, I can make no forecasts. We will play the cards as they fall. Now I will prepare my case. The court calendar has scheduled the summons for the second day of October, a Tuesday. You have military duties to fulfil until then; I dare say. I will ask you to attend me here one month before, on the fourth day of September. I can go over our case, and we can discuss what avenues to go down."

Arthur thanked him, left his office and walked back to the Castle. The following morning, he bade his friends farewell and headed off to Athlone.

For the next four weeks Arthur was the living example of an efficient adjutant. It provided him with something to do and prevented him thinking too much about Mary and his brother. When he returned to Dublin, he went to see Mr McBride, as arranged.

"Major, welcome back to Dublin. We have some information on your brother's claim. He has a pair of witnesses, who saw you and the lady spending the night together. That seems to be the only evidence at the moment, but we need to see who is on the bench. We believe he will call some character witnesses, too. Some of our judges are excellent and honest. They will make a judgement based solely on the evidence before them. However, some are exactly the opposite. Some are entirely venal and corrupt."

"What is the procedure?" asked Arthur.

"You will be in court, as will I. You will sit with me. The bench will read the claim, and ask Mr Molloy to open his case and to outline his evidence. I will describe our defence, and the judge will ask Molloy to produce his evidence. I will be able to cross-examine any witness and challenge that evidence. The judge will then deliberate and give his judgement. It is not a question of guilty or not guilty; it is a matter of the amount of damages if he finds the case is proved."

"Do we have a chance?"

"We always have a chance. It depends on the judge, and whether I can cast sufficient doubt on the evidence."

Two days before the hearing, Arthur returned to Dublin. That evening, he went to Gardiner Row and asked the butler if Robert was there. The servant admitted him and showed him into the library. A few minutes later, Robert entered with a quiet smirk on his face.

"Robert, why are you doing this?"

"Why? Because I can. That is all. I can do anything with the strumpet who, unfortunately, is my wife."

"That is no answer. What do you hope to gain? I am your brother, after all."

"And that is why it hurt so much. You – my brother – could do this to me."

"This is still no answer. Men and women fall in love all the time."

"Not my woman – and not with my brother."

"So you are determined to go ahead? Nothing can change your mind, even though you gain nothing of use from this action? Even though the affair will be plastered all over the broadsheets?"

"Gain nothing? My dear Arthur, I gain everything! Your destruction! Your misery. I gain the knowledge that you and that harlot will never, ever know happiness again. Now do you understand?"

Arthur shook his head in disbelief while Robert summoned the butler to show him out.

At the Court, Mr McBride and Arthur took their place before the Bench. Robert and Mr Molloy were present behind a desk some feet away. The court was packed. Such an unusual case attracted more than the usual number of onlookers. Eventually, the court was full, and the beadles closed the doors.

A door opened, and the clerks entered in procession, followed by a tall man in a full-bottomed wig and robes. John McBride groaned audibly, and Arthur looked at him.

"Pray stand for Lord Justice Carter," called the clerk.

Mr McBride turned to Arthur and whispered, "I am so sorry, sir! Lord Justice Carter is the worst judge we could have hoped for."

Arthur looked at Robert, who returned his gaze and gave a thin-lipped triumphant smile.

The judge read out the introduction to the case.

"A claim for damages on the grounds of criminal conversation, made by the Right Honourable Robert, Earl of Belvedere, against Arthur Rochfort, Major in His Majesty's Army. A claim, in that the defendant has committed adultery with the wife of the plaintiff. Mr Molloy, what evidence are you able to offer to support this claim?"

"My lord, we have witnesses to the event."

"Mr McBride, you are appearing for the defendant?"

Arthur's lawyer rose to his feet and answered in a sonorous tone, "I am, my lord."

"Will you be offering any evidence on your client's behalf?"

"My lord, my client contests the claim, but we have no evidence of our own to present to the court."

"Very well. We will proceed. Mr Molloy, do you call your witness."

The clerk rose to his feet. "Call Seamus Barry!"

A door opened, and a junior clerk repeated the summons. A man, sitting on a bench outside, rose to his feet, hands grasping his hat and entered the court. An usher showed him where to stand, and pressed a Bible into his hand.

"Do you, Seamus Barry, swear on the Bible that you will tell the truth, the whole truth, and nothing but the truth?"

"I do, sir." The witness looked around. He was a man in his forties, of medium height, with pale red hair, and he looked terrified. He looked vaguely familiar to Arthur.

"Are you Seamus Barry?" asked Mr Molloy.

"I am, sir."

"And are you the landlord of the Royal Oak Inn, at Enfield in the County of Meath?

"I am, sir."

Now Arthur knew where he had seen the man before.

"How many years have you been the landlord of the Royal Oak?"

"For five years, sir. Since before the Year of Slaughter."

"Have you seen the gentleman in a military uniform over there before?"

"I have, sir."

"And where did you see him?"

"At the Royal Oak, sir."

"When would that be, Mr Barry?"

"I've seen him a few times. He is a regular client of mine."

"And when was the last time you saw him?"

"This year, sir, in the summer."

"Was the gentleman alone?"

"This time? No, sir. No, he had a lady with him."

"Did the gentleman take a room for the night?"

Mr McBride was on his feet. "My lord, Mr Molloy really must stop leading the wit-ness."

"Thank you, Mr McBride. Mr Molloy, you may carry on."

"Thank you, my lord. Mr Barry, permit me to ask a different question. What did this gentleman do?"

"That time, he rented a room for the night."

"For both himself and the lady?"

"Yes, sir. My wife served them dinner in the room."

"And they spent the night together in the room?"

"Indeed they did, sir."

Mr Molloy turned to the bench. "My lord, I have no more questions."

"Very well. Mr McBride, do you wish to cross-examine this witness?"

Arthur's lawyer stood up, replied that he did, and went over the innkeeper's evidence, but without being able to shake him in any of the facts that he had stated. After twenty minutes, he turned to the judge. "No more questions, my lord."

"Thank you, Mr McBride. Mr Molloy, your next witness."

"Call Sarah Barry!"

Over the next fifteen minutes, the publican's wife answered Mr Molloy's questions in a faint but steady voice. The questions and responses were exactly the same as her husband's. Mr McBride spent a further ten minutes questioning and probing, but was unable to shake her.

"Mr McBride, will you be calling any witnesses?"

"No, my lord," said the lawyer, slowly shaking his head.

The Clerk rose and called on everyone else there to do so. Lord Justice Carter announced a break for lunch.

After lunch, Mr Molloy announced that he would be calling a character witness.

"Call Doctor Delaney!" went the cry. An elderly gentleman in clerical garb took the stand and was duly sworn in.

"Doctor Delaney, were you Dean of the cathedral here in the year of our Lord 1736?"

"I was indeed, sir."

"Tell the court, if you would, of the character of the plaintiff."

The doctor replied at length. "Why, I have known Lord Belvedere for many years. I conducted his wedding myself in the cathedral. I know him to be a fine and upstanding member of the community. His word should be regarded as inviolate."

The judge invited Mr McBride to question the Dean, but there was little that he could ask when set against a simple declaration from such a senior churchman.

"Members of the jury, you have heard the evidence of two witnesses, and no less a personage than the Dean of Christ Church has stood as a witness to the upstanding character of the plaintiff. No rebuttal of their evidence has been offered. Accordingly, I direct you to find the claim proved. I will retire to consider the question of damages."

The clerk stood up and intoned, "All rise!" The court rose while Lord Justice Carter left for his chambers.

Once the door closed, Arthur turned to his lawyer. "I am

ruined." He looked back at his brother who sat there with a triumphant smile on his face.

"We must await the judge's ruling. Damages for criminal conversation are impossible to predict. These are not ordinary or frequent cases, so there is nothing to guide us."

They repaired to a nearby inn, although Arthur could not eat anything. All he could think of was Mary, and how vindictive his brother was being.

After lunch, they didn't have long to wait. The court rose while Lord Justice Carter took his place and prepared to read his findings.

"It is my decision that the claim is proved for the plaintiff. The defence has offered no evidence. We now come to the matter of damages. I have given this considerable thought. I consider the extreme damage to the plaintiff's feelings and reputation by this event. This is made worse by the fact that this betrayal involved the plaintiff's own brother. Accordingly, I have determined that the amount of damages is to stand at twenty thousand pounds. Also, the defendant will pay costs for the plaintiff amounting to fifty guineas."

Chapter Nineteen

AN IMPOSSIBLE TASK

Everyone in the court gasped. No one else in court, including the lawyers present, had ever heard of a judge awarding such an amount before.

"I base this award on the terrible damage to the plaintiff's reputation. The lady concerned is his wife and the mother of his children. I also acknowledge the outrage to the plaintiff's feelings and the blow to his honour and family pride. The way in which his own brother, his own brother, mark you, has used his relationship forms part of his conduct. I, therefore, rule that his conduct has severely aggravated the injury to the plaintiff."

The hearing concluded, and the judge swept out. Arthur and Mr McBride went back to St Stephen's Green. Arthur was in a daze. Once the two of them were closeted together in Mr McBride's inner office, he spoke, in a voice full of despair.

"What is to become of me, Mr McBride? What do I do now?"

"Well, the first thing is to pay my bill and Mr Molloy's costs. Seventy-five guineas is not too hard a sum, and it is important to get costs paid first. You will be given some time to pay, say four weeks. Then you will be expected to make payments to the court."

"And if I can't pay?"

"The tipstaffs will come for you and take you to Debtors' Prison until you do pay."

"My only hope is that Robert will come to his senses."

Arthur pulled a purse from his coat and counted out seventy-five guineas. Mr McBride put it away inside his desk and assured Arthur he would pay Mr Molloy on his behalf.

"Major, I can give no specific advice, but you need to take a day away from this place, and discuss matters with your man-of-business. You have an estate, I know, and you have your commission. Both are worth something. Unfortunately, as soon as I saw Lord Justice Carter on the bench I knew our cause was lost. He is celebrated for his venality. I have little doubt that your brother has come to a suitable arrangement for him to enforce a judgement of this size. There have never been damages this large in Dublin, I know."

Arthur walked disconsolately back to the Castle.

The next day, he called at his man-of-business's office. That gentleman, Mr Whelan, confirmed that he would act for him. As a start, he advised Arthur to sell out. His infantry commission as major would raise over two thousand pounds.

"Very well, Mr Whelan, please contact the commission agents and put my commission up for sale. What about Belfield House?"

"Ah, yes. Your estate. I will find the deeds and make a start on finding a purchaser. You are aware, of course, that this will take some time?"

"I am indeed, Mr Whelan, but I have little choice. I am going back to Athlone to tell my colonel I am selling out. I will try and put Belfield House in some order while I am there, and then come back to Dublin. I must tell the Castle what has happened as well. Tell me, what happens to the funds when you receive them?"

"I must pay them into the court. They then pay them to your brother, and they will keep an account until the damages are paid in full."

"Mr Whelan, I have to tell you that I do not have anything that I can sell to increase my assets up to twenty thousand pounds."

"Major, do you have any jewellery, any paintings, and valuables you can sell? Do you have any money in the Funds?"

"Nothing that will come close to this figure."

Arthur left Mr Whelan and headed back to the Castle.

There, he drafted a letter to the garrison commander in Dublin.

He headed back to Athlone and brought Colonel Monroe up to date. The colonel was sympathetic and understood Arthur's position, both as a friend and as a brother officer. He released Arthur immediately with sad regret.

Arthur collected his possessions and arranged for them to be brought to Belfield House by a carter as soon as possible. After loading his horse with a portmanteau and some provisions, he left, taking his other horse on a rein behind him.

He arrived at Belfield House in the afternoon and found disaster awaited him. Thieves appeared to have ransacked the property while he had been away. Some furniture, some spare clothes, some paintings and other valuables, all were gone. Furnishings were missing, even some of his dining and kitchen equipment. He managed to find a lamp and some candle stumps and struck a faint light. Tomorrow he would have to ride into Mullingar and report the theft to the magistrates.

At the courthouse in Mullingar, he found the magistrate in his office and told him of his discovery.

"Major, you have my sympathy, but I can offer little hope. We have had a spate of thefts. You say the house was empty?"

"Yes. It has been empty for some time."

"There is your answer. I will note the loss. You are too far outside Mullingar for my watchmen. How long ago do you think this happened?"

"I have no idea. It could be some weeks ago."

"I'm sorry not to be more help. If you talk to the colonel in the barracks, he may be able to send a patrol out. You should not hold out any hope, though."

In Dublin, Robert was at dinner with some friends. One of those attending was Lord Justice Carter, and Robert took the opportunity to pass him an envelope. The judge placed it deep in his coat pocket, without opening it.

"Thank you, my lord. A most satisfactory outcome, I'm sure you agree."

"Oh, indeed. A most pleasant dinner also. I will watch and

wait to see my brother fail to raise the damages."

At Gaulstown, Mary was settling into a routine.

If her imprisonment was irksome before, it was doubly so now. The cook, Mrs Clohessy, was, at best, incompetent. The only maid left was a slattern, and Mary felt herself under continuous observation by the two guards. She would walk up and down in the long gallery on the first floor to take some exercise. She started to wash her own clothes, as the damage being inflicted on them by the maid's attentions would soon have left her naked. Fortunately, she still had access to the library. Books provided her only escape from her unbearable existence.

At first, her spirits had sunk into the depths of depression. Not only was she suffering a cruel imprisonment, but she was also deprived of her children. The thought that anyone would meet out treatment like this to anyone – let alone his wife and the mother of his children – seemed unimaginable.

After a while, she once more determined not to allow Robert to break her. Whatever indignity and suffering he forced upon her, she would endure it. She would survive.

Arthur had visited his man-of-business several times. He had also told him about the robbery from his house. Mr Whelan was sympathetic, but reminded him that the court took no notice of such events. They cared only that the cash be paid.

A month after the hearing, he was at the Castle when a messenger told him he was wanted at the gatehouse. Next to the soldiers on guard duty were two officials, plainly but identically dressed.

"Major Arthur Rochfort?"

"I am he. Who wishes to know?"

"We are tipstaffs of the court, sir, and we have a warrant to take you to the Debtors' Prison."

Arthur felt a cold feeling in the pit of his stomach. Deep down he had known the moment was inevitable, but now it had arrived. Any question of flight was useless. He felt as if he was trapped in the wheels of a giant mill.

"Very well, gentlemen. Please allow me five minutes to pack and say my farewells."

"Certainly sir, but we must be with you at all times. We are now responsible for you, and if you escaped, we would be held at fault."

Arthur and the tipstaffs went up to his room, and they watched him pack. Five minutes later the small procession crossed the yard and walked out of the Castle.

It only took five minutes to walk to Newhall Market. When they arrived, the tipstaffs stopped before a large wooden door and knocked hard. The door opened immediately, and they were shown into a tiny office. An elderly fat man in a dirty shirt, with grey, unkempt and greasy hair, was sitting at a battered desk.

"Name?" he called.

The senior tipstaff replied, "Arthur Rochfort."

The warder wrote Arthur's name and the date in a ledger and signed a note for the tipstaffs, who turned and silently left the room. Arthur could hear the front door close behind them with an awful finality.

"I am the Warder, Mr Collins. You are Arthur Rochfort. Twenty thousand pounds. Do you have money for rent?"

Arthur was surprised at the man's tone. He hadn't expected to be made welcome with open arms, but this offhand remark, addressing him as if he were a commodity rather than a person, was Arthur's first experience of the dehumanising effect of prison. He wasn't sure if he had heard the Warder correctly.

"Pardon, sir?"

"Do you have money for rent? While you are here, you must pay a Gaol Fee of three shillings and eight pence for every day, and if you want a bed, another shilling. In advance. You can send out for extra food if you have the money. If you cannot pay the fee, you sleep on the floor, and I add the Gaol Fee to your debt."

"So I must pay for being in here?"

"Of course. This is not a hotel. Prison is not a free

197

establishment."

"Here is twenty pounds. I will have more when needed. What rules are there in this place?"

"If you pay and have credit, you can leave during the day. You can bring in food. You can work to reduce your debt. You can see your man-of-business or your lawyer. If you are not back in here at sunset every day, the tipstaffs will find you, and you will then be held in the cellars, in chains. You do whatever I tell you, but pay your fees and your life here may not be too bad. With a debt such as yours, you will be here for many years."

Arthur's heart sank. He left the Warder's office, and a turnkey took him to a small room with a bed in it. The door had no lock or catch. A three-legged stool stood in a corner. There was no window, but a grille set with bars high in the wall let in a few feeble rays of light.

Arthur unrolled his baggage. He found a candle stump in the corner of the room and put it to one side for his first night. His stay here was going to be more complicated than he thought.

Robert appeared one day at Gaulstown. He ordered Mary to come into the garden.

"I have some news for you. I'm sure you will enjoy it!"

"What news? Are you going to release me?"

"Alas, no. You will be delighted to hear Arthur is currently languishing in the Black Dog, in Dublin."

"What is the Black Dog?"

"Well, from its name, you might think it was an inn. It used to be, but now it is serving a much more useful purpose. It is the Debtors' Prison."

"What is Arthur doing there?"

"There is the small matter of him owing the court, and thus owing me, the sum of twenty thousand pounds."

"Robert, what have you done to him? Why have you done this? He is your brother, for God's sake."

"I took him to court, to claim damages. For Criminal Conversation. For your benefit, I can tell you, this means I sued him for having sex with you, my wife. The judge could only agree what a terrible, terrible thing this was, how my own brother had dragged my name through the mud, and what an insult this was to my reputation. He awarded me damages to the tune of twenty thousand pounds."

"But he doesn't have anything like that. He is an army officer and a younger son."

"I know. Delightful, isn't it?"

"How can you hate like this? How could you do something to your brother and wife?"

"Madam, I have little or no feelings for either you or my brother. You could both die tomorrow for all I care."

"Will you leave me? I wish to go inside. You will excuse me while I get out of the sun."

"Of course, madam. I am delighted to be the bearer of such good news."

"You are enjoying this. The discomfort, the hurt, the humiliation, are you not?"

"Madam, I am. It amuses me, and I wish you good day."

With that, Robert walked her back to the house. The sound of the door closing shot through her heart like an arrow.

That year, the harvest failed again.

Arthur was now accustomed to the vagaries of life in a Debtors' Prison. He saw a constant passage of debtors and whores entering the Black Dog. Many of them were not only in debt or riddled with disease, but also starving. Their loans had become due, and they found themselves tossed into debtors' prison.

He soon discovered that access to the privies was available only to those who could rent a room. All others had to use what shelter they could. Those people who could not pay for food had bread and water, and sometimes oatmeal and potatoes. Arthur arranged to have a meal sent in from one of the local inns. As a soldier, he had experience of life on campaign, so managed to procure what he needed to make his stay at least bearable. He found it tragic to see some people manage to raise the money to clear their debts, through family or friends, but who then found themselves unable to leave because they could not pay the Gaol Fee.

Arthur could at least leave the prison during the day, so he could make a short visit back to the Castle to sell his two horses. Like others before him, he found the Black Dog an expensive place to be imprisoned. During the famine winter, the cost of food rocketed as the full extent of the potato blight became apparent.

Food (or lack of it) was not the only problem. With the lack of sanitation or fresh air, disease spread like wildfire, and there Arthur made another macabre discovery: there was no medicine available in the Black Dog. An inmate could call a doctor if he could pay, but all the others had to take their chances. A debtor might be healthy one day, and next day leave on the parish cart.

That winter was a terrible time for Arthur. His man-of-business had sold Belfield House and his Major's commission, for him. Arthur knew he had reduced his debt by some eight thousand pounds, less the accruing daily Gaol Fee, but the money he had from the sale of his hunters started to run out.

From time to time he had had visitors from among his friends in the army, but unfortunately, they gradually moved on from Dublin to fresh postings elsewhere.

In April 1749, the time came when he had barely any coins left at all. When the Warder came to collect his rent, Arthur protested that he needed a little time to borrow what was required.

The warder was impervious to supplications like these. He heard them every day.

"One week, Rochfort. That is all." He turned and left Arthur facing desolation.

The following day, Arthur left the gaol and went to the Castle. By dint of waiting around by the gatehouse, he eventually caught sight of Colonel Monroe and beckoned him over. The two of them repaired to a nearby inn, and Arthur told the colonel the extent of his problems.

The colonel was appalled, both at the conditions in the gaol that Arthur described, and by Arthur's appearance. While he was clean, his clothes were worn and mended. Worse, though was his physical appearance. His face was gaunt and sallow, and his eyes, once so famously blue and laughing, were deep-set and dull as if a light had gone out in them. The clothes were hanging off him.

"I have an idea. There are several of your old colleagues coming to Dublin in the next week. It is insupportable for one of our friends to be forced to exist in this way. We know the reputation of the Black Dog. It is a vile place. I want to collect a subscription for you. At least we can keep you out of chains."

"Colonel, I cannot tell you how grateful I am. It truly is hell in there."

"Arthur, I cannot imagine how any man could treat his brother like this. Robert's reputation does not improve. I see him in Mullingar from time to time. He rarely has contact with the Army now. His time as Muster-Master is over. Now, how much money do you have on your person now?"

"Three and a half pence, exactly," replied Arthur.

"Well, here is three guineas. It should keep that monster from you for a few days while I organise this subscription."

Back in the Black Dog, Mr Collins was clearly amazed when Arthur handed him three guineas.

"Where did you get this from?" he snarled. "Did you rob someone?"

"Thankfully, no. It seems I still have one or two friends in this city."

Ten days later, a servant came for Arthur to tell him that someone wanted him outside. At the door, he found Colonel Monroe, who shook his hand and led him back to the nearest inn.

"Arthur, it seems you still have many friends. I have the sum of forty-eight guineas for you in a mixture of coins and banknotes. Is there anywhere you can keep it safe?"

"I have a trunk in my room. I can lock it in there. I will pay my rent for the next three months straight away, as well."

"Keep it safe. You look terrible, but I imagine many of your fellows look worse."

"Colonel, I am lost for words. I can only thank you and everyone."

The two friends embraced, and the colonel returned to the Castle. Arthur headed back to the gaol via a small detour to leave most of his funds with his lawyer. As soon as he got back to the gaol, he immediately paid Mr Collins for the next two months' cell rent.

The warder gave him a searching look and placed the money in a strongbox.

"Your friends are generous, Rochfort. But mark my words: their generosity won't last long."

Chapter Twenty

JEALOUSY IS SUCH AN UGLY THING

Robert sat on a bench in his garden. Before him, a series of terraces led down to the south and gave him a clear view towards Lough Ennell. The only thing obstructing the view was the old family home of Rochfort House.

Robert was feeling good. Life was treating him well, although a nagging doubt lurked in his brain.

His wife was still his prisoner in Gaulstown. His brother was still alive but safely locked away in Debtors' Prison. He was spending more than half his time in Dublin, where his latest mistress provided all the physical diversions he craved. Political duties in the Irish Parliament kept him busy as well. It was an excellent place to meet people. He would arrange business dealings while always moving to increase his fortune and power.

Robert's treatment of Mary was well-known to society, and as a result, many houses and dinner invitations were closed to him. But Robert didn't care. His fortune was large enough to ensure that if he wanted female company, he knew where to find it.

He sat in the evening sun and looked down the terraces. Something was upsetting him, and he still couldn't think what it was. He heard the door open and close, and seconds later a waft of perfume reached him.

"Come and sit down my dear," he said to his latest mistress.

She was in her thirties and had been a widow for several

years; an intelligent woman, with a grasp of what could make her irresistible to men. Robert was not her first patron, but she could see a future by his side measured in years rather than months. She was curious about her lover's home, on this, her first visit.

"How far is it to the lake?" she asked.

"About a quarter of a mile. You could walk it in a few minutes."

"What do you do when you are here?"

"What any gentleman does in the country. Some hunting, a little fishing, some shooting."

"Don't you ever get bored?"

"Not usually. Up to now, I've been working as well, so I've been away in Athlone, or in town here or back and forth to Dublin."

"Whose is that house over there?"

"That's George's house. My youngest brother."

"It looks terribly grand. Imposing, I think, would be the word."

Robert looked at her. "More imposing than Belvedere?"

"Well, it looks bigger. Didn't you tell me that you built your house as a hunting lodge?"

"It was. My old house is eight miles away and is inconvenient and expensive to maintain. I built this as a replacement."

"It's beautiful. The gardens and the lake are both lovely views. You must be delighted with it. It is such a pity the eye is drawn to your brother's house, instead of down to the lake."

Robert's face darkened, a sure sign of his anger. Without a word, he got up, went into the house and shut himself in his study.

The following morning, Robert was already eating breakfast when she appeared.

"I have ordered my carriage. It will take you back to Dublin."

"But I thought you wanted me to stay—"

Robert cut her off. "I have no wish to have odious

comparisons made in my own home."

"What do you mean?" She looked shocked and upset.

"Perhaps I should be grateful and thank you for pointing out the shortcomings of my house. Pray, don't concern yourself. I will take proper steps, so no other visitor will feel so incommoded."

"Do you want to see me again?" she asked.

"I don't believe that I do. Now if you will excuse me, I have some business to attend to."

With that, Robert walked out and returned to his study, where he started to make some sketches and wrote a letter to Mr Castel.

His mistress finished her breakfast and climbed the stairs with a heavy heart. An hour later, the butler knocked on her door and told her that the carriage was waiting.

As the carriage moved off, she turned and looked back at Belvedere, and over to Rochfort House. She sighed to herself, musing on the strange nature and temperament of her recent protector.

"Never say die," she said aloud, and put all thoughts of Robert behind her.

Some weeks later Robert strode out of his new Dublin mistress's house. A chill was in the air, and the leaves on the trees were already turning brown. The streets were quiet, owing to the early hour. Some carts rumbled in from the countryside with vegetables for the market, and grain for the merchants. A light breeze blowing in from Dublin Bay carried the scent of the sea. He heard the seagulls as they wheeled and dived, seeking out rubbish from the market, and saw them swoop on anything that looked edible from the brown waters of the Liffey.

Life for Robert was indeed good. He felt a glow of self-satisfaction. He had spent two months in London. He had been summoned to Whitehall again. There, to his amazement, he had learned that Mr Stafford had died the previous winter. Stafford was the one person Robert feared, and he felt as if a heavy load had been lifted from his shoulders. Robert had also been introduced to His Majesty the King at a ball. He smiled at the memory. Having the monarch as godfather to his son and heir could only be good.

He walked into Gardiner Row, and his valet appeared silently from the servant's quarters. Robert handed him his coat.

"A bath and shave. Quickly, now!"

"Certainly, my lord," and the valet disappeared to the kitchen. Robert climbed the stairs to his bedroom, where a chain of maids brought buckets of hot water up to the room. Once shaved, dressed and enjoying the autumn air, Robert left the house and headed towards the Castle.

The new occupant of the Castle, Lord Stanhope, was a stranger to him. Robert thought it only proper for him to call and leave his card. He knew that their paths would cross eventually, and assumed that he would get on with him in much the same way as he had with his predecessor.

Robert sent his card up via a servant and sat down to wait. After an hour spent glancing anxiously at his pocket watch, his good humour had evaporated into a vile temper. He bellowed his displeasure to a passing servant, who assured him that he would take his concerns to His Excellency's private secretary.

An hour later still, the Lord Lieutenant's secretary arrived, apologised, and asked Robert to follow him up.

When Robert entered Lord Stanhope's office, he approached his desk and immediately started to protest at being kept waiting for two hours. He felt he was being treated like an ordinary tradesman.

Lord Stanhope raised his head slowly and looked at the figure stood before him.

"I do not see you, my lord!"

"What? What do you mean, you do not see me?"

"I do not see you, my lord, and I will not see you until you address me in the manner you would address His Majesty, in whose place I stand."

Robert looked stunned. Gone were the days of easy familiarity, access and easy conversation he had enjoyed with

Lord Cavendish. Sensing what was required, he drew his feet together, stepped forward and executed a low bow.

"Robert Rochfort, Earl of Belvedere, Your Grace."

"Thank you, Rochfort. Welcome to Dublin. Why are you here?"

"Why, Your Grace, to pay my respects, and to meet you, as His Majesty's Lord Lieutenant."

"You have our thanks. However, I must advise you that the world has changed here. Part of my role in Dublin is to remove or replace those officers who owe their position to friendship with officials."

"My lord, I can only assure you that I have always strived to serve His Majesty. I would ask that Your Grace examines the muster records for the Midland counties of Ireland. I think you will find them most satisfactory."

"Most satisfactory? I think not. It seems to me that you, sir, have done little or nothing apart from building your new house. To say nothing of your appalling treatment of your brother."

Robert's face paled as he saw his world of privilege and power slipping away from his grasp. He tried another tack.

"Your Grace, you must know that His Majesty is a friend, and he will not be pleased at how you propose to go on here."

"Rochfort, know this and know it well. His Majesty is no longer your friend. He is no friend of mine either, so I regard any former friends of his with great suspicion. Why do you think he stood as godparent to your son? It was simply because he needed your political support. Now he needs this no longer. This does not entitle you to call His Majesty your friend. My advice to you is to return to your house, put your affairs in order, and stay away from the Castle. You are no longer welcome here. Your position as Muster Master for the Irish Midland Counties is already forfeited. We have come through the Scottish uprising. The land is peaceful. I wish you good day, my lord."

Robert, now almost in a daze, executed another bow, turned and left. Once out in the street, he entered an alehouse and called for a tankard of porter. It took only a few seconds for him to drink this, and he called for another, and a bumper of brandy to go with it. After ten minutes of hard drinking, his temper had cooled. He left and crossed the Liffey Bridge back to Gardiner Row.

Once inside, he shouted at the servants before retreating into his study. He had an urgent need of more brandy. As he drank, he cursed the fates that had brought him to marry Mary.

Surely this was her fault...

Chapter Twenty-One

LIFE AS A DEBTOR,
AND A SLOW DECLINE

Christmas in Debtors' Prison was a day just like any other.

Those with funds could eat. Those without would starve if they couldn't survive on potatoes and oatmeal. Loaves of bread would arrive and be thrown among the prisoners. Those who could fight would weigh in and grab a loaf.

A curious sense of honour prevailed in the cell. Nobody ever took more than one piece of bread.

Arthur, while his funds lasted, could have food sent in. A bowl from one of the local inns could be arranged through the Warder or his wife. These two always took half of the cost as a commission. Everything was available in the Black Dog, for a price. For some of the inmates, the prison provided a refuge from their creditors. They could not be pursued there. Sometimes it was more of a punishment for them to be released and to be at the mercy of their creditors again.

The worst thing was the boredom. Arthur would talk for hours if there were a fellow inmate who would oblige. Sometimes there was nobody to talk to, and there was never enough light to read the occasional broadsheet or Bible that made their way into the prison.

Every winter, disease struck. The turnkeys were forever bringing up bodies from the lower reaches of the building. Those with no money at all, and who lacked the possibility of ever leaving, could find themselves chained up in the cellar, which was the only part of the building used as a privy.

Arthur himself was lucky to escape with a mild fever. No doctor was appointed or allowed in the Black Dog without payment. If a prisoner were ill, he would likely die. As each winter ended the outbreak of illness passed, and the flow of bodies from the prison slowed again to a trickle.

In Arthur's second year there, tragedy struck. One morning, a turnkey came to his room. "Mr Collins. Now!"

Arthur followed him to the Warder's office. Mr Collins gestured to him to enter. "Rochfort. Twelve thousand guineas, and no more funds."

Arthur started. He knew that this day would come sooner or later. As an inmate, he was never given any schedule, and the calendar of payments seemed to operate purely at Mr Collins' behest. There was no rhyme or reason.

His face fell, and he pleaded with the Warder.

"I need a week to raise more funds."

The Warden failed to react. He never even turned his head to look at him.

"Denied. Take him away."

Arthur was shocked at the complete indifference of the Warden. It was another example for Arthur of the dehumanising effect of prison.

Two turnkeys marched Arthur out of the office and down two floors to one of the large open rooms. There, one of them attached a chain to his wrist and stapled the other end of the chain to the wall. All this had happened before Arthur had any chance to react.

That night, a basket of bread, a bucket of water and a pot of boiled potatoes were delivered to the cell. As soon as it was put down on the floor, there was a mad scramble for the food. Arthur was still in a state of shock and made no attempt to eat.

"You'll eat soon enough," a voice called to him.

Arthur looked at his neighbour. "What do you mean?"

"You won't eat today; you may eat tomorrow, but in two days you'll fight for every scrap. You need food to survive." His neighbour was a small, stick-thin little man. "My name is

Josiah. Josiah Twenty-three Guineas, as Collins would say."

"How did you end up here?" asked Arthur.

"I was a tailor. I would make coats for grand gentlemen who did not pay their bills. Eventually, a haberdasher had me put in here until I paid what I owed him."

"How long have you been here?"

"This time, only six weeks. It's not so bad. My wife and family are working to pay the debt, and I will be out before too long. I can go out in the day to work, too. Collins makes me pay for the privilege, but it helps reduce the debt. A tailor friend gives me some work. It all helps."

"What about living here?"

"You are lucky. There is a little space today. You wait, though. Collins will put another half dozen people here inside a month. The space you have, you hold. If you have room to lie down, you fight to keep it. Can you fight?"

"I could. I fought in the Army."

"If you've been in the Army that will help. It is different down here. How long were you upstairs?"

"Over a year. I managed to sell a pair of horses, and that paid my Gaol Fees and rent."

"Can you raise no more?"

"Not a penny. My debt is too high to ever pay. I will die here."

"Why, how big is your debt?"

"Twelve thousand guineas," replied Arthur.

Josiah's eyes opened wide. "How in God's name did you do that?" he asked.

"Oh, it was bigger. When I came in here, it was twenty thousand pounds. After selling my house and my commission, I now owe about twelve thousand guineas."

"Can you not borrow from your family?"

"It was my family who put me here. The debt is to my brother. He is my only creditor."

"That's a terrible thing, for a brother to do that. How did it come about?"

"I fell in love with his wife, and she with me. My brother found out and sued me for damages."

211

Josiah whistled under his breath. "Now that is an expensive mistake to make."

"It was no mistake. My brother has a heart of stone. He never loved his wife, not even for a moment."

Over the next few days, Arthur found how grim life could be. He found he had to fight for his space on the floor, and the scraps of straw they had to sleep on. Bound by his chain, he had to use the central gutter for his bodily functions. As Josiah had foretold, by the third day, he was fighting for his bread and for a pannikin of water. Also, as Josiah had said, the population of the cell regularly increased.

Those who had paid their debts and Gaol Fees would be taken away and released without ceremony. Others, the old and the sick, would spend their last moments there, with no hope of a priest to ease their passing. The turnkeys would collect their bodies and carry them to the door to be collected by the local gravediggers.

As the days passed, Arthur could feel himself sinking. A career in the Army had indeed helped – sleeping rough and poor food held no horrors for him – but he gradually grew weaker, and the light started to go from his eyes. He thanked the gods that at least Mary couldn't see him in this condition.

After four months in the cell, his friend Josiah was called to the door. As he left, he turned to Arthur and wished him luck. "They've got me out. I'll be fine now. Good luck, and stay alive. Who knows what the future may bring."

Arthur watched Josiah walk towards his freedom. Having lost the only person he could call a friend, he felt lower than ever.

Years of living alone at Gaulstown, with its leaking casements and cracked, draughty walls, had brought a considerable change in Mary. The confinement and monotony had drained the colour from her cheeks. Never plump or full-figured, she was now stick-thin. She took to her bed and asked Mrs Clohessy to bring her some tea.

It had taken many months, but Mrs Clohessy had at last

unbent and smiled with her. She had a taste for an occasional gin, and she knew that Mary was aware of this. She also knew that Mary hadn't told Robert, and for this she was thankful. As time went by she relaxed and started to talk to Mary, but always when they were alone. Gradually Mary got her story from her.

"I lost my man and three babes in the famine, ma'am. Truly, it was the Year of the Slaughter for us. They lie in a grave together at Rockfield. We had a small farm and a cow, and we could manage. Then the cold came, the cow died, and we lost everything. Your brother-in-law, Mr George, was our landlord, and his agent came demanding a new high rent. We had nothing, so we had to go. He had some bully-boys with him who threw us off onto the highway. So, we walked."

"Where to?"

"We wandered, and we carried the babes. We tried to head for the road at Rochfortbridge. The cold came back, and one morning the babes never awoke. We were in a deserted byre, and when my man found the babes lying still and cold, he gave up. 'Twas as if a light went out in him. The next morning, he was lying cold under a blanket next to me."

"What did you do?"

"I laid them out in the byre and closed the door. Then I walked. I walked back to Rockfield and the priest there gave me shelter. His housekeeper had died in the cold too, so I took over."

"I am so sorry. I had no idea."

"Why would you?" replied the housekeeper. "Why would you be interested in the likes of us?"

"Perhaps because I'm a mother. I've lost my babes, too. Not like you, but thanks to my husband, they are lost to me."

The two of them shared a cup of tea in the kitchen, knowing they shared more than motherhood.

"Are they still there, in the byre?" asked Mary.

"Indeed they are not. When the winter ended, the priest arranged for a parish wagon to come with me and we brought them back for a proper Christian burial. They are at peace now."

Over the following months, the two women drew closer. They were too conscious of their positions to become friends, but they understood and valued each other.

Initially, Mrs Clohessy's cooking abilities were limited in the extreme. As a farmer's wife, most of her cooking was based on potatoes and oats. Only sometimes did they have meat, and generally that would be a rabbit caught in a snare on the farm. Mary, slowly but surely, managed to expand her choice of meals, and the quality of life for everyone at Gaulstown improved. When the groom made his weekly trip into Mullingar, he would carry a shopping list written by Mary. Gradually, the bill of fare improved, with cheese, beef, pork and mutton appearing in season.

Every week, Mr Flynn would send some staple foods out to the house, delivered by a local carter. What arrived depended on what was available in the market that week. Apart from this, the only persons to visit Gaulstown were Flynn, and Robert himself.

Mr Flynn would attend every month and pay the staff (a maid, who helped Mary when she could, a groom-cum-gardener, and the two guards). Mary would speak with Mr Flynn when she could, but felt desperately restricted in what she dared say to him. After she had been at Gaulstown over a year, he started to unbend. When she had been there two years, he became much friendlier. Although always guarded in his approach, he seemed to become more helpful.

Mary could have no way of knowing how his loyalties to Robert could be distorted by his loyalty to much more powerful persons. Mr Flynn was not going to tell her who his real masters were.

Every time Robert came to Gaulstown, he would make her walk in the garden. To prove his power, he made her walk twenty paces in front of him. They would make two circuits around the garden before returning to the house when her confinement would resume. When Robert was there, she would keep her eyes downcast and avoid eye contact. She knew he thought she was totally subservient, but try as he might, he couldn't crush her spirit. As soon as he had left, her face would light up again. She would march into the kitchen and share a cup of tea with Mrs Clohessy.

She had lost any idea of not undertaking tasks considered below her station. The staff were too few in number, and the terms of imprisonment Robert imposed on her effectively applied to them all.

Over the course of time, Mary's good-heartedness won over all the staff, apart from the two guards, who remained suspicious and distant. The house staff and Mary, on the other hand, banded together to form a conspiracy to improve their lot as much as possible. Under Mary's supervision, they cleaned and maintained the rooms they were living in. With the groom, they carried out some repairs to keep the living area weatherproof.

Their pace of life was governed by the seasons. One day was much like another, particularly for Mary. The one single unbreakable rule was that she could not leave Gaulstown. The boundaries of the garden were her prison walls. She could not even go outside without being escorted by one of Robert's bully-boys.

Mary's days crawled by, month by month. In her second year, with Christmas approaching, her thoughts turned even more to her children. Whenever she saw Robert, she asked about them, but without any response. There could be no letters. She had no keepsakes of their passing years. No milk-teeth or locks of their hair. Nothing to bridge the growing void in her heart. While her dreams at night were still of Arthur and of lying in his arms, during the day her thoughts always turned to her son and daughter. How tall were they? Had they had the croup? What sort of people were they growing up to be? She had tried asking Robert for these details, but had been rebuffed again and again.

"Their welfare is none of your business, madam," was his response. "I'll trouble you not to bring this subject up. You may only speak to me when I speak to you first. Do you understand?" Robert stood over her in the drawing room, with eyes as hard as flint. A disdainful smile appeared to be forming on his lips.

"Oh, I understand only too well, sir. I understand you have a heart of stone."

Mary lowered her eyes to her lap, and Robert turned and walked out. She lifted her face, and a glint of utter determination filled her eyes. She would not be beaten!

Chapter Twenty-Two

A GAOLER BY ANY OTHER NAME

For Robert, the time was dragging. Since his interview with the new Lord Lieutenant, his social engagements had all but disappeared. He still returned to Dublin every few weeks, but when he went to the Castle, he found his presence barely tolerated.

He tried hosting dinner engagements. His guests almost all concluded that they had urgent business elsewhere. After two attempts, at both of which he had been left with a small number of guests he despised, he abandoned any further attempts.

Carnal pleasures were still available to him, for a price. He renewed his acquaintance with the bawdy-houses of earlier years. In some of them, he found a few of the older women remembered him from his youth. They hadn't aged well. He mentioned this to the madam.

"Well, you haven't aged that well yourself, my lord," was her reply.

"What exactly do you mean by that?" His eyes and face darkened.

"Well, look at you. You've got the look of a man who has seen a ghost. You look like a man who has seen the bottom of too many brandy bottles, and you look like a man who has no friends!"

Robert got up from the sofa and walked out of the brothel into the cold Dublin air. By the time he had walked back to Gardiner Row, his brain was seething with the injustice of it all. He was an earl, for God's sake. How dare people take

217

against him?

The following night, he walked over to Dublin Castle and into the officer's mess. None came over to welcome him, even some he recognised or knew by name. He sat alone at a table, and a mess servant came over to him.

"Brandy!" he barked.

The servant withdrew without a sound and produced as if by magic a large glass full of the spirit with a jug of water. He put these on the table and withdrew.

As Robert sipped at his glass, a tall figure appeared by his side, and without asking him, seated himself at the table. The stranger announced himself.

"My lord, I am Colonel Wilson, the new commander here, and the Mess President."

"Hmmph. Pleased to meet you, Wilson," Robert grunted.

"It is my unfortunate duty to inform you that you are no longer welcome in the mess. I'll thank you to finish your brandy and leave."

"Supposing I don't? Supposing I refuse? What will you do?" Robert snarled.

"I, sir? Nothing. However, these gentlemen will be forced to eject you."

Robert looked around and saw three large sergeants standing by the mess door. Even through a haze of brandy, Robert knew that he had been outmanoeuvred.

Another cold walk over the bridge and through the streets of Dublin saw him home.

The following morning, he shouted at the servants to pack. They were returning to the country immediately. He was damned if he would stay and be publicly humiliated a day longer. Back at Belvedere, he could watch his new building project take place.

Some months previously, he had decided that he needed a wall that would blend in with the ruins of some of the old castles in the area. It must be high enough, and long enough, to block out entirely the view of George's house. Furthermore, it must look 'right'. It must seem as if it had been there for several hundred years.

He had drafted a letter to Mr Castel, requiring his immediate attendance with a view to another commission, then had settled down to dream of his new folly.

His dream was rudely interrupted two weeks later when he received a short note from Mr Castel declining the commission. The note also advised that Mr Castel would be unable to undertake any work for at least two years.

Robert was incandescent with rage. He walked over to his brother's house, something he had not done for many months. He was used to seeing the traces of wooden scaffolding, but he had taken no interest in the rebuilding of the house. George was at home, and Robert joined him in his study and started ranting about the ungrateful attitude of the professional classes. After ten minutes, George had had enough.

"Robert, will you please tell me what your problem is?"

"It is Castel, the architect. He has refused to work for me."

"I happen to know he is committed to a large project elsewhere. He also wants to return to his native Germany."

"What possible project could he have more important than mine?"

"Well, he has been working for me, and now the Master of Trinity has engaged him to build some large buildings for the University."

"You mean that Castel has designed all this?" Robert gestured around him.

"Indeed he has. His work is now finished, and the final set of building work is being undertaken by my own stonemasons. In six months, it will be finished, and I will have a country house to rival yours. Once more, Rochfort House will be the pre-eminent house in Westmeath."

Robert stared at him, snapped his walking stick between his hands, threw the pieces to the floor and stormed out.

Once home he shouted for brandy and sat down to think. Eventually, he decided that he needed to be in Dublin.

Next day he made an early start. A long, uncomfortable journey through a rainstorm did nothing to improve his temper. As soon as he arrived at Gardiner Row, he threw off his cloak and demanded food. After he had eaten, he wrote a short note to his man-of-business, Mr Coote, advising him that he would call on him before lunch on the following day.

When he called, Mr Coote was all obsequious attention. It was many months since he had seen his client, and he was curious why he was there.

After exchanging the usual compliments and greetings, Mr Coote asked Robert to explain what he wanted.

"I need a new wall building at Belvedere."

"Of course, my lord. But what do you want from me? Building a wall is a task beyond my abilities."

"I need an architect."

"My lord, you had an architect. Mr Castel is as well-known as any in Ireland."

"Mr Castel is, unfortunately, not available. I need another."

"I see no problem, my lord. There are many highly skilled architects here in Dublin. I will prepare a list of candidates and will call on you next week. You can then tell me whom you wish me to engage. While I make my list, can I ask you, my lord, to let me have some details about this wall? How long, and how high, for example?"

Robert agreed and returned to Gardiner Row. He made a rough sketch of what he thought he wanted and sent it round to Mr Coote's office that same day. As he had little technical knowledge, he could do little more. He had also failed to take any proper measurements.

Mr Coote called at Gardiner Row the following week. Seated in Robert's study, he apologised and explained that there was only one architect who was prepared to go to County Westmeath and build a wall. What he could not explain was that Robert's reputation had preceded him. Several of the architects Mr Coote had consulted had refused point blank to work on the Belvedere estate. Others had no interest in the building of a wall, especially when hearing that his lordship had only recently completed building his new home.

Mr Coote produced a piece of paper with several names on it. All had been crossed out, save one.

Robert's face darkened. He snarled at his unfortunate guest. "Coote, you told me you would have a list I could choose from."

"I did, my lord. Unfortunately, it seems that all the local architects are engaged. I do, however, have details of a Mr Wright, who has recently arrived from England and appears to have the requisite qualifications and experience. He is also anxious to build a reputation in Ireland. Most importantly, my lord, he is available."

"Then engage him, and tell him to come to Belvedere early next week."

Robert returned to Belvedere the following day. Over the intervening days, he paced out some distances to give himself some idea of dimensions.

The following Tuesday evening, his visitor arrived and presented his card. Robert read: *Thomas Wright of Durham, Architect*.

"Mr Wright, Welcome to Belvedere. I have a room for you. We will meet tomorrow morning, and I will tell you my requirements."

Thomas Wright followed the butler to a small guest room. The groom brought his luggage up some minutes later, and he unpacked the tools of his trade: drawing instruments, a large board, two quires of folded foolscap paper, a measuring chain and a yardstick.

Nobody came up to him, so he made his way downstairs in the gloom to the kitchen. The housekeeper was happy to serve him, and sat with him by lamplight to talk about Belvedere.

"Do you have any idea what his lordship expects of me?" asked Thomas.

"Not a notion, sir, apart from him wanting a wall building, so he doesn't see his brother's house. He's a jealous man, is his lordship. Did you hear about his wife?"

Thomas, only newly arrived from the north-east of

221

England, had not heard of the scandal that had enveloped Dublin some years earlier. The housekeeper was only too happy to advise him of what she knew.

"But what about his brother?" he asked.

"Which one? His lordship has two. He hates them both with a passion."

"Why would he do that?"

"Pure jealousy, I believe." The housekeeper pulled her chair closer to Thomas, leaned towards him and dropped her voice to a whisper. "Even though Mr Robert got the title, his younger brother, Mr George, got the bulk of their father's fortune. He's been very successful building it up. They do say he's not above bending the rules as well. Mr George is a hard, hard landlord, as my family know."

"And the other brother?"

"Ah. That's Mr Arthur. Mr Arthur got the looks, and he got the manners to go with them. A lovely, lovely man. He made one mistake, though."

"Yes?"

"Well, he fell in love with his lordship's wife. And she with him, I understand."

"What did his lordship do?"

"Locked them up. He has locked his wife up in the old family home at Gaulstown, and he had Mr Arthur flung into the Black Dog in Dublin. A terrible place, to be sure."

"What, pray, is the Black Dog?" asked Thomas, his interest piqued by these revelations.

"For sure, sir, you are a stranger here. The Black Dog is the prison in Dublin where they put the debtors. His lordship sued his brother, and the judge awarded him with more money than Mr Arthur, or any ten men, could ever pay. So he is in the Black Dog, and there he stays. 'Tis a foul and evil place indeed."

"His lordship sounds a terrible man to cross."

"He is indeed. He has money and position, and he has powerful friends, and he makes his own rules. So, you be careful how you deal with him."

"I will, and thank you for the advice. If I could, I'd get on the first boat back to England, but that's not possible until I get some work and get paid."

With that, he took a candle from the kitchen and made his way back to his room.

In the morning, he went down to the kitchen, where the housekeeper made him breakfast. It quickly became apparent that this was how he was to comport himself during his stay at Belvedere. Not a servant, but not a guest either.

He waited until mid-morning when Robert summoned him to his study. He told the architect what he had in mind and took him out to the front of the house to show him the view.

Spread out in front was a series of terraces and lawns stretching downwards towards a circular drive. Beyond that was a stretch of parkland, suddenly interrupted by a new-looking manor house, built of the same grey stone as Belvedere.

"Is that the house?" asked Thomas.

"Indeed it is. It was built where our old house used to stand. My brother hired my architect and built a house like that to annoy me."

"Quite so. It looks similar in design. Now can your lordship show me exactly what you had in mind?"

"I want a wall. I want you to design me a wall that looks like an old ruin, and it needs to be big enough so that I don't have to look at that house!"

"Very well, my lord. I will spend the rest of this week drawing and measuring. Can we meet this time next week, and I will show you some designs?"

"Very well. I will leave you to your work," said Robert, bringing the meeting to a close.

They met in the dining room a week later. On the table was a series of plans, showing walls of differing sizes, heights and widths.

Robert took one look at them. "These are too small!" he spluttered, his voice sharp with annoyance.

"How do you mean, my lord?"

"I want a large wall. A wall that will completely hide the

view of that house. A wall that will look magnificent. Now, do I make myself clear?"

"I believe so, my lord. What type of wall was it you had in mind? I imagine you want more than a plain straight wall."

"Of course I do. I don't need a fancy architect to build me a simple wall. I told you, it is to be magnificent!"

"It will be necessary to build more than just a wall, my lord. There must be something to support it. A stable block or similar, or a house or barn. Something behind the wall to stop it from toppling over."

"Then add a stable block. If it's on the other side of the wall, my brother can enjoy the sight of it."

"My lord, if you walk with me, I can make some suggestions, and you can guide me if they meet with your approval."

For the next hour, Robert and the architect walked, pointed, measured and discussed. At last Thomas had a proper idea of what his strange employer wanted.

Inside another week, he had a set of drawings, outlining the new wall. In its new form, it was to be over sixty paces wide, and one-third of that in height. The style was to be something between a ruined cathedral and a castle. There would be ruined windows and arrow slits and the remains of battlements.

"Now you are showing me what I want," exclaimed Robert. "Tomorrow we will go into Mullingar and talk to my agent."

Over the next month, Thomas worked daily to produce a full set of working drawings. He made the trip to Mullingar several times, where Joseph Flynn put him in touch with two men who, he said, were skilled masons. They had both worked on Belvedere, and on the new Rochfort House.

At the end of that time, Thomas returned to Dublin, leaving the masons with a proper understanding of their task. They had no idea why Robert wanted such a wall, but it meant work and pay for them, and for a large pool of labourers from Mullingar.

Over the coming months, foundations were dug, stones were purchased, and gradually the wall began to grow.

Chapter Twenty-Three

STONE WALLS DO INDEED
A PRISON MAKE

Winter had arrived. Gaulstown, with its draughts and leaking roofs, was a hotbed of colds and agues.

Mrs Clohessy had a stock of country remedies for such illnesses. The kitchen was hung with bunches of herbs and wild plants. She would cook, chop and mix them with various materials into different nostrums and unguents.

Mary was sick enough to take to her bed, and Mrs Clohessy, who assured Mary that she never ever got ill, kept her dosed with foul-tasting medicines.

"Hold your nose and drink it quick, ma'am, it'll do you good," was her constant cry.

Mary preferred a mixture of honey, herbs and brandy with some hot water. With the aid of this, she made a quick recovery, and Mrs Clohessy turned her attention to the other staff.

They soon learnt to assure her that they were all in the pink of health. The threat of her medicines was enough to frighten away any fever.

By the time Christmas arrived, Mrs Clohessy had a much better grasp of cooking. The waggon would come back from the market well-laden. The staples were still potatoes, bread and oatmeal, but now they had meat, and the groom kept chickens. They didn't starve, although any addition, such as a rabbit, was welcome.

Christmas Day brought a welcome surprise for Mary. She heard unfamiliar voices on Christmas morning. Robert's carriage had arrived in front of the house. She looked around nervously, but much to her delight the coach doors opened. George and Jane, followed by a stiff and ageing Nurse, stepped down from the carriage.

Mary burst into tears. It was two years since she had seen her children. She had had Robert's casual assurance that they were well. She had tried asking Mr Flynn on his calls to Gaulstown, but he knew little more.

Nurse brought them to her, and Mary opened her arms. "Do you remember me? I'm your mother."

"Of course, Mama," said Jane.

"Give your Mama a kiss, children," instructed Nurse. Both the children slowly came towards her. Mary could hold herself in check no more and swept them into a fierce embrace.

After hugging them to her as if her life depended on it, she released their hold. Jane looked at her, and moved forward herself and hugged her mother. Nurse herself was crying by now. George returned her embrace and then moved out of her reach. Mary took them all into the drawing room. Mrs Clohessy appeared, evidently having heard visitors.

"I'll be getting some tea, and something for the children, ma'am," she announced, and disappeared towards the kitchen.

"Nurse, how is it you are here?"

"I'm sure I don't know myself. His lordship came into the schoolroom this morning and told me to make them ready for a trip. I asked him where to, but he didn't reply."

"How long are you all here for?" asked Mary.

"Only until the afternoon. We must leave and get back before sunset. The coachman tells me that we should go soon after three o'clock."

Mary instantly calculated. She had them for just over two hours. Mrs Clohessy arrived at that moment with tea, and with some buttermilk for the children.

"Why is he doing this?" Mary asked Nurse.

"I'm sure I don't know, ma'am. You know yourself we

never know why he is doing what he does. His lordship follows no rules. Do you know about his wall?"

"Wall? What wall?"

Nurse told her of the construction. The whole household knew that his lordship was building a new wall so he would not have to look at Mr George's house. It was said it was because trees would take too long to grow.

There followed two emotion-packed hours for Mary. Gradually, the children lost their fear of her. In the middle of the afternoon, and replete with tea, buttermilk and cake, the children happily embraced their mother when it came time to say goodbye. None of them knew when Robert would permit another visit.

That night, for the first time in over two years, Mary went to bed with a smile on her face. What, she asked herself, would the New Year bring?

At Belvedere, Robert was inspecting his wall.

"How much longer?"

"Oh, about thirty feet, sir."

"No, how much longer will it take you to finish this wall?" shouted Robert.

The masons came over to where he stood. "What was it you were wanting, my lord?"

"How much longer is it going to take you to finish the wall?"

"Well, that would depend, my lord."

"Depend on what?" Robert's humour was rapidly disappearing.

"We have a problem with the stone, my lord."

"What problem?"

"There isn't enough of it," replied McCabe, the older of the masons.

"What must we do?"

McCabe explained the problem: a shortage of suitable stone. The output from the local quarry was already used, and it would take many months before a proper supply of dressed stone blocks would be available. Ever since the famine, there was less labour around to undertake hard, backbreaking work for little reward.

"Tell me, McCabe, could you use stone from an old building?"

"Indeed, my lord; that would be grand!"

"I own a small manor-house. It's no longer required, and it would give me a certain satisfaction were it to be demolished."

Robert told them where the property was, and by the end of six weeks, the labourers had removed everything of value from the house, including stone, lead sheeting and sound pieces of timber. Everything was loaded onto carts and waggons and carried to the building site at Belvedere. After this, the work on the wall continued apace.

In form, it looked like a mixture of castle and cathedral. Timber scaffolding surrounded the structure. A team of horses stood by with their driver to haul blocks via a pulley to the top of the wall. Robert counted twenty labourers working with the masons. They were mixing mortar, carrying stones and climbing up and down the long ladders tied to the scaffolding.

Of Belfield House, nothing remained except a pile of broken stones and unusable pieces of wood.

"Burn it," was Robert's last instruction when he rode out to inspect his now-cleared estate. No trace remained of Arthur and Mary's presence.

Once the pile of remains was alight and burning, he left the labourers to carry on with their work and rode over to Gaulstown. Sitting on the top step was one of his guards. The man looked bored but stood up as soon as he recognised Robert.

"Is she inside?" barked Robert.

"Is who inside?" the guard asked.

"Her ladyship, you idiot!" Robert strode through the front door and into the drawing room. Mary was standing inside. She had heard his voice and was wondering what fresh torture Robert had come to inflict on her.

"I thought you might be interested in some news."

Mary's face lit up. "News? News of whom?"

"I'm sure you remember my younger brother's home?"

"Belfield House? Of course."

"Well, I'm delighted to tell you that it is no more."

"What do you mean by that?"

"Precisely what I say. If you look out of the front door, you will see the smoke from its remains. When the court seized my brother's house, I bought it for a song, and now I have destroyed it."

"Why?"

"Isn't that obvious? I will leave no visible trace that reminds me of the pair of you rutting like animals."

Mary shrunk at this description, so different from the reality.

"It is now part of my wall."

"Your wall? What wall?"

"Oh yes. I have built a wall. A wall to shield my view from brother George's house. I now have a clean, unobstructed view of my own creation. From the house to the wall and across to the lough."

Mary shook her head in bewilderment. "I don't understand. Why would you destroy Belfield?"

"Because I could, Madam. That, and because I wanted the stone for my wall. I bid you good day." With that, he turned on his heel and strode out to his horse.

Mary stared after him. "Stones for a wall?" she whispered. "Your heart is truly made of stone."

Eighty miles away in Dublin, Arthur, lying on some scraps of straw, turned and shifted his position carefully. He was still shackled to the cell wall, and he could feel himself, day by day, sinking into the very fabric of this hell-hole.

He was well-practised at seizing his rations as soon as they were thrown to them. This was generally little more than bread, potatoes and water. Sometimes one of the Dublin charities would supply something palatable, perhaps a stew with some cheap cuts of meat.

The one thing they had in the cell was water. A trough in

the room was kept full and fed by a system of lead pipes. His clothes were in rags, but he was at least moderately clean.

And he had learnt to fight. His time in the Army served him well, but to survive in the prison, he had had to beat off several attacks. Power in the cell came through violence. He had also had to fight off occasional attempts on his person at night. Sometimes this was for robbery, but more often by an unchained prisoner seeking sexual favours.

After a year, the other inmates and the turnkeys knew to keep away from him. "Leave Rochfort alone, and he behaves," was their motto. They knew he would fall in the end. Nobody could ever pay a debt as large as his.

Arthur had his mind fixed on surviving. He knew he needed to keep alert and strong, so he ate whatever he could. The cold and damp in the cell affected everyone, especially in the winter. He had seen many people die in there; no doubt he would see even more if the winter was harsh.

The debtors were a mixed bunch. Most of them seemed to be small traders who had not been paid. Their suppliers would make them bankrupt, and they would be committed to the prison. They would stay there until their families had managed to raise the funds to free them.

Sometimes the amounts were derisory;less than ten pounds. On two occasions, he saw the same person admitted and released, only to be made bankrupt again and reappear in the prison.

News was hard to come by. The outside world barely impinged on the lives of the prisoners. Their only worry was when their families could raise the funds for their release. The other inmates' concerns and interests were rarely his. Sometimes a professional man would enter the prison: a lawyer once, and an actor. Unfortunately for Arthur, he never saw another military man. Any chance to talk on any subject was meat and drink to him. There was nothing left to do in the cell. There were no books, and no light bright enough to read by anyway.

Christmas for Arthur was a day of better food from the

local church. A stew of mutton and vegetables provided a festive note to the day. A young priest also came into the cell to say Mass and to preach. The congregation hung on his every word, even those who were Protestants. There was no religious divide in the prison; their situation was too dire to allow such niceties.

Arthur knew enough of the liturgy in Latin for it to make sense. He felt no qualms about following a Catholic service, and had been to many over the years. Now, it provided an hour's release from the boredom that hung over the gaol.

With nightfall, the cold and damp returned, and the prisoners huddled together for warmth. After a day of change, life returned to its stultifying routine. For Arthur, the only purpose was to stay alive.

Arthur thought of Robert only rarely. It was if he had played his part in Arthur's life and had left the stage. Mary, though, was in his thoughts every night. If he dreamed, it would be of her. He still loved her, with every fibre of his being. And although he had heard nothing of her since the day of his incarceration, he knew she still loved him.

Chapter Twenty-Four

IN WHICH ROBERT CLIMBS, AND COUNTS THE COST

Robert was unhappy.

He had his new home. After almost a year, his wall was complete. He had his view, unobstructed by the sight of his brother's enormous house. He had a mistress in Dublin. Despite all these things, he felt something was lacking.

He knew that he would never be received back at Dublin Castle again. He had lost any patronage he might have had from the King. The new Lord Lieutenant had seen to that.

He barely gave Mary a thought. He saw his children on rare occasions in passing, but hadn't spoken to their nurse for several months. The nursery was in the attics at Belvedere. It was enough that they were there.

As for Arthur, he was as good as dead.

In the fading light, Robert walked over to his wall to admire it. He noticed some of the construction details for the first time. There was a series of protruding blocks and holes that formed a rough but sound set of steps and footholds to allow a man to climb up the wall. The stubs of some of the construction timbers were still fixed in some places. There was no handrail, but they seemed serviceable, if not apparent to the uninitiated. He put his foot on the lowest step and climbed. The darkness and a certain natural caution prevented him from trying to climb more in the dark. He cautiously retraced his steps to the foot of the wall and walked back to the house, then turned to look at his recent ascent from the top terrace. A large glass of brandy helped him sleep that night.

He returned to the wall for an inspection in full daylight. In the sun, the steps were clear, once one knew where to look. This time, he looked carefully where he could see his way. The steps and handholds seemed serviceable, if narrow. They had been put there to provide strength and to assist in building the wall, rather than to aid access.

He climbed slowly and steadily, pausing before each new step to examine it and to see where the next step was positioned. The only thing to differentiate the steps from a regular staircase was a certain unevenness in the rise of the tread.

In less than five minutes, he was as high as the steps would take him. There was a ledge running part of the way along the wall, like a firing-step in a fort. He found he could walk a short way along the ledge, and from this position, in the bright light of morning, he could look right over his own house. He could see Mullingar to the north-east. In the opposite direction, he had a perfect view of George's new house, and right across the lough, between the trees, to the far shore. Robert grunted in satisfaction and made his way slowly to the ground again. The climb and descent were easy, providing he took care.

Back in the house, he ate a late breakfast and called for his horse. An hour later he rode into Mullingar and dismounted outside his agent's office. Mr Flynn was in, and a clerk showed Robert into his inner sanctum.

"Good morning, my lord. To what do I owe the pleasure?"

"Good day, Flynn. I am going to Dublin next week, and I'll see my man-of-business while I am there. My wall is now finished, as you know, and it is time to settle accounts. I need a full set of the bills for the wall, and anything outstanding for the rest of the estate, ready for me to take with me."

"Of course, my lord. I will have them with you for next Wednesday."

"How are matters at Gaulstown?"

"As they should be, my lord. I have changed one of the guards. The first man fell ill. The new guard seems entirely satisfactory."

"And my wife?"

233

"She seems resigned to her fate, my lord. She appears thin and pale but in good health. I am no doctor, of course. She seemed much improved after her children's visit at Christmas."

"That visit was made for their benefit, Flynn, not hers. Their nurse requested it and seemed to think it necessary. I'm not inclined to repeat it."

"My Lord, might I ask what you intend to do with her ladyship? Eventually, that is?"

"No, Flynn, you may not ask. I can tell you that I intend to bury her when she dies. That is the sum total of my plans for my wife."

"I apologise for my impertinence, my lord."

"I should think so. We will review the procedures at Gaulstown when I return. Is the place still as leaky as ever?"

"I understand so, my lord."

"Good. When she has died, I will demolish it and rebuild it for my son."

With an air of quiet satisfaction, Robert rose and strode out of the office.

On Tuesday of the following week, Flynn appeared at Belvedere as ordered. He handed Robert a large sheaf of papers in two leather satchels. Robert looked at him quizzically.

"There seems to be a lot of papers here?"

"Indeed there is, my lord. There were still some bills outstanding from the building of Belvedere, so I have put them all together. Also, my lord, I will need some operating funds on your return. May I suggest the sum of fifty guineas?"

"You may suggest all you wish. I agree to nothing without examination of the costs and invoices."

"Of course, my lord. I wish you a safe trip and satisfactory meetings."

The following morning saw Robert on the road to Dublin. There were matters he needed to deal with there. He led a second horse laden with a portmanteau and the satchels of papers, covered in oilcloth in case of rain.

234

Dublin was grey and damp. The cold of the autumn rose from the river and kept the few pedestrians moving at speed. A penetrating wind made sure this was no weather to dawdle.

Mr Coote welcomed him into his office and shut the door. After greeting Robert and taking the satchels of papers from him, he suggested they adjourn to a spare room. There, a large table would allow them to spread out the papers, and, in the words of Mr Coote, make some sense of all this paperwork.

Robert sat there for over an hour, while Mr Coote went through the papers, sorting them into piles. From time to time, he would enter the figures from the papers into a large ledger.

"Coote, how much longer will this take?" Robert asked, unable to keep silent anymore.

"Oh, not too much longer, my lord. I can't be too precise, but I expect to have things arranged properly in the afternoon."

"This afternoon?" Robert's voice rose several tones.

"Indeed, my lord. I did say it would not be too long."

"It is too long for me. I will return in the morning. This is ridiculous." He turned on his heel and marched out through the office into the street.

Outside, rain was pouring down. Robert's temper was already in shreds, and by the time he had walked back to Gardiner Row, he was in a foul mood.

The servants heard Robert's return, and all decided to stay out of his way as much as possible until his temper had cooled.

After lunch, Robert left again, this time to a tavern, where he spent the rest of the day. A visit to Mrs Gleeson's establishment (one of Dublin's finer bordellos), and several large glasses of brandy, restored his equanimity. He returned home at midnight. His valet was still waiting up for him and saw him undressed and into bed.

The next day, nursing a hangover and feeling the effects of the previous night, Robert called on Mr Coote again. His temper showed no improvement because of his headache. He put this down to having drunk from a dirty glass in Mrs Gleeson's.

This time Mr Coote was ready for him. All the papers, together with several ledgers, were already spread out on the table.

Mr Coote took one look at Robert and sent one of his clerks to the nearest coffee shop. Robert had the appearance of a man in urgent need of coffee. Five minutes later, the clerk returned with two steaming cups. As soon as Robert had finished, Mr Coote decided it was time to get proceedings under way, and plunged into the bills for the wall. He spoke clearly and expressively for an hour. Robert's attention, while cursory at the start, soon became more acute.

After an hour, Mr Coote took off his pince-nez and carefully placed them on the table.

"And that, my lord, is it. To summarise, your wall has cost more than nine thousand pounds. To be precise, the sum of nine thousand, six hundred and eight pounds, twelve shillings. Also, there are unsettled accounts from the construction of your hunting lodge. These make a further four thousand three hundred and twenty-four pounds. A grand total of thirteen thousand, nine hundred and thirty-two pounds, and twelve shillings."

Robert swallowed. This was far more than he had expected to pay.

Mr Coote continued, "This figure is greater than the sum I am holding for you here, my lord, by more than two thousand pounds."

"What?" exclaimed Robert. "How is that possible?"

"Your receipts from rents have plummeted in the last years, my lord. A lot of your properties are not producing any rent at all. I believe you will need to sell some of your holdings at the Bank of England."

Robert's face went white. With this news coming on top of his hangover, he looked – and felt – wretched.

"Arrange it, if you must. Make payments from what I have on deposit as best you may. I will return to Belvedere tomorrow and speak with my land agent. I need to find out why the rents have fallen. Flynn is generally reliable, but it seems he has a soft spot. A soft spot which he will lose forthwith."

Two days later, Robert was sitting with Joseph Flynn and the estate ledgers in his study at Belvedere. Together they went through the list of properties. It soon became evident that there were far fewer of these than Robert expected.

"Where have my farms gone?" he demanded.

"My lord, you sold a lot of them after the famine."

"But the farms I sold were worthless. Falling down and unworkable."

"Indeed, my lord. I see from the records that many of them were sold to nominees. Most of them are now in the hands of your brother."

"Good luck to him. They are worthless."

"My lord, they might have been worthless then, but not now. Mr George has grouped several of the properties together, to make much larger estates. Some of these he has sold off, especially to gentlemen coming from England and wanting to buy a property."

"Is there any way of reducing our expenditure here?" Robert asked.

"That is not for me to say, my lord. It does not appear to me that your expenditure is excessive, save for the matter of the wall. I would suggest that all will come right with time, providing you avoid any more building ventures."

After Flynn left, Robert's thoughts turned towards his brother George. He became almost incandescent with rage. How dare he, his own brother, buy his proprieties and plot against him? The fact that George appeared to have acted entirely within the law simply didn't enter his head.

The following morning, he decided once and for all to have it out with George. He collected a walking stick and left the house for the short walk over to Rochfort House. The butler admitted him to George's study, where his brother joined him.

"How dare you?" Robert shouted. "How dare you?"

This was the first time Robert had called on his brother for over six months. George had been puzzled as he watched the wall go up. When he eventually heard the supposed reason for Robert building it, he was quietly amused. He had no interest whether his house had an unobstructed view of Belvedere or not, but he did have difficulty understanding why Robert should object to his extending Rochfort House.

His voice grew icy as he replied. "I dare because I can. This is my house, and I will extend it as I wish."

"But you bought my farms without telling me?"

"That, Robert, was simply good business. Nothing more nor less. Now, if you have no further business, I have work to do. I'll leave you to admire your wall."

Robert's face grew redder, and it seemed as if he might explode. He raised his walking stick but thought better of it, turned and marched out of the house. As he walked, he promised himself never to speak to George again.

Chapter Twenty-Five

A GLIMMER OF HOPE AND DESPAIR

Arthur was suffering from the ague yet again. The combination of winter chills, noisome atmosphere and poor food had left him badly weakened. Nothing changed in the cell unless the turnkeys came in to remove a body, or another unfortunate joined the throng of debtors.

A senior prisoner by now, Arthur was no longer shackled to the wall, although the other end of the chain was still attached to his wrist. He had raw sores where the manacle had rubbed right through the skin.

On occasions, he would find the place next to him occupied by someone with a tale to tell. Most debtors only had one story: how their creditors had conspired against them. How, when they managed to find enough to pay their creditors, they would go back into business. Every time they assured their cell-mates that this time they would not return. For some of them, it would only be a matter of months before they reappeared in the cell. His friend Josiah, the tailor, made another appearance that year and stayed in the cell for a further five months. His business was good, but payments from his lordly clients were delayed. The same haberdasher as before had him committed to the Black Dog. Eventually, some of his clients paid their bills. His family paid off the haberdasher, and Josiah walked free for the second time.

After Josiah had left again, it was hard for Arthur. Every few months he would find an occupant he could converse with. He was desperate for news from outside. Always, when asking about Mullingar, he would draw a blank.

At the end of his third year in the Black Dog, an actor sharing the cell mentioned that one of the local gentry in Westmeath had built an enormous wall. Built, he had heard, to improve the view. Little more information was forthcoming.

The prisoners were fortunate that year. Charities made larger donations of food. Some meat and vegetables appeared in the monotonous stew in the prison. Even this was an improvement on the plain oatmeal gruel, bread and potatoes that were their usual fare.

Arthur was now one of the longest surviving debtors in the prison. His hold on life was remarkable, and brought him some grudging respect from the turnkeys. His thirst for news drove him to question every new prisoner who came into the cell.

"What is happening in the world?" he would ask. "What is new in Dublin?"

Most of the time he got little response. Few debtors had any great knowledge of the world. Sometimes he would get news of the wars, and of the famines. Sometimes a handbill or broadsheet might appear in the prison, and Arthur would fall on it to read in the limited hours of daylight.

In May, a turnkey came to the cell and called his name. "Rochfort! You are wanted!"

Arthur was puzzled, but had little choice but to go with them.

They took him to the Warder's office. Sitting there was a half-forgotten figure.

"Major Rochfort. I am John Meagher, lawyer to Lord Molesworth."

"Your servant, Mr Meagher. I remember you. Not happy memories, I must confess."

"Indeed, Major. I wish it were a happier time. Mr Collins, leave us, please. I would talk in private."

The Warder got up and left with a surly expression on his face. Mr Meagher pulled his chair nearer to Arthur.

"Major, please listen carefully. Lord Molesworth has instructed me to render you some reasonable assistance while you are here."

"How did Lord Molesworth know I was here?"

"His tailor seems to be the source of the information. His lordship contacted me. I made enquiries and found that you were still alive and incarcerated here. I am to make regular payments to the Warder so that you have a room and bed. Mary, Countess Belvedere, was a favourite of her father's. He would do right by her. Naturally, no word is ever to be mentioned of these arrangements. Should they become public, they will cease immediately."

"I understand, of course."

"Good. I will also arrange for some clothes for you. They will be used, but clean and serviceable, and better than the rags you have now."

Arthur looked down at his feet and the rags that hung from his legs. "Mr Meagher, I don't know what to say."

"There is nothing to say, Major. Now I must away and wish you good fortune, or, at least, better fortune than you have had over recent months."

"Before you go, sir… What of Mary? Is she still alive?"

"I'm sure I don't know, Major. Her father didn't mention how she was. As far as I am aware, she is still being confined by her husband. Quite legally, I must add."

"Thank you, Mr Meagher. Again, I don't know what to say!"

"Then I'll say goodbye. Mr Collins?" he called out. The Warder came back into the room.

"The Major is to be accommodated on a bed, and in his own room again. You will be paid, of course, and here are the fees for the next month. My clerk will return and make regular payments on Major Rochfort's behalf. Do you understand?"

Mr Meagher left, and when the turnkey returned, the Warder instructed him to remove the shackle from Arthur's wrist. The skin underneath was raw and scarred. He descended to the large cell and collected his pitiably few belongings: a plate, a mug and a frayed blanket. The turnkey took him up to the top floor and showed him his bedroom. It stood alone, close to his previous room, and had a similar small barred window high in one wall.

Later in the day, the turnkey brought a parcel for him. This proved to be the promised clothes. They comprised coarse but serviceable breeches, a pair of linen shirts, and a short woollen coat; all used, but ideal for life in a Debtors' Prison. A pair of stout leather clogs was included. Arthur stripped, threw off his rags and washed himself from a bucket of water. He sat and let himself dry off before dressing himself in his new clothes.

For several minutes, he sat on the bed and allowed the sense of free movement of his limbs and of feeling clean wash over him. For the first time since he entered the Black Dog, he felt things might be looking up. A surge of hope ran through his veins, if only for a few moments.

Then the awful realisation of what the future held came back to him. He knew, beyond a shadow of doubt, that he was doomed to die there.

Chapter Twenty-Six

WINTER IS COMING

"Mrs Clohessy?" Mary's voice rang down the corridor towards the kitchen. "Do we have anything we can use to stop these draughts?"

"Precious little, ma'am. There's nothing in the store that would do."

"Can we get anything at the market?"

"We could if we had the funds. Mr Flynn is giving us so little to live on these days. I hear his lordship is short of money."

"How so?"

"Well, when I talk to my friends on market day, they all say that he has put the rents up again. And he has told Mr Flynn to be much more particular in collecting. There are a lot of tradesmen waiting to be paid for their work on his precious wall."

"And the children?"

"Nothing, ma'am, but I did hear they are missing their mama. A friend of their nurse told me."

"Last Christmas he sent the children to me for an afternoon. It was the first time I had seen them for some years."

"I remember, ma'am. It was good to hear young voices in the old house."

"I must hope and pray he repeats it this year. He has refused to acknowledge any request. Now he doesn't listen to anything I say."

"Ma'am, I don't think his lordship listens to anyone at all.

At least nobody that we know."

"That may well be true. Nevertheless, I will write to Mr Flynn and ask him."

One morning in November, Mary was, once again, lost in a black world of despair when Mrs Clohessy knocked at her bedroom door.

"Ma'am, begging your pardon, but there's a visitor for you. 'Tis Mr Flynn himself."

"Mr Flynn? Why is he here?"

"To be sure, I don't know, ma'am, but he was most insistent about wanting to see you."

"Tell him I will be with him shortly." As Mrs Clohessy went down to attend to their visitor, Mary forced herself out of bed and slowly began to dress.

Thirty minutes later, she went downstairs to find Mr Flynn drinking tea in the drawing room.

"My dear Mr Flynn. To what do we owe this call? You've never asked to see me before."

"Madam, should anyone ask, I haven't made any call on you at any time. However, I feel you should know that your children's nurse, Miss Prior, will be leaving Belvedere. I believe that his lordship intends to send them both away to school. The governess has already been given notice."

"When is this to happen?"

"Immediately after Christmas, my lady."

"Do you know why he is doing this?"

"His lordship has not taken me into his confidence on this. I would think it is because the children are getting older and he has no wish to be bothered recruiting a tutor."

"And Nurse?"

"I have no information on Miss Prior, my lady. I imagine his lordship will just dispense with her services."

"I'm so sorry. I can only hope she can get another position. But the children?"

"My lady, I'm sure that will not be on his lordship's mind."

"Mr Flynn, I can stand anything his lordship does to me, but he cannot punish the children."

244

"My lady, who will stop him?"

"I will. If I do nothing, I will curse myself to the end of my days. Say nothing of this to my husband, I beg you. But, Mr Flynn, what of his lordship? Does he seem happy? Content?"

"My lady, with his lordship, who can tell? I do know that he has lost the favour of His Majesty, and with that, the friendship of many people. Right-thinking people do not like how he has treated you or Mr Arthur. They say that these are not the actions of a gentleman."

"There's nothing I can do about that, but my children are different. Tell me, is he spending his time in Dublin or here?"

"To be sure, I don't know. He makes regular visits to Dublin; that I do know."

"What is my husband doing over the Christmas season?"

"I have no idea, my lady."

"Do you think you could find out for me? In a discreet manner?"

"I can try, my lady. I will make some enquiries, and I will return before Christmas."

The weeks passed. Mrs Clohessy found some old blankets in the market, and Mary and the housekeeper did their best to stop the icy wind blowing through the ill-fitting doors and windows. Some of the cracks in the walls were large enough for them to put the tips of their fingers in.

November had faded into December, and preparations were being made for Christmas in all the homes in Mullingar. All the homes, save one.

Two weeks before Christmas, as Mary and Mrs Clohessy were sitting in the kitchen, a visitor arrived. Mr Flynn had brought a Christmas gift for the house and its staff: a large basket of food and some fabric. This could be sewn into underclothes and work-wear for the few staff still at Gaulstown.

"My lady, you asked me to find out what your husband plans for himself for Christmas. I have made some discreet enquiries. It seems he is spending Christmas at Belvedere. I believe he has invited a large number of guests to a party."

"Do you know how many?"

"I'm afraid not, my lady."

"Then thank you for this information. I must decide on what I might do."

"You can rely on my discretion, ma'am. I trust you to be careful in your choice of action. I do hope that all in the house have a good Christmas."

"And the compliments of the season to you also, Mr Flynn."

With that, the land agent made his farewells and left for the cold ride back to Mullingar.

Chapter Twenty-Seven

A SEASON OF ILL-WILL

For several days, the grooms at Belvedere had been busy delivering invitations. Robert was holding a party. By inviting the great and good of County Westmeath, he planned to show his power and influence.

Despite his recent financial problems, he was determined to put on a dinner of the highest order. He consulted with the butler and housekeeper to decide on a suitable menu and selection of wines and other drinks, and employed a clerk for the Christmas period to cope with the task of writing the invitations and guest list.

He invited everyone he could think of that he considered worthy of visiting Belvedere. With over a hundred guests invited, he was looking forward to an evening such as Belvedere had never seen. His plan was to impress George with his power.

The replies, when they arrived, were mixed. Many couples pleaded prior engagements. There were some acceptances, but fewer than he hoped. Of those who accepted, some were those over whom he had some political or financial hold. Others were frankly curious.

At Gaulstown, Mary was making her own preparations for the party. The exact date and time, three days after Christmas Day, were common knowledge. Her plan, desperate as she was, was to confront Robert at the party and demand access to her children. One morning, she was talking with Mrs Clohessy over a cup of tea at the kitchen table.

"Mrs Clohessy. You are aware how concerned I am for my children."

"Yes, ma'am. You've talked of little else for these weeks past."

"Mrs Clohessy, I must see my children. Do you understand that? I must try and stop Robert sending them away."

"Ma'am, I understand. I'm not going to be telling anyone about this, but you must take the greatest care. Only think what his lordship might do."

"What can he do worse to me? He has imprisoned me for all this time. I'm at my wits' end. I don't know if what I plan will work, but I must do something. I am not going to let Robert destroy me without a fight."

"We will need to do something about the guards, ma'am."

"I know. They are still Robert's men. They must know nothing. My chances of success are small, but they are as nothing if they found out."

"Ma'am, there is one thing that might work. It is the Christmas season, so if I present them with a bottle of strong spirits each, then they will drink it and fall asleep for sure."

"What spirit would do that to a man? Where could we get it anyway?

"Your ladyship is thinking of spirits like brandy. We don't have the money for such, and that is for sure." Mary's face fell.

"I can get a couple of bottles of poteen, though."

"Would that get them drunk enough?"

"Ma'am, a bottle of poteen each and they will sleep for two days and two nights."

"How can you get the stuff?"

"Ah, ma'am, I have my sources. I know who to ask in the market."

"Do we have the money?"

"That's no problem. 'Tis not expensive."

"How can I get to Belvedere? It's a good hour's ride away."

"The groom can leave a horse saddled. He's a good man and will do what I ask. It'll have to be a man's saddle, though."

"It's many years since I rode astride, but I haven't forgotten how. I must pick out a dress that will fall on either side of the horse."

"We will need a good moon, ma'am, and a clear sky. 'Tis a five-mile ride near enough."

"If the weather stops us, all we will have wasted is two bottles of your spirit. If it works, I can change my life, and the lives of my children."

"And if it fails, ma'am?"

"I am beyond caring. There is little more that Robert can do to me. It could be bad for you if I fail, though."

"Don't worry about that, ma'am. I've friends enough to help me these days, and, thanks to you, I'm a good enough cook to get a job in an inn or small house. There's always someone looking for a cook or housekeeper."

"Very well. Let us prepare."

Mary got up from her chair and left to allow Mrs Clohessy to cook dinner. Sitting in the drawing room, she went over in her mind, again and again, what she proposed to do.

The next time Mrs Clohessy went to market in Mullingar, she paid a call on a certain stall. When she left a few minutes later, her basket contained two bottles of clear spirit, covered discreetly with vegetables

At Gaulstown, Mary sorted out the few clothes she had left. Many were unsuitable, and others were too worn. One or two were little more than rags. Eventually, she found a white thin silk dress with full enough skirts so that she could ride a horse. She had no suitable coat, and she silently prayed for a dry night.

The day of Robert's party dawned cloudy. Some showers during the night disappeared, and a breeze blew most of the clouds away. Mrs Clohessy's two bottles found their way into the hands of the two guards. Mrs Clohessy had sampled a small drop and declared it to be a fine spirit, with a kick like a thoroughbred horse.

The hours passed. After two hours, the guards were singing lustily. Mrs Clohessy could hear them from the kitchen. After four hours, there was no sound from their quarters. She put her head around the door and saw them lying insensible on the floor.

She went back to the drawing-room and told Mary. The clock showed seven o'clock.

"Take your courage in both hands, my lady. It's now or never. You'll not be alone on the road."

Mary looked puzzled. "Whatever do you mean?"

"Simon, the groom, will ride there with you."

"But he works for Robert. He will betray us."

"Indeed he won't, my lady."

"Why wouldn't he?"

"Because his wife, Sarah, used to be your maid."

"I remember Sarah. I remember telling her to marry for love."

"Well she did, and Simon is her widower. Sarah died in childbirth four years ago. Even in these troubled times, they loved each other deeply. They went and worked over in Rochfortbridge after leaving here, and Simon came to work here when he heard there was a vacancy for a groom."

"How strange, that I should find him here. Sarah was a sweet girl. I hope their time together was happy."

"Enough talking, my lady, it is time to get you on your way. Simon is waiting outside the front door. Those two yahoos are dead to the world."

Mary went out of the front door and found Simon mounted on one of the house's hacks, and leading a mare with a side-saddle on it.

"Good evening, my lady. It is good to see you out."

"Hello, Simon. Mrs Clohessy was telling me about you and Sarah. I am so sorry."

"Don't apologise, ma'am. We had two wonderful years, and she gave me a son, even if I lost her."

"Where is your son now?"

"With my parents. He's a fine little mannie, so he is."

"I'm glad you are with me, Simon. The ride will be easier now."

Mary kicked the mare into a trot, and the pair headed towards the gate to Gaulstown. The sky was cloudy, but the moon was full enough to give light to see the way.

"Ma'am, we will head north and west to the Rochfortbridge road. That will be easier in the dark. You stay close to me, now. We'll be going slowly. I'll not be letting you fall on a night like this."

There was a cold breeze blowing. It had rained earlier, but for now that had passed. There were plenty of gaps between the clouds, and they could see the stars, and the clouds scudding across. Simon kept the pair of them moving at a fast walk.

At Belvedere, the party was in progress. The lack of guests had annoyed Robert, and he didn't hesitate to show his annoyance to his staff. More of his guests had sent their apologies. From an invitation list of approaching a hundred, it appeared he would have just over fifty guests on the night.

On the evening itself, several more had failed to appear or had sent a note of apology to Belvedere with a groom. The servants were busy rearranging the tables and chairs for the reduced number of guests. Finally, only fourteen couples were sitting down to dinner. Tables had been arranged in both the drawing and dining rooms. Extra staff had been engaged. A waggon had already set off back to Mullingar with half a dozen extra footmen whose services would not be required.

Robert was inwardly seething. In compensation, he had indulged in several large glasses of brandy, and was happy to tell anyone who would listen what he thought of those people who had, as he described it, 'let him down'.

By the time dinner had finished and the remaining guests were sitting together in small groups, Robert had reached that stage of drunkenness where he was becoming noisy and belligerent. It became apparent to all who were sober that the party was over, and they started to rise. Robert saw them and shouted.

"Wait, everyone! I have something to show you."

The guests turned and looked at him.

"Come with me," he ordered, and marched out of the front

door onto the terrace.

"Look at my wall!" he declared.

Everybody looked as instructed. The last rain shower had passed by, and the moon shone brightly on the pale stonework. The guests looked their fill at what was an incredible piece of architecture: part castle, part church, part manor-house. The origins of the wall were unclear to all, save perhaps the architect. By now, the remaining guests were standing in pairs on the terrace in front of the house.

Robert, some two levels of the terrace below them, turned and shouted, "Come and watch!"

Obedient to their host's call, the guests followed him down the steps and across the grass to the wall. There, to their horror, Robert started to climb.

One of the guests came towards him and protested. "Robert, you can't. You've had too much to drink. Come back into the house, the ladies are getting cold."

"What, sir? You tell me what I can and can't do in my own house?"

With that, he turned back to the wall and resumed his climb. He appeared to be familiar with the wall, and didn't hesitate in finding footholds and handholds. If the truth were told, he had climbed the wall regularly. He derived a perverse enjoyment in climbing it and looking out over his brother's house and over the lough. There was no building like it in the whole of County Westmeath.

On and up he climbed, and within two minutes had arrived almost at the top of the wall. He had found a place where he could stand and rest. He stood now and turned his eyes towards Rochfort House, where windows were glowing from the lamps inside. George and Alice were among those who had refused his invitation.

He turned and looked down at his guests, all of them looking up at him with fear in their eyes. It was a look that Robert valued. As a measure of his power, he wanted to see that fear.

Mary and her groom kept moving at a fast walk towards

Belvedere on the Rochfortbridge to Mullingar road. Simon insisted that they could not risk using lanes and bridleways at night. But as it was the Christmas season, the roads were virtually deserted.

For the first hour the weather was kind to them, but then the showers started. The rain felt almost cold enough to freeze. The horses didn't like it, but Simon reassured them and murmured in their ears. His familiarity and confidence seemed to extend to the animals, and they became calm again.

After what seemed like an eternity they passed through the gates of Belvedere. Mary was wet and freezing. As they approached the house, they saw the guest's carriages. The grooms had left blankets on their horses and had retreated to the stables.

Unseen, the pair reached the head of the line of carriages. Simon dismounted and lifted Mary from her saddle. It was her first ride in several years, and she was stiffer and in more pain than she thought possible. But she was not to be put off, and passed the reins to Simon.

"I do not know what will happen here. If I am not back in an hour, or when the last guest leaves, then you are to ride back to Gaulstown. Do not try to follow me."

She ran her fingers through her hair and brushed the raindrops off. The damp made the thin silk dress cling to her body and was almost transparent. She noticed the people standing on the terraces looking at the wall before them. One or two of the guests were carrying lamps, but the clouds obscured the moon from time to time, making it difficult to see any detail.

Taking a grip on her fears, she walked around the corner of the wall and up towards the house.

Robert, perched precariously at the top of his wall, saw their heads all turn to look at the creature who had walked into view. The rain and brandy were enough to cloud his vision. All he saw was a dishevelled but ethereal figure in white. He shook his head in disbelief.

The apparition looked up towards him. Her mouth opened.

"Robert," she screamed, "I want my children!"

He recognised the voice immediately.

"You!" he breathed, and stepped forward.

The guests nearest the wall both heard and felt the impact. All of them instinctively took a step back. The ladies present turned to their partners, who put their arms around them to shield their eyes from the view.

Colonel Bryant, who was there on his own, ran forward and knelt at Robert's side. He didn't need the services of a doctor to know that Robert was dead. He called out for the butler to bring some footmen to carry Robert's body indoors, then went over to Mary and took his coat off to put around her.

"Is the tyrant dead?" she whispered, as the guests started to make their way back to the house.

"Most certainly, my lady. Now come inside with me."

Shielding her eyes from the sight of Robert's body, he escorted her back into the house to sit before the fire and dry out. The housekeeper arrived and sent a maid for a blanket.

Colonel Bryant took charge of the situation. The local magistrate was there with his wife.

"Mr O'Neill, I think you saw what happened. This will be recorded as a terrible accident. There was no arguing with Lord Belvedere when his mind was taken with something."

The magistrate, an elderly man who knew the Colonel and Robert well, could only agree. He had noticed the amount that Robert had been drinking, and had been among those who tried to persuade him not to climb the wall.

Colonel Bryant asked Mary to retire to a spare bedroom, but not before she had the butler send word to Simon that all was well and that she would be staying the night.

Robert's body was laid out in his own room, where it could await the services of the Protestant minister from Mullingar.

Chapter Twenty-Eight

THE MORNING AFTER

In the morning, Mary rose early. Her dress was still damp, but dry enough to put on. She knocked at the nursery door and went in. She found Nurse, blithely unaware of the events of the previous night.

"My lady! You have surprised us. Children, do you remember your mama from last year?"

In less than a minute, the children, now eleven and twelve, were in their mother's arms.

"Children, I have some news. Your father has had an accident. I am very much afraid he won't be coming to see you anymore."

They looked at her, and Mary explained what had happened.

"I want you to stay with Nurse for a few minutes. I will be back later."

Mary went downstairs and sat down for some breakfast. She knew she would have to break the news to her brother-in-law.

That event happened sooner than she expected. The butler appeared at the dining room door.

"Mr George Rochfort, ma'am," he announced.

George entered and came across to her. His face wore a scowl, and he looked worried. Anything like this could disturb his business plans.

"A bad business, Mary, a bad business."

"It was an accident, and, perhaps, fortunately, it was

witnessed by the magistrate and by Colonel Bryant, among many others. My husband was the author of his own downfall."

"Yes, well. I will be only too happy to take over the running of my brother's estate for you."

"That won't be necessary. I have sent a groom to Mullingar for Robert's lawyer and my husband's land agent. Now, if you will excuse me, I have much to arrange. I will let you know when proper arrangements have been made for Robert's interment."

Pearce, the butler whom she had appointed after the death of old Mr Danvers, showed George to the door and came back to her.

"Ma'am, no groom is going to Mullingar." He sounded puzzled.

"I know, Pearce; I just said that to Mr Rochfort to get rid of him. It is good to see you again, even if under such strained circumstances. I am going to write letters to Robert's lawyer and Mr Flynn. Can you arrange to have them delivered forthwith? I need to go to Gaulstown and then return here. My groom will come back with me."

"Of course, ma'am, right away, to be sure. And, ma'am, it is good to see you again."

"Why, thank you, Pearce. Can you arrange a carriage for me while I write these letters?"

"Right away, your ladyship." He turned and went out of the dining room with a large smile on his face.

Mary wrote two short notes and gave them to Pearce. By this time, a carriage was ready. One of the maids found her a cloak, and with a blanket over her knees, she made a comfortable and fast trip back to Gaulstown.

The two guards appeared, filthy and unshaven. They went to grab hold of Mary, only to find themselves assaulted on all sides. Mrs Clohessy attacked them with a poker from behind, while Simon and the coachman came at them from the front. Mrs Clohessy turned to them and snarled, "Get out of here. You are finished. If you show your face around here, I'll report you to the magistrate."

They took one look at the faces confronting them, glanced at each other, then turned and fled.

"Ma'am, what has happened? I can see that things are mightily changed around here."

"Indeed they are, Mrs Clohessy. My husband died in an accident last night. He got drunk and tried to climb his ridiculous wall. He fell and broke his neck. Oh, Mrs Clohessy, it is over! I have my children. I can't thank you enough."

"Are you going back to Belvedere? You will need clothes and things."

"I will indeed. Can I ask you to pack me a portmanteau or trunk? The coachman will take it and put it in the carriage. I will take everything I need over to Belvedere."

Two hours later, she was dressed in her most serviceable dress. Such few clothes as were still suitable to wear, along with her personal effects, had been put in the carriage.

She arrived back at Belvedere as the sun was setting. It was cold, and a damp wind blew from the west, off Lough Ennell. She was glad to arrive and to get into the house. A maid rushed forward and took her bags. Mary's first thought was that she would have to get used to having a maid again. She was so used to dressing and looking after herself.

An hour later she came downstairs in the cleanest and best clothes she could find. Pearce entered the drawing room.

"My lady, your letters have been delivered. The gentlemen concerned will wait on you here tomorrow morning."

The following morning the local priest and his vergers came to remove Robert's body and prepare for a burial service. She told the priest that there would be no eulogy, and only family members and staff would be present.

As the priest and his sad entourage left, Mr Flynn and a worried-looking gentleman in glasses arrived. He introduced himself as James O'Connell, Lawyer of Mullingar, and lawyer to his lordship for his local business dealings. The three of them sat around a table in the dining room.

"Gentlemen. You know of course of the dreadful accident that took place two days ago. We now have a new earl, who is still a minor. He is my son, and I will fight like a lioness to protect him and my daughter."

"My lady, I have little doubt you will. I do not wish to take up more time today than is essential. We will be spending a lot of time together over the next weeks. I have his lordship's Will here. His lordship evidently didn't countenance dying for many years, as he had me redraft his Will three years ago. His entire estate passes to his children. The bulk of it is left to his son, and a parcel of property and some funds to his daughter. He expected, I am sure, that they would have reached their majority before he died. To summarise, you, as their mother, act for them. It is for you to administer their estate and to pass it over to them when they marry, or when they reach full age."

Mr Flynn leant forward and spoke with an air of authority. "My lady, we have to get through this week, and only then will we be able to address any questions respecting the estate. Now, is there anything else you need urgently?"

"Nothing where you could help me. I must go into Mullingar to see a dressmaker. I desperately need clothes of all sorts, not just mourning clothes."

"Of course, ma'am. I also have some funds for you should you need. The portion settled on you by your mother has accumulated. It is not large, but you will have no reason to be short of money. For the moment, though, rest easy. These days will be difficult enough."

"There is one more task for you, Mr Flynn. I wish you to call the builders back. They must arrange the wall so that no one can ever climb it again."

"Ma'am, I understand your concerns entirely. I will contact them directly."

Two days later, Robert's funeral took place at All Saints' Church in Mullingar. The church was full, but any mourners were there more out of curiosity than any affection for the late earl. George was there, and Alice, both dressed appropriately in black, as was Mary herself. The local seamstresses had toiled relentlessly to make suitable mourning clothes. Interment took place under a leaden sky, with a sharp cold breeze casting a damper over everyone's spirits.

"Say goodbye to your father, children," Mary whispered, and they both murmured a quiet farewell to a father who had never shown them a single sign of love.

As they walked away from the grave, the breeze blew away the clouds, and the sun came out. Mary felt her heart lift. This might almost be a sign.

An hour later, she was sitting in Mr Flynn's inner office.

"Mr Flynn. I look on you as a friend, and I feel I need a friend at a time like this."

The land agent smiled and nodded. "Your ladyship does me honour. I am delighted that you consider me your friend. I will always do what I can to assist you, ma'am."

"Mr Flynn, you must not think me indelicate, with my husband barely cold in his grave. You know – better than most, I believe – the real state of our marriage."

"That is so, ma'am. The late earl's policies and practices were not ones to commend themselves to most people."

"There is one person whose name has not come up since my husband's accident. That is his brother, Arthur. Do you know if he is alive, or where he might be found?"

"Ma'am, I do not, for sure, but I can make enquiries. The last I heard, he was cast into the Black Dog, the Debtors' Prison in Dublin, after your husband made him bankrupt. However, this is a matter of the law. With your permission, I will consult with Mr O'Connell as to how to proceed."

"I know a little of the matter. My husband would delight in telling me how he had managed to destroy his brother. I know nothing of the Black Dog, save that it has an evil reputation."

Later, she sat with her children and Nurse, determined not to speak evil of their father to Jane and George. They would find out eventually, in the fullness of time, what manner of man he had been.

Chapter Twenty-Nine

TANGLED WEBS

Mr Flynn was as good as his word, and the first week in January, Mary was taking breakfast when the butler announced his arrival. He was accompanied by Mr O'Connell.

"Invite them in please, Pearce. I'm sure they would welcome some coffee."

The two men entered and sat with Mary while a maid poured coffee. Once she had left the room, Mary rose from her chair and closed the door for some privacy.

"Mr Flynn, tell me you have some news?"

"Indeed I do your ladyship. It is mixed news, but there is some good."

"Tell me, please. My heart is breaking."

"Of course, ma'am. Mr Arthur is still in the Black Dog Debtors' Prison, and he is still alive."

"Can I go to him?"

"No ma'am, not yet. I said it is mixed news. Mr O'Connell is in touch with a Mr John McBride, who was the lawyer for Mr Arthur. They are establishing what needs to be done to have him released."

"Can we do anything in the meantime?"

"Very little, it seems. Mr McBride is aware of your wish for a speedy resolution."

"Do we know how my brother-in-law is? I fear for him in there."

"Mr McBride is arranging for a physician to attend Mr Rochfort. We must apply to the court for instructions. Your ladyship, I must warn you that these things do take time. The law grinds fine, but it does grind exceeding slow."

"I see. Thank you."

Joseph Flynn sipped his coffee appreciatively. "Ma'am, there is something else. Mr O'Connell and I will need to consult your husband's private papers. There are matters concerning the building of this house and his wall, and some sales of land and property we need to check and resolve."

"Mr Flynn, I will put my husband's study at your disposal. You and Mr O'Connell may come and go as you please. I can do little myself over the next weeks. I believe you will understand why I will be keeping in mourning for as short a period as possible."

"I understand fully, my lady. I propose that Mr O'Connell and I try to prepare the papers for your signature and that we meet every week. We can then bring you up to date on progress."

Mr O'Connell added, "I will also make sure Mr Coote, his lordship's man-of-business in Dublin, and Mr Molloy, who has been acting for the family there, are kept in the picture."

Over the next days and weeks, Mary found her time all too occupied. She had to receive visitors, all of whom called to leave their cards and condolences. Many of them came purely to see the widow who had been kept locked away for so long. Few indeed were genuine friends of her late husband. Some callers offered her the hand of friendship and some practical support, but it was difficult. She could not tell anyone of her love for Arthur. There would be a time, and hopefully soon, when she could shout it from the roof-tops – but not yet.

The days and weeks dragged on. Some weeks later Mr Flynn could tell her that Arthur was indeed alive, but still in a pitiable condition. He was being attended by a physician and was receiving some medicine and proper food, but the conditions in the Black Dog were so extreme that he would not be able to recover until he had left the prison. Although Robert was now dead, the debt owed by Arthur had not, unfortunately, died with him; it was now owed to his estate.

Then Mary had a brainwave. Mr Flynn and Mr O'Connell had taken to visiting her every Friday with papers for her to sign, and she raised the subject with the lawyer during one of these weekly visits.

"Mr O'Connell, I have a question. While I know nothing of the law, I can only go on what my husband and the likes of yourself and some others have told me."

"My lady, I will try to answer your question as best I can."

"Mr O'Connell, when my husband sued Arthur in court, the Court awarded him damages, did it not?"

"Indeed ma'am. The sum of twenty thousand pounds."

"And, as Arthur was unable to pay this amount, Robert had him committed to the Debtors' Prison?"

"That is so, ma'am."

"Well, if Robert had him committed to the prison, surely I, on behalf of the new earl, can cancel the debt and have him released."

"Ma'am, you raise an interesting and valid point. I must consult some colleagues before I can give you a definitive answer. As it happens, I am in Dublin next week and will speak to some friends on this matter. The curious circumstances surrounding your late husband's actions make this more complicated. However, I see no reason why we should not make progress. Have faith, ma'am, and I will return as soon as I have some news."

"Thank you, Mr O'Connell. You have given me hope."

The lawyer produced some more papers for her to sign, then took his leave. He promised to return as soon as he had more information.

The following Friday dawned bright with a hard frost. Mary waited, watching the clock hands creep around past ten o'clock, her visitors' usual arrival time. As every minute passed, her concern grew.

Before noon, a solitary horseman approached. As soon as Mary heard his horse's hooves on the gravel, she sprang up and darted to the front door. Pearce was there before her, and he pulled the heavy door back to reveal the figure of Mr Flynn climbing the steps.

Mary's face fell.

"My lady, have you had some bad news? Why so sad?"

"Oh, Mr Flynn, I do apologise, I was hoping Mr O'Connell was back from Dublin with news of Mr Arthur."

"Ma'am, I haven't seen him at all this week. I am sure he will come to see you as soon as he gets back."

Mary clasped her fingers together in frustration, before escorting Mr Flynn into the drawing room for another round of reports on properties and rents. These were taking a familiar turn; whenever they met to discuss these things, there was invariably a shortfall. It was evident, from what the land-agent reported, that no one had made a systematic check on holdings and rents for some years. To say the records were in a mess would be to severely understate the case. Mary made a note to discuss the matter with Mr O'Connell when he next appeared at Belvedere.

Late in the afternoon, she heard voices in the entrance hall. She hurried downstairs and found Mr O'Connell with the butler.

"Mr O'Connell, what news? Tell me you have some news before I go mad!"

"My lady, I do have news, and good news at that."

Mary hurried the lawyer into the drawing room. "Now tell me, or I will die of worry."

"Ma'am, we can apply to have Mr Rochfort released."

"What must we do? Tell me, please."

"To summarise, we must make an application to the court. This process is simple but protracted. I will draw up the papers, and you will sign them. I will then submit them to the court."

"Thank God! Do you know how Mr Rochfort is? His state of health?"

"He is alive, and his health may best be described as fragile. Ma'am, I will not hide the hardships he has faced in that hell-hole. Happily, he is now getting proper food and a doctor's care."

"When can I see him?"

"Ma'am, I beg you not to attempt to see him until he is out of there. No decent lady should ever set foot in the Black Dog under any circumstances."

Mary had to be satisfied with these limited tidings, and the lawyer departed on his horse for Mullingar.

All next week, she had to contain her impatience. There were days she thought she would explode. Every time she heard a horse's hooves or a carriage outside she would jump up and hurry into the hall in the hope it was Mr O'Connell with some news.

On Friday, her prayers were answered. Mr Flynn and Mr O'Connell presented themselves. The lawyer produced several sets of documents, which she signed and Mr Flynn witnessed.

"When will you take these to Dublin, Mr O'Connell?"

"Ma'am, I will be going on Monday. However, there is another matter which is causing us concern. There seems to be a gross discrepancy between the estate records and the rents received."

"Sir, I am aware of a problem and discussed it briefly with Mr Flynn, but I have no idea of its cause."

"These are many. I must tell you that it is becoming clear to us that fraud is being committed on a massive scale. It could have been going on for years. When I am in Dublin, I will speak to his late lordship's bankers. I need to see the patterns of payments and receipts."

Mary spent a better weekend. With the news that Arthur could be released, even though no date was specified, her heart sang as she walked through the garden. A spell of warmer weather had bought the first flowers of spring out. Mary happily picked bunches of crocuses for the house. She could feel the change of the seasons.

"This year," she promised herself, "will be different!"

Chapter Thirty

FROM THE DEPTHS

Arthur was ill once again. A fever had raced through the Black Dog, and half of the inmates were sick. The worst were suffering from the flux as well as fever, and several bodies had been carried up from the lowest floors of the prison. At least now he had the luxury of a bed and blanket, but the longer he stayed in prison, the weaker he became. When the fever struck that winter, Arthur felt the effects more than most. His pleas for help were met with complete disinterest.

This time, he was reduced to shivering under a rough blanket, between bouts of diarrhoea and copious fevers and sweats. He turned his face to the wall and prepared himself for death. He found himself dreaming, and his thoughts alternated between his memories of Mary, and his terror at knowing he would never see her again.

That week the Warder had a pair of visitors. The first, a large, imposing gentleman, introduced himself.

"You are Collins, the Warder?"

"I have that honour, sir, and welcome to the Black Dog. Who might I be addressing?"

"My name is McBride. I am a lawyer in this city. This gentleman, Mr Christie, is a doctor. We are here to see Mr Arthur Rochfort, a gentleman in your care."

"No doctors in here, sir. We do not allow it."

"Mr Collins, we know your reputation and practices. We also know that you allow anything within these walls, for a price. I must advise you that we will pay you two guineas for

Doctor Christie to examine and treat Mr Rochfort. I can also tell you that Mr Rochfort will be leaving this hellhole shortly."

"Mr Rochfort is not going anywhere until he, or indeed you, sir, have paid his Gaol Fees."

"Ah yes. The Gaol Fees. So, tell me, Mr Collins, how much does Mr Rochfort owe in Gaol Fees?"

"Well, sir, he has been here a long time now. I have to pay the turnkeys, and for the upkeep of the gaol from these fees, so you'll understand there will be a substantial amount to pay."

"How much, man? Spare me your ramblings."

"Well, sir. One thousand and forty-three days, at two shillings and sixpence a day. This makes a grand total of one hundred and thirty pounds, seven shillings and six pence. However, for prompt payment, I will say one hundred and twenty guineas."

"That is ridiculous. How dare you demand a sum like that?"

"Sir, you wrong me. I pay rent to the City for the privilege of running this fine establishment. Gaol Fees are a settled way of doing business. I do nothing against the law or custom here, sir."

"I will pay you one hundred guineas, provided Mr Rochfort is fit and healthy on his discharge."

"You drive a hard bargain, sir. Yet I am too old and too tired to fight over this. The doctor may attend him directly." He gestured for one of the turnkeys, who stepped forward and led Mr McBride's companion to Arthur's room.

Dr Christie found Arthur comatose on his bed and quickly bent to examine him. Taking his handkerchief from his pocket, he wiped Arthur's face. Arthur's eyes fluttered open.

"Who are you?" he whispered.

"Quiet now, and rest. You are sick, sir. You must save your strength." The doctor opened his bag and produced a bottle of medicine and a smaller bottle of pills. Using a spoon, he managed to get Arthur to swallow some. Arthur spluttered violently and retched. The doctor managed to get him to sit up a little and spooned another dose of medicine into his mouth. This time, he gave him a cup of water to wash it down and induce him to take two of his pills.

"Mr Rochfort, you are a sick man. You need proper food and care. Now I want you to sleep, and I will return tomorrow. Do you get food?" Arthur nodded weakly. "Try to eat, and I'll see you in the morning.

He left Arthur and went back to find Mr McBride concluding his discussions with the warder.

"Mr Rochfort is seriously ill. Why have you not had him examined by a doctor?"

"We do not provide doctors or apothecaries in the prison, unless they are prisoners themselves, of course."

"Doctor Christie will attend Mr Rochfort every day," Mr McBride snarled. "Here is another guinea. Do not even attempt to tell me that this is not enough. And you can abandon any ideas of trying to extort any further funds."

The Warder led Mr McBride and Dr Christie out into the fresh air. The two men inhaled deeply, trying to dispel the noxious airs and fumes of the prison.

"How is he, Doctor?"

"He will live, though he is gravely ill. I think the long stay in that place has affected him very badly. Much longer, and he might well have died. As it is, he will need an extended period of nursing to recover properly."

"So the sooner we can get him out of this place, the better."

Three days later, John McBride lodged a writ with the High Court in Dublin, duly attested, to say that the damages had been paid and that Arthur Rochfort could be released. On leaving the court, he collected Dr Christie and two servants. Together they went to the Black Dog. Twenty minutes later the servants carried Arthur as gently as they could to a waiting carriage. In his office, Mr Collins counted and recounted his guineas, before locking them away in a strongbox.

Half an hour later the carriage had crossed the bridge and stopped outside Gardiner Row. The butler was at the door, and he ordered two more footmen to lift Arthur into the house.

Mary watched, her face strained with emotion and tears of

worry, as the servants carried Arthur's senseless body upstairs to the master bedroom and laid him on the bed. There, Dr Christie and a footman removed Arthur's clothing and shoes and consigned them to the fire. The oldest maid in the household, who remembered Arthur as a young child, helped the doctor to wash and clean Arthur's body. His body bore the scars of his long period of imprisonment. He was rail-thin, his skin had an unhealthy pallor, and his hair was pale and lank.

Doctor Christie left Mary with a bottle of laudanum drops, with strict instructions how she was to use them.

"Give him one or two drops if he is in a lot of pain. But he is very frail, so too many drops might kill him. The best thing you can do to restore his health is to care for him. Good food, in small amounts. Soups, gruel, eggs and the like, but never too much. I have given him some of the laudanum to help him sleep tonight, and I'll return every day to check on his recovery."

Mary stayed sitting by Arthur's bed, watching the shallow breathing and slight rise and fall of his chest. Her memories came flooding back. When they met. When they first kissed. When they realised that they loved each other. She looked at his face, so pale.

Going over to him she kissed him, as delicately and tenderly as she could, before moving the candle, so it didn't shine on his face. Pulling the curtains, she left him to sleep. Lying in her bed that night, as she drifted off to sleep, she allowed herself to remember his body when they were lovers.

Chapter Thirty-One

A NEW DAWN

Arthur's eyes flickered open. He blinked at the light and struggled to focus. Mary was sitting by his bed, and he felt the warmth of her hand as it slipped into his.

"My darling. You are free now. It's over."

For the first time since entering the Black Dog, he could feel the terror ebb from his body. He started to relax. Mary was talking to him, quietly and in a low voice. He couldn't understand her words, but he knew he was safe. He fell into a deep and relaxing sleep.

He woke again that evening, to find Mary at his side again. "How long have I been here?" he asked.

"A whole day. Now don't talk. You must eat. You can only get well if you eat well."

"I would like that. I feel – hungry."

"Nurse is here, with the children. She wants to help look after you." Mary called out quietly, and the once-familiar face of Nurse came into view.

"I'll look after you, Mr Arthur. Don't you worry."

Arthur managed a wan smile, and Nurse held a handkerchief to her eyes, wiping away tears of relief.

A housemaid entered with a tray, and Mary and Nurse lifted Arthur into a sitting position. Over the next half hour, they took turns feeding him from a bowl of broth and spooning a lightly boiled egg into his mouth. After this, Arthur looked tired. Mary kissed him and left him to sleep again.

He was still sleeping when she looked in to see him later. She smiled, kissed him on the forehead, and went to her own bed.

Despite wanting to assert his independence, Arthur had no defence against the combined wiles of Mary and Nurse. He soon began to feel better. Dr Christie came every day in the first week, and then announced he would come only every three days.

On Monday of the second week, Arthur demanded to get out of bed. Dr Christie looked at him from under his eyebrows. "Do you feel you can?"

"I feel I must try!" insisted Arthur. "I feel like a caged animal stuck in here."

Mary hastily summoned a footman, and he and the doctor supported Arthur as he swung his legs gingerly over the side of the bed. As his legs bent and his feet touched the floor, he felt how weak he was and leant on them both. After a few moments, he found himself on his feet. The doctor allowed him to walk to the other side of the room before they turned him around and slowly walked him back to his bed. By the time he was lying against the pillows, he had broken out into a slight sweat. He felt the muscles in his legs spasm. He took a deep breath and forced himself to relax. Turning to Mary and the doctor, he forced a tired smile.

"Thank you. I managed it. Let me try again tomorrow."

"Of course, Mr Rochfort. That is exactly what I want you to do. Do make sure you have someone to support you." The doctor rose to leave, "Oh, and please, do not try this alone. You now have an inkling of how weak you are. Keep eating well. You will be able to do more every day, I promise you."

Over the course of the next two weeks, Arthur's strength slowly returned. He was still as weak as a kitten, but he could get out of bed and walk around the room.

Three weeks after, a caller arrived at Gardiner Row. Minutes later, an elderly gentleman was shown into Arthur's room. Mary was sitting there sewing while Arthur dozed.

"Father? What are you doing here?"

"I heard that Arthur was released from the Black Dog, and I came to see both him and you."

At the sound of voices, Arthur stirred and awoke. "Lord Molesworth. I cannot thank you enough."

Mary looked at the pair of them, astonished.

"My darling, I owe my life to your father. He paid for food and a bed for me while I was in prison."

Mary leapt to her feet and ran into her father's arms.

"Mary, you must know, I did this for your mother. I loved her deeply, and she was torn from me by fate. I knew you loved Arthur, right or wrong, and I knew I couldn't live with myself if I stood by and did nothing. Although I must warn you, your stepmother doesn't know anything of this."

"Don't worry, Father. Your secret is safe with us. Suffice it to say that both of us will be eternally grateful to you."

"The little tailor told you, I heard," Arthur added. "He was a good man. I would be dead without your help, I am sure."

Eventually, Dr Christie pronounced Arthur fit enough to be moved to the countryside. The move was accomplished more easily than expected thanks to an improved road and a comfortable carriage. Even so, Arthur was visibly tired when they arrived at Belvedere. This time, they did not stop at the inn at Enfield. After their betrayal by the innkeeper and his wife, Arthur was determined never to stay there again.

Once they arrived at Belvedere, the place of life slowed perceptibly. Arthur graduated little by little to being able to come downstairs and to walk in the garden with Mary. The children, still favourites of Arthur's, were bound to lift his spirits, and his recovery continued apace.

One sunny day, Mary took Arthur down the steps and across the lawns to see the infamous wall. In its shadow, he turned to her and took her in his arms again. Their kiss, desperate and hungry after so long apart, showed every ounce of passion in their bodies. To kiss and hold each other in the shadow of Robert's folly seemed to lay his brother's ghost forever.

That night, Arthur came to her room, and they made love with an urgency that surprised them both. They lay in each other's arms, satiated. After a short sleep, Mary stirred, and her hands explored Arthur's body. He responded at once, and Mary felt him hardening beneath her hands. With a sense of urgency,

271

she pulled him into her. She had a desperate need to be held. A need to be loved.

Later he woke again to find her sobbing quietly.

"My darling, what is it?" he whispered. "You are safe now."

"I know. I was crying because I'm so happy."

Later that morning they had a pair of visitors. Mr Flynn and Mr O'Connell arrived with a large portmanteau of papers. The butler announced their arrival to Arthur and Mary in the drawing room.

"Gentlemen, it is good to see you again," Mary smiled. "It seems that your efforts were successful."

They looked over to where Arthur sat, smiling, on a sofa. "So I see, my lady. May we say how happy we are." Mr Flynn turned and looked pointedly at Mr O'Connell, who was holding a large folder of papers.

The four of them adjourned to the dining room and seated themselves at the table. Mr O'Connell looked earnestly at the three of them.

"My lady and gentlemen, I am sorry to bring such a quantity of papers to you. However, it seems that Mr George Rochfort has been undertaking a significant number of fraudulent activities. Mr Flynn has visited a large number of properties, and we have found evidence of fraud. It seems that his late lordship's tenants have been paying their rents to your brother George rather than to the Belvedere estate."

"Mr O'Connell! How and why has this happened?"

"The reason why is easy to fathom. Mr George has been rebuilding Rochfort House. These things take a deal of money. I also happen to know that he has lost several large contracts to supply His Majesty's Army. It seems that the prices he was charging the commissary bore no relation to the prevailing prices in the market."

His three listeners were still looking puzzled. He continued.

"The method seems to have been simplicity itself. Your late husband, the earl, has himself needed funds over the last three years. The wall may look magnificent, but so is the cost of such construction. To help in paying, his lordship sold several of his farms to his brother, who in turn resold the farms as larger estates. But, and here lies the nub, he has never paid for these properties. His lordship handed over the deeds to the properties on a handshake, expecting to receive payment through his man-of-business. But this simply never happened."

Both Arthur and Mary were shocked into silence. No one spoke for over a minute, and the expressions on their faces changed from astonishment to shock and anger.

Mary spoke first. It was her son's estate now, and she would fight to keep it as it should be.

"What can we do to get this money back?"

"I cannot advise going to the courts. To sue your brother-in-law will be difficult, and will not be popular."

"I will not do it! There has been enough of the courts between brothers in this family."

"Very wise, ma'am. You can manage without these funds. A quiet life will help. I don't know what your plans are for the next year, but I would warn against any extravagance."

"Mr O'Connell, we have no plans at all. Mr Arthur's health is still not yet restored. We expect to live quietly for the next few months. If all goes well, we plan to marry this time next year. While we care nothing for society's opinions, we have no plans to launch ourselves back into a social whirl."

Mary felt Arthur slide his hand into hers under the table. She smiled at him, and the love in her eyes was clear to the others in the room.

"Gentlemen, what do we do now?" she asked.

"You need to tell Mr George that you know of his conduct. After that, we will see what he says. Taking no action means he gets to keep all these properties. The title for them has been transferred. We should, I think, try to regain them. This especially when they have not been sold on."

"Very well. I will call on George as soon as I can. Even though you know that I do not intend to use the law, he does not know that. Can I rely on your support in this?"

"Of course, ma'am. We will be happy to accompany you."

273

The following Wednesday, Arthur and Mary, together with Mr O'Connell and Mr Flynn, presented themselves at Rochfort House. George was clearly astonished to see them.

"Good Lord. What are you doing here? How did you get out?"

"Good morning, George, and how are you?" replied Arthur, a sardonic smile making his eyes twinkle.

"What? How am I? Why do you ask?" blustered George, clearly discommoded by their arrival.

Mary stepped forward. "George, all these gentlemen are here on my behalf. My behalf and on that of my son, the Earl of Belvedere."

George looked concerned. "You had better come with me. I'll call my wife, and she can entertain you to tea, Mary."

"I don't think so. This is a matter that affects me directly."

They followed George into his study, which was lined floor to ceiling with books and boxes of documents. Mary wondered idly how many of the papers in the boxes related to properties that belonged rightly to her son.

They sat around George's desk, and Mary introduced Mr Flynn and Mr O'Connell. George immediately looked worried. Arthur said nothing during these exchanges, but Mary knew that he was watching George intently.

Mr O'Connell rose to his feet. "Mr Rochfort, I am afraid to say that we have evidence of a substantial number of frauds carried out by yourself or your agent."

George resorted to more bluster. "Fraud? What are you saying? How dare you accuse me of fraud in my own house?"

"Mr Rochfort, we dare because we have the proof. You still owe the late earl's estate a sum of more than eight thousand three hundred pounds."

"Impossible. I owe nothing! Get out of my house!"

"Mr Rochfort, we have proof here," replied Mr O'Connell, producing a sheaf of papers. "We have here a list of properties which you purchased from the late earl, at, I must say, remarkably cheap rates. Payment for these properties has never been received. It seems his lordship's man-of-business was never informed of the sales."

George stared for some moments at the paper he had been given. Mary's voice broke his concentration.

"George, the situation is clear. The choice is yours. You will transfer the title to these properties back to the Belvedere estate immediately."

Mr O'Connell passed him another, shorter list. These were the properties that had not been sold.

George took it and read it, and realised immediately that it represented a considerable gain to him. He was not being asked to repay any rents received – at least, not yet.

"Why should I do this?" George continued. "I only have these wild accusations so far. I need time to examine your claim."

"You may have one week. There is no mistake in this, sir. If you transfer the listed titles to the Belvedere estate as we require, her ladyship will take no further action. Should you fail, however…" Mr O'Connell let his silence speak for him.

The visitors rose and left the room as one, leaving George sitting, fuming, and looking at the list of properties he had lost.

Chapter Thirty-Two

TIME, THE GREAT HEALER

That summer was the first summer of happiness and contentment Mary and Arthur had known for many years, and their first as a couple. They were both determined to make up for lost time.

The only souvenirs Mary wanted from her first marriage were her children. She loved them with a fierce passion. She was determined to show them the love denied to her after her own mother died.

Her feelings for Arthur had never wavered, even in the darkest hours after he had been shot, and during the long period when he was away in Gibraltar. Even when he was in prison, and while there was no news or information at all, there still flickered a flame in her heart that insisted he could still be alive.

Arthur's feelings for her had never fallen, never diminished. In his darkest nightmares, lying in chains in the filthy hovel that was the Black Dog, he knew that Mary loved him. He also knew that his own feelings for her had never wavered.

During that spring, they renewed their love. Every day was a journey. They remembered all the incidents of their meeting and of their all-too-brief times together before Robert's discovery of them. Every night was a sweet exploration of each other's bodies.

Life was peaceful throughout that summer. George decided that it would be prudent to spend some considerable time at a property he had bought in England. Between them, Arthur and

Mary built up a small but understanding circle of friends, several of them from the garrison. Mary had an innate sweetness of character. Robert's awful reputation and his treatment of her, and Arthur's extraordinary ability to make himself agreeable to all, combined to conquer any doubts their friends might have had over their relationship.

The following spring, the bells in the Protestant church in Mullingar rang out a short but joyful peal. Arthur and Mary walked down the aisle and out of the church door as man and wife.

That night, as the last of their wedding guests left in their carriages, they turned to each other and embraced with tenderness and passion.

"Happy?" asked Arthur.

"Oh, yes, my darling," replied Mary. "Happy at last."

THE END

Afterword

WHAT REALLY HAPPENED

Robert Rochfort was a truly evil man. In reality, he accused Arthur and Mary, on no evidence whatsoever, of "Criminal Conversation". He imprisoned Mary at Gaulstown for over thirty years, and he sued Arthur for damages. As in the story, he was awarded £20,000 – a record amount which has never been surpassed.

He did condemn Arthur to Debtors' Prison, where in fact he died.

The circumstances of Robert's own death are not clear. He may have been murdered by his tenants.

From *The Annals of Westmeath* (James Wood, 1907)

*The second Earl of Belvedere died in 1814,
and having no issue, the title became extinct.
With his death, the Rochforts are cleared out
of Westmeath, root and branch.*

*They were a wicked race, and to this day
the name is loathed and execrated in this county.*

Fantastic Books
Great Authors

CROOKED
CAT

Meet our authors and discover
our exciting range:

- Gripping Thrillers
- Cosy Mysteries
- Romantic Chick-Lit
- Fascinating Historicals
- Exciting Fantasy
- Young Adult and Children's Adventures
- Non-Fiction

Visit us at:
www.crookedcatbooks.com

Join us on facebook:
www.facebook.com/crookedcatbooks

Made in the USA
Columbia, SC
03 October 2017